The RED WOMAN on MARS

AF621881

Also by Claire Barner

Moonrising

The Red Woman on Mars

A Novel

CLAIRE BARNER

DIVERSION BOOKS

Diversion Books
A division of Diversion Publishing Corp.
www.diversionbooks.com

Copyright © 2026 by Claire Barner

All rights reserved, including the right to reproduce this book or portions thereof in any form whatsoever. No part of this publication may be reproduced or transmitted in any form or by any means, electronic or mechanical, including photocopying, recording, or any other information storage and retrieval, without the written permission of the publisher.

Diversion Books and colophon are registered trademarks of Diversion Publishing Corp.

For more information, email info@diversionbooks.com

First Diversion Books Edition: July 2026
Trade Paperback ISBN: 979-8-89515-151-8
e-ISBN: 979-8-89515-152-5

Design by Westchester Publishing Services
Cover design by Jonathan Sainsbury // 6x9 design

Printed in the United States of America
1 3 5 7 9 10 8 6 4 2

Diversion books are available at special discounts for bulk purchases in the US by corporations, institutions, and other organizations. For more information, please contact admin@diversionbooks.com.

The publisher does not have any control over and does not assume any responsibility for author or third-party websites or their content.

To Rufus,
the love of my life

"Till this moment, I never knew myself."

—Jane Austen, *Pride and Prejudice*

CONTENT WARNING

This novel contains content that may be troubling for some readers, including on-page graphic violence, painful medical procedures, pregnancy symptoms, malnutrition, discussion of sexual assault, domestic violence, miscarriage, abortion, and a brief mention of suicide.

PROLOGUE

Seven years, three months, and eighteen days into Vivian Bowen's indefinite detention at the Sumter Refugee Camp, she finally found an escape.

In her family's government-issued tent, Vivian was curled up on her cot lost in a novel when a sharp, acrid smell reached her nostrils. Was the stew bubbling over? Vivian tucked her book under one arm and went to investigate.

Outside, dark smoke snaked up to the sky, originating from a small fire spreading on the tent's canvas surface. With a steady stream of cursing, Vivian grabbed the basin of suds used for washing dishes and poured it over the fire. A hiss erupted as water doused the flames.

Vivian stared down at the ruined corner of the tent, chest heaving. A ragged hole the size of a dinner plate marred the bottom corner. How much would a proper repair job cost them? More than the meager savings her family had stored in the jar hidden at the bottom of their clothes bin.

Ringing laughter made Vivian whirl around. Max Rinaldi stood several feet away, his meaty hands on his hips and his head thrown back in amusement. Vivian's whole body went rigid. She took two shaky steps toward him. "Are you insane or just stupid? You could've burned down half the camp."

"Nah, these tents are barely flammable. Took me forever to get yours to light." He let out another peal of laughter. "You should see your face!" His eyes traveled slowly down her rail-thin body. Vivian crossed her arms over her oversized T-shirt, one hand still clutching her book. "I can't stop thinking about the way your tight ass felt pressed against my thighs last week." He idly pulled a sharp white shank out of one pocket and twirled it between his fingers.

"I hate you." Vivian touched one hand to her throat involuntarily, feeling the lingering scab from where that shank had cut her.

"There she is," he murmured. "I know you'll be a hellcat in the sack."

"Leave me alone." Vivian shifted uncomfortably. The normally noisy camp was eerily quiet. Typically, her neighbors would be outside, tending cooking fires, hanging laundry, kicking soccer balls, and trading gossip. But now, not a single person was in sight. No one would be coming to her aid today.

"I'm here to make sure our message from last week stuck. No more stealing from my brothers and me."

Vivian eyed the marred tent and swallowed her rage. Even if she found the accusation of stealing ridiculous, the memory of how easily Max had overpowered her the week before was too fresh to argue. All she and her friends had done was collect extra cans of beans and boxes of pasta to ensure the camp children were fed during shortages. But hoarding food was a strategy the Rinaldi brothers used to keep control of the camp, and they weren't willing to give up any power.

"No more," she agreed.

"You could use protection, Vivian. A girl like you has no sense for the proper order of things. I could make it real comfortable for your parents. And what's your sister's name?" He snapped the fingers on his free hand. "Delilah. She's growing up to be quite the vixen. I bet she's going to need looking after."

"Keep Delilah's name off your lips," Vivian retorted before she could stop herself. She was going to get herself killed if she didn't learn to keep quiet.

"A hellcat," he repeated. Vivian wanted to slap the smirk off his mouth. "What's this book you're holding so tightly?" With one quick movement he snatched it from her hand. A few of the edges of the ancient yellowing pages crumbled to the ground. He flipped to the front cover. "A Regency romance?" He raised his eyebrows at her. "Didn't know that's what you were into. I could rustle up a top hat if that's what turns you on."

Vivian was going to murder him. She was going to take that stupid shank and shove it directly into his throat and then stand over his bleeding body as he took his last gurgling breath.

If only she wasn't so frail.

Max opened the book to the middle. "'He freed one breast from the tight confines of her corset and brought his mouth to her aching nipple.' Very nice."

Vivian's face was hot, and she felt the sting of unwanted tears threatening to fall. "What do you want with me? Why are you really here?"

"Relax, Vivian. I'm no rapist."

Just a bully and a thief. An arsonist. And probably a murderer.

"I could give you this." He traced one meaty finger down the page. A few more yellowing pieces floated down onto the hard-packed dirt. "I heard a rumor that the Martians have built their whole society around a Regency fantasy. I think we could manage a little roleplay in the bedroom."

Vivian gritted her teeth. "No, thank you."

"Fine." He shoved the book back at her, and Vivian staggered as she caught it with one hand. He pulled an imaginary hat off his head and gave her an elaborate bow. "Pleasure to see you, my lady." Max Rinaldi sauntered away, his hands in his pockets and thumbs through his belt loops.

Vivian let out a slow breath as she watched his retreating back. At least her parents hadn't been around to witness the confrontation. Even defeated as he was, she didn't think her father could have swallowed Max's behavior. And Delilah, always eager to make dangerous men happy, probably would have started flirting.

"You seem to have a problem on your hands."

At the edge of the next tent stood a woman. Her elegant navy pantsuit and black leather valise conveyed quite clearly that she was not a refugee. A missionary? The rare government representative?

"I have it under control," Vivian snapped.

She'd handle Max Rinaldi.

Somehow.

The woman came closer. "A man like that isn't going to let up until he gets what he wants. He may not have any power outside the walls of this camp, but in here, he'll always find a way to assert his power over you."

"And?"

The woman flashed a badge. "I'm with the Arcadia Group, representing the interests of the Martian dome on Earth."

Vivian jerked her head. This was a new one. "Hello."

"How would you like a ticket out of here, Ms. Bowen?"

"Mars?" Vivian hadn't been outside the high walls of the Sumter Refugee Camp since she was a teenager. People like her were lucky to get a work permit for a factory in Charlotte, not travel to another planet.

"I'm looking for women just like you. Women who are interested in the adventure of a lifetime."

"Women," Vivian repeated skeptically. "Only women?"

"To be precise, healthy cis women who have no kids, partner, or addictions. Ages eighteen to twenty-five. A surprisingly hard set of criteria to fill."

"To do what?"

"Marry a Martian and have their children."

Vivian barked an involuntary laugh. "I'm not having children."

The woman tilted her head, taking in the tent community. People were starting to emerge from their homes now. A few cooking fires had been relit, and one girl who couldn't have been older than fifteen sat on a stool outside her tent with a baby nursing at her breast. Two skinny half-naked toddlers ran screeching in between the tents with no minder in sight.

"Of course you don't want children *here*. Who would?" She gave a flick of her fingers, as if dismissing the refugees en masse. "The wealthy Martian oligarchs of the Arcadia Dome are seeking a group of Earther women to travel to Mars to marry them and bear their children."

"Like an arranged marriage?" She looked down involuntarily at her historical romance novel. Some things were better off staying in fiction.

"Not exactly. You'll have the choice of a spouse. In fact, you'll be courted. You know the Martians—any excuse for a ball with them."

Vivian did not, in fact, know anything at all about the Martians. "Not interested."

"This is a job, Vivian. You'll be paid." And she named a sum so outrageous Vivian opened her mouth in shock. It was more money than she could hope to acquire in a lifetime. Enough to buy a permit to leave the camp for good. But perhaps not enough to buy three permits.

"I have a sister," Vivian ventured. "She's turning eighteen in two weeks."

"Delilah is welcome to join you. I do have a quota to fill."

Vivian touched her throat. What was preferable? To get in bed with Max Rinaldi or an unknown Martian? There would inevitably be a baby either way. Birth control was illegal in the Carolinas, and Vivian wasn't fool enough to trust Max to pull out. If she stayed and acquiesced to the dubious protection Max offered, would she end up a tool of the brutal gang that ran the camp, turning on her own friends and their children? And Delilah—Vivian couldn't bear to see the light go out of her sister's eyes. They'd both been lucky to stay under the radar of the Rinaldi brothers and their men for all this time. If Vivian hadn't been arrogant enough to believe she could get away with changing the camp's status quo, she might have escaped their notice longer.

But to leave the camp for good, with Delilah by her side. To earn the funds to buy her parents a way out. Hadn't she been dreaming of a chance like this for seven years?

"Alright," Vivian said slowly. "I'm in. Take me to Mars."

After seven years, three months, and eighteen days, Vivian finally found an escape—into a gilded cage.

CHAPTER ONE

61 Sols to Presentation Day

Did I just trade one hell for another?

Bright garish colors, pungent smells, and the unfamiliar burden of gravity assaulted Vivian as she took her first steps on the surface of Mars. She pushed the unwelcome thought away and straightened her spine. Letting her eyes adjust to the full sun, she watched the willowy Martians moving confidently through the expansive redstone plaza as they perused the merchant stalls selling cultured beef kabobs, recycled electronics, flavored water, wide-brimmed hats, and vibrant clothing. Even in the shuttleport, close to the dome's edge, the translucent barrier soared double the height of their lanky forms.

Her friend Luz slipped beside her and squinted up at the Martians. "They don't look like aliens."

"You know they aren't aliens," Vivian retorted, trying to reassure herself. She watched a Martian with pale skin stretched over his cheekbones make a strange languid gesture to his companion with one unnaturally long arm. "We share the same genetic sequence."

"I know, I know. It's the low gravity making them all seven feet tall." Luz gave a Martian man purchasing a kabob an appreciative once over. "They remind me of pro basketball players. I've fucked a pro ball player or two in my time. The height difference matters less when you're lying down."

Vivian's cheeks darkened. After nine months confined together on a transport ship, Luz's crass sense of humor still managed to unsettle her. She attempted to match her friend's disinterested tone. "I'll keep it in mind."

Stepping away from Luz, Vivian located one of their Earther escorts from the ship. His muscular arms crossed over his chest as his eyes darted around the crowd. "Are we required to go to a customs checkpoint?"

He shrugged, barely looking at her. "We're expected. I imagine they'll want you lot behind high walls as soon as possible."

Vivian glanced around the crowd uneasily. What had the man so tense? Their group of thirty disheveled young women clad in spacer jumpsuits weren't the only Earthers in the shuttleport. Earthers staffed many of the merchant stalls and some stood behind Martian individuals or couples, bearing their purchases.

"I've never been valuable goods before," Luz muttered in her ear. "It's rather refreshing."

Delilah sauntered up. "Viv, isn't this place wonderful?" Her sister grabbed her arm playfully. "Look at those stunning hats." She pointed at a pair of Martian women with bright cloche hats adorned with chartreuse ribbons. "We must get our own, of course. Everyone is wearing one, and we'll need to fit in with the locals." She raised a finger again and made a face of disgust. "Except him."

"Don't point," Vivian chastised as she followed Delilah's gesture. And flinched, staring.

This Martian looked like an alien.

Augmented tech covered the man's tall Martian form, glittering from the silver circular attachment on the right side of his bald head to the shiny silver rings on his fingers. His heavy scarlet robes were cut too short for his tall frame and flapped absurdly above his tiny, booted feet as he parted the crowd on his way toward them.

Giving a small bow in their direction, the man said in a high, thin voice, "Red Mothers, I am honored to welcome you on behalf of the great Constance Yarrow, Secretary of the Arcadia Dome and my patron. I am Wim Adair, reverend of the Intelligence, and your guide in this new land."

Vivian had no idea what it meant to be a reverend of the Intelligence, but she was not going to allow herself to be intimidated by her first Martian encounter. "Pleased to meet you." She hefted her slim bag over her shoulder and stepped in front of the other women to offer her hand.

Wim bowed to her again instead of taking her hand. "Lesson the first, my dear: Earthers and Martians do not shake hands. Your strong grip would quite overwhelm us."

Vivian quickly put her hand down. Should she have already known that? She knew so very little about Martian customs.

"Come, ladies," Wim called, tapping two fingers on each hand together. "You must be exhausted by your ordeal. I am here to escort you to your new home." He turned to the guard and said in an undertone, "Keep a close eye out, if you please. I don't want any trouble."

What kind of trouble? Vivian wondered. This place was supposed to be a new chance for her and Delilah. If she'd made a mistake, it was too late to turn back. The increasingly disturbing combination of propositions and threats from Max Rinaldi in the days leading up to their departure flashed through her mind.

"Make way!" Wim's reedy voice came out booming as he activated an augmentation at his throat. "Make way for the Red Mothers."

Vivian threaded her arm through Delilah's and gave her a reassuring smile. Her sister beamed in response. As Wim led their group through the busy plaza, the crowd parted before them, murmuring. The glances they gave the women were mostly curious, not hostile. Some even smiled or shouted words of welcome. Tension dripped out of Vivian's body as she forced herself to greet the friendly faces with an answering smile.

Until her gaze caught on one Martian in the sea of goodwill who didn't look pleased to see them. The man wore a double-breasted burgundy tailcoat over light-colored trousers. His long arms crossed over his chest, and his black top hat did not conceal the look of anger in his dark eyes. Vivian returned his glare until he looked away.

"Who was that?" she asked Wim.

Wim followed her gaze and scowled. "Don't worry about him, my dear. Counselor Dorsey is not on the approved list, as much as it pains his aunt, my mistress Secretary Yarrow."

"Why did he look so angry with us?"

"Leave be, girl," Wim snapped. "We did not pay your way here to ask questions."

Vivian felt an uncomfortable jolt of recognition at his dismissive tone. She swallowed a tart reply and bowed her head in a picture of meek acquiescence.

"Fucking men," Luz muttered behind her. "The same on every planet. You need to watch yourself with that one, Viv baby. Your curiosity is going to get you into trouble."

"I'm not going to let him intimidate me." When she'd accepted this role, she'd vowed to herself that she'd never again allow petty men grasping at power to assert control over her. "This place is a new beginning, and I intend to make my own way in the world." If she could convince Luz of her self-confidence, perhaps she could convince herself.

Luz snorted. "Never stop dreaming, Viv."

After threading through the bustling shuttleport, Wim directed the group of women to climb a one-story platform and board an elevated caterpillar train that transported them on thin arching rails above the heads of the pedestrians. The clean and comfortable train car held two adjacent rows of silver benches. Delilah rose on her knees and eagerly pressed her face to the window. Sensing the curious eyes of the other passengers, Vivian repressed her desire to join her sister in staring at the view and focused on projecting a cultivated and incurious air.

In less than ten minutes, they arrived at their stop. From the train platform, Vivian could see over the high walls into a grouping of modest buildings. Small, sculpted trees lined the curved redstone walkway enveloping an open lawn dotted with incandescent boulders in shades of indigo and violet.

After ushering the women down from the platform, Wim led them to the towering gates. "Welcome to your new home," he said grandly, pressing his palm to the door key. The steel door swung open at his touch. When the women were inside, Wim dismissed their escort.

The gates swung shut and locked with a sharp click. Vivian's muscles tensed at the sound. The interior of the gate had no palm lock or handle.

I'm not trapped. I'm not a prisoner.

Her breath came too fast, and the pace of her heartbeat felt alarming.

Delilah slipped a hand into hers. "We can climb these walls," she whispered in Vivian's ear. "This light gravity makes us superheroes."

Vivian huffed a laugh. "Superheroes?" She focused on the pressure of her sister's hand. Vivian was supposed to be the strong one. She was supposed to protect her baby sister like she'd done her whole life. Not fold immediately upon arrival.

I'm safe. I led us to safety.

She took a breath and let it out slowly, mentally counting backward from ten.

"Keep up, girls," Wim commanded.

Delilah tugged on her hand, and Vivian allowed her little sister to lead the way. Ten paces. Twenty. They reached their destination—a squat building adjacent to the compound's high walls.

Inside, the building contained a row of clean utilitarian bedrooms, each with two twin beds and a narrow closet, a shared bathroom with stalls and a row of showers, and a kitchen and dining area large enough to fit all thirty of them.

Vivian flashed to the rows of hammocks the thirty women had slept in on the weightless ship, and, before that, to the one-room tent she'd shared with her parents and Delilah. At the camp, the walk to the filthy bathrooms took ten minutes and could be so dangerous after dark that Vivian had learned years ago to monitor her water intake carefully after sunset.

"It's not much, I'm afraid," Wim bemoaned, oblivious to the way the women's eyes fixed on the bowl of real apples, oranges, and bananas. "The Intelligence asks you to consider this place your temporary base until you select a partner."

Vivian drifted to the kitchen. The sink turned on at her touch, letting out a stream of clean water. She opened the large refrigerator and stifled a gasp. Packages of fully cooked cultured meat, soy cheese, leafy vegetables, and berries greeted her. Vivian opened the cabinets to find sandwich bread, pita, bowls of potatoes and tomatoes, cooking oil, and spices. Her thin frame trembled, and she blinked back unwelcome tears.

Wim's augmented eye swiveled to her face, unnervingly out of sync with his human one. "I will leave you to select bedrooms and settle yourselves. The clothier will be by this afternoon to take your measurements. I will return in one sol."

When they were sure he'd departed, the women fell upon the kitchen, laughing as they haggled over food. Vivian wasn't much of a cook and allowed Luz to take charge of her meal. Soon, the two women were seated at a side table away from the group, eating large bites of pita sandwiches with juicy cultured chicken, crisp tomatoes, and crunchy romaine lettuce.

"This tastes like my favorite street vendor in Manhattan," Luz said around a mouthful of food. She closed her eyes. "Forty-Fifth and Ninth. When I was a dancer, I'd get shawarma every night before my shift. Until the flood."

"I didn't know you danced," Vivian said. "Were you ever on Broadway?"

Luz pressed her lips together in amusement. "Viv, honey, it wasn't that kind of dancing."

Vivian flushed. "Oh, of course." She was always stepping in it with Luz, unable to fully mask her naïveté.

"I don't know if these Martians are going to fall in love with you or eat you alive." Luz curled her full lips in a smile that mixed mockery and affection. Her friend was exactly what Vivian wished she could be. Confident, pragmatic, worldly. Gorgeous, with a full head of straight dark brown hair, glowing tan skin, and a lush curvy figure. Luz might have ended up the same as Vivian—trapped in a camp after losing her home to a storm—but before that, she'd seen the world. She'd *lived.*

"If we have food like this every day, it doesn't matter. As long as Delilah makes a good match, and we both can send enough funds home for our parents to buy their way out of the camp, I'll be fine." Vivian looked over to Delilah where she stood on the other side of the room, playfully popping grapes into her friend Camille's mouth.

"What do you want for yourself?"

Vivian shrugged. "I don't care." And she didn't. Her only goal was finding someone who made her skin crawl less than Max Rinaldi.

"You must have some preferences. Men, women, other genders?"

Vivian rubbed her shoulder uncomfortably. "Men."

"I won't ask tall or short," Luz continued. "Or hefty, muscular, or lean. These Martians seem to come in one body type. Do you think their cocks are proportional to their heights?"

Laughing involuntarily, Vivian pressed her hands to her flaming cheeks. She wished she could dash off a glib, unruffled response instead of giggling like a schoolgirl at the word "cock."

"What do you look for in a man? Someone who can make you laugh? Or can take you on a nice date? Someone good in bed?" Luz waggled her eyebrows at Vivian.

"Stop it!" Vivian snorted and nearly spit out a mouthful of water. "You know I have no idea." The only experience she had with men was avoiding them—or trying to. She remembered the expressive brown eyes of the glowering Martian that Wim had called Counselor Dorsey. He'd been glaring at Wim, she realized suddenly, not her. There was something appealing about the angular planes of his face, so different from an Earther man.

"You did think of something. I can see it in your expression."

Vivian shook her head. "It doesn't matter. I'm here to find stability, not love."

CHAPTER TWO

60 Sols to Presentation Day

Vivian stared at the stranger reflected in the mirror. Her long curly brown hair was done up in an elaborate coiffure, and her dark eyes sparkled with the aid of cosmetics. The clothier, an artificial construct with a polite but firm personality, had insisted upon preparing the women's hair and makeup itself, moving efficiently from one to the next with steel limbs and inhuman speed.

The dress the clothier had foisted upon her was a floor-length cream ensemble studded with embroidered flowers and a silk bow at the back. The modest neckline covered her breasts, and the full capped sleeves hid her shoulders. She looked like a heroine from one of the ancient paperback Regency romances she'd find in Sumter's donated library. The fluffy fabric felt so different from the polyester jumpsuits she'd been issued for the voyage or the threadbare secondhand clothes available at the refugee camp. She'd never worn dresses at Sumter. Dresses attracted the wrong sort of attention from the bored men prowling the camp. Now, she felt confined and hampered by the unfamiliar skirts.

Once the women's appearance was deemed acceptable by the clothier and it had departed, Wim entered their dormitory, his single human eye alight with anticipation in his long narrow face. "Excellent. I find it a pleasure to see you clothed in the style of our culture. You will do us a credit." He pressed his long-fingered, ringed hand to his chest and gave a little bow. "Today, the great Constance Yarrow, Secretary of Arcadia and my esteemed patron, has honored us with a luncheon hosted in the banquet hall to introduce you to Martian society. My lady, in her wisdom, has heeded the will of the Intelligence to allow you a plethora of opportunities to obtain a satisfactory partner." Wim bustled around the room, passing out slim black earpieces and silver headsets with petite rectangular screens that came in front of the left eye. "The Intelligence has identified optimized matches, and these devices will guide you to interact with the guests determined to be most compatible with you as a spouse and co-parent."

Delilah placed her headset on her head and twirled like it was a tiara. "The perfect accessory to compliment my outfit." She gave an exaggerated curtsey as the headset wobbled, and several of the other women smiled fondly.

Vivian took hers from Wim automatically and stared down at it with a frown. "What's the Intelligence?"

Wim's brow furrowed. "Surely you must know of the Intelligence?"

"An AI," Camille offered. "When the tech billionaires came to Mars a couple hundred years ago, they created the Intelligence to help them build the domes."

"Very good, Miss Harris." Wim gave her a little bow. "The Intelligence has always guided Mars." He put his fist to his forehead in an unfamiliar gesture.

An AI was going to play matchmaker? *Ridiculous.* Vivian wrinkled her nose. "What if we select a partner who isn't an optimized match?"

"Ah, I don't think that's a likely outcome, my dear. The Intelligence is powered by the wisdom of the whole of human history and is never mistaken. Your optimized matches have compatible values, temperaments, and sexual proclivities. All potential partners have been screened to confirm they're of appropriate social standing and have sufficient income to support a wife." Vivian watched him glance at Luz as he said, "They've been vetted against risk factors such as mental health defects, a tendency toward sexual violence, experiences with trauma, and other suboptimal traits."

Tough, unflappable Luz shivered at his words.

Vivian thought of her friend Evie from the camp who had gotten pregnant through rape and still loved her baby fiercely with every fiber of her being. "Experiences with trauma?" She blurted out. "Mental health defects? You think people who've had a hard life shouldn't become parents? What does that say about us, then?"

"Ah, you are to be our new resident skeptic, I see," Wim said through clenched teeth. "My esteemed lady does relish a challenge. The Intelligence guides us to optimize our limited resources here on Mars. A lesson Earth could badly use."

Luz shot her a look that clearly said, *Shut up, Viv.* "We are new here and eager to learn."

Vivian clamped her jaw on further argument. Right, she needed to be careful here. Her position was precarious, and her parents' future hung in the balance. Sumter had taught her self-preservation was often achieved through silence, but it galled Vivian to simply swallow her objections and go along without debate. How could she ever find a new beginning if she couldn't speak her mind?

"Just so, Miss Flores." Wim nodded to Luz in approval. "Red Mothers, it's time to find your partners."

The compound wasn't much larger than a couple of football fields, encompassing their dormitory and several additional buildings hugging the high walls. The middle of the space was wide and open, their path lined with sculpted mandarin orange trees. Instead of grass, Wim explained, creeping thyme served as a ground cover, requiring minimal water and enhancing the air quality. The thyme bloomed an amethyst hue, bathing the afternoon walk in color. Large boulders dotted the ground cover, their shimmering colors exotic to Vivian's Earthborn eyes.

In a matter of minutes, they arrived at a square white building with open arched French doors. The harmonious sounds of instrumental music wafted toward them. Vivian raised her chin and stepped inside.

The party was already in motion. Long-limbed Martians wearing formal clothing and elaborate head coverings gathered in small groups conversing, casually holding vibrantly colored stemmed glasses in their long, elegant fingers. The women wore dresses similar to Vivian's, tailored to their long slim bodies, and wide hats adorned with real flowers. The men wore brightly patterned vests under sober well-cut tailcoats with shiny black top hats. The sumptuous decor matched the Martians' clothing. Tall stalks of irises and lilies covered every surface, and crystal chandeliers brightened the room in a shimmering rainbow of light.

Earther servers clad in simple black uniforms moved quietly and efficiently through the crowd. They were the only other Earthers in attendance, Vivian realized with unease.

"The Red Mothers," Wim announced, his voice artificially amplified. He gave a little bow in the women's direction.

The Martians murmured among themselves, looking Vivian and the other women up and down with frank appraisement. Some lowered their headsets onto their left eyes, and Vivian observed how they considered each woman in turn, eyes flicking over the data.

"Don your headsets and earpieces, if you please," Wim commanded the women in a low voice. "And no drinking, ladies. We would not want to get sloppy. First impressions are critical."

Delilah stifled a giggle.

Vivian stepped further into the room and pasted a smile onto her face. Her hands shook, and there was a leaden weight in her belly. A bearded Martian man nodded to her. Next to him, a copper-haired austere woman looked down her aquiline nose at Vivian.

"Mr. Nakamura is a close ally of my lady Secretary Yarrow and a noble patron of the arts," Wim's voice came in her ear. Vivian jerked in startlement. "An excellent choice for a spouse, if overly pretentious." On the far side of the vast room, Vivian could see Wim in a crowd of Martians, gesturing with one ringed finger. "Miss King has excellent credentials, but, in my humble opinion, is haughty and discourteous." The earpiece, Vivian realized suddenly. Was Wim's commentary pre-recorded?

"Vivian Bowen." The man stepped forward and swept off his top hat to bow, revealing straight black hair down to his shoulders. "I see you enjoy reading. Poetry?"

Mitzi King—head of the Arcadia Banking Group and Council Minister of the Treasury, her headset supplied—let out a huff. "Poetry? Don't be ridiculous, Ren. She has an eighth-grade education."

"And nearly a year of high school," Vivian corrected softly. To the man, she said, "I prefer fiction."

"Oh, lovely!" His light brown eyes crinkled in a smile. "What kind?"

"The Bronte sisters, Alcott, Austen." A half-truth. She wasn't about to mention the mental escape she'd found in romance authors writing about the same period hundreds of years after those women had died. And here she was, in an uncanny Martian re-creation of the Regency era. She didn't remember any of her books describing the dresses as quite so cumbersome and restricting.

Mitzi snorted. "Earther drivel."

Ren frowned reproachfully at his companion. "You could show a modicum of respect to our new friend, Minister."

"I could, but why bother?" Mitzi said to Ren without looking at Vivian. "Her sexual preferences don't include women."

Ren turned to include Vivian in the conversation. "The Intelligence believes a healthy sexual relationship is a key factor in a successful marriage and serves to reinforce the co-parent bond." To his credit, he delivered the information while keeping his eyes on her face.

Even so, Vivian repressed a shudder of revulsion. The AI cared about the sex life she'd have with her new husband? Would it . . . *monitor* her somehow?

"I—I thought we were to conceive children in-vitro," she stammered.

Vivian had only just arrived at this party, and her head was already swimming with confusion. What had she been told when she signed the contract at the camp? Martian doctors would retrieve eggs from her body and later implant a genetically modified embryo with her and her partner's genetic material.

"Of course you will. That's why you're here, isn't it?" Mitzi's voice held a trace of impatience. "But the Intelligence wants us matched on sexual compatibility anyway. Even if it doesn't have a body of its own, the Intelligence understands how decent sex can ease the tedium of marriage." Her thin lips pressed in a smirk. "Who am I to argue with the wisdom of the Intelligence?" She fixed sharp eyes on Delilah, already basking in the attention of a group of admirers. "I'll try her."

Vivian breathed through a tightness in her chest. Across the room, Delilah let out a sparkling peal of laughter, and her new Martian suitors smiled at her enthusiasm. Vivian would not allow her sunny, bright-eyed little sister to choose someone who regarded marriage as tedious.

Before Mitzi could approach Delilah, Ren grabbed her arm and nodded to the arrival of a new group. "Would you look at that," he remarked to Mitzi in an undertone. "I didn't expect Dorsey to allow his pets to come out and play."

"Fucking hypocrite," Mitzi hissed, the tendons on her long neck protruding. "So much for his sanctimonious bitching in the last Council session. If Yarrow wasn't protecting him, I'd crush him like a bug."

Vivian swiveled and adjusted her headset to observe the three newcomers. Caspian Hayes was rated a 60-percent compatibility match. He held a seat on the Council, invested in the terraforming industry, and maintained a community hospital with his sister Ivey, the headset helpfully informed her. His rosy face held an open, affable expression as he took in the room with pleasure.

"Mr. Hayes is a well-respected member of society, but I believe he is too easily influenced and weak-minded," Wim's pre-recorded voice chirped in her ear.

Ivey's pinkish skin and sandy hair resembled her brother, but her cynical detached smile did not. Even though her sardonic expression appealed to Vivian, the headset warned that Ivey was only a 20-percent compatibility match. Why did the Intelligence put so much stock in co-parenting with a sex partner? She wasn't attracted to Ivey, but she might enjoy raising children with a girlfriend who shared her sense of humor.

"Despite her altruistic pursuits, Miss Hayes is insufficiently respectful to the superior intellect of the Intelligence," Wim opined. Were any of the potential spouses good enough for Wim's exacting standards?

Next to Ivey stood the disagreeable man she'd seen at the shuttleport the day before. The headset flashed a warning. *Xavier Dorsey. Unsuitable Match. Do Not Engage.* Putting the headset down on a side table, Vivian looked at the man with both real eyes. He was startlingly handsome with rich brown eyes and dark skin. His open jacket revealed a brocade vest of silver and navy that hugged his trim torso. Vivian hadn't been sure she could be attracted to the stretched-out Martian physique, but Xavier's tall, elegant body made her mouth run dry.

Until he ruined it by scowling at all in attendance and heading immediately for the bar.

"Mr. Dorsey may have honorable connections to her ladyship, but he is blasphemous, disagreeable, hubristic, supercilious—" Vivian pulled the earpiece out of her ear and dropped it in an abandoned champagne flute.

Across the room, Xavier accepted a glass of white wine from the Earther bartender. He angled his lean body forward across the bar and said something that made the bartender flash his white teeth in a laugh and lay a hand on Xavier's forearm.

What caused the Intelligence to label Xavier Dorsey as unsuitable? Was he an unsuitable match for all the women or just for her? And why had he been watching them at the shuttleport?

"I do hope you'll come to agree with me," Ren said to her.

Vivian jerked her head away from watching Xavier to realize Mitzi had left their side, and Ren had been speaking to her. "Of course," she replied automatically.

"Good, good. That is the foremost reason why I adore Martian poetry," Ren continued, oblivious to her distraction. "Let me introduce you to the works of Kenji Nakamura, my great-great-grandparent. They reclaimed the ancient method of Haiku, traditionally used to mark the seasonal changes of nature, and applied it to the harsh Martian landscape." He closed his eyes and pressed a long-fingered hand to his chest. "Stillness and quiet / A ship scatters sand and rocks / Crash! Silence again."

Vivian waited for the rest. Ren peaked his eyes open. "What do you think?"

"Oh." Vivian attempted a smile. "Very nice. Thank you."

"That's Kenji's gift. So simple, so profound. Please allow me to bestow another upon you."

When Vivian was able to escape Ren reciting Martian poetry at her, she found herself in an equally tedious exchange with a man describing the distilling process for making Martian vodka. In detail.

Then, a Martian man and woman approached her, holding hands. Vivian hadn't returned her headset to her eye and didn't catch their names. "As you can see," the man said with a half-smile. "I am already wed. Reverend Adair has assured us that the Intelligence welcomes triad marriages for Red Mothers."

"I've heard that Earthers have particular views about monogamy." The woman leaned forward with bright eyes. "But I can promise you, I don't mind sharing. Triads are common here. Martian women have often had to share their husbands with Earther women if they want children. I want to raise the children who will break the Martian dependency on Earther mothers once and for all."

Concealing her surprise, Vivian murmured, "I am open to all arrangements."

Had she known this possibility? So eager for the opportunity to leave the camp, she hadn't asked enough follow-up questions of the recruiter. Why hadn't she taken the time to read more about Martian culture on the ship, instead of losing herself in Earther romance novels? Now that she was here, everything was happening bewilderingly fast. Vivian took a deep breath and tried to steady herself.

None of it matters, she told herself. *As long as we're safe.*

She found herself alone at last and looked around for Delilah. Her sister was engaged in a lively conversation with Caspian, one hand holding her hat in place as her beaming face angled up to look at him. Unwillingly, Vivian's eyes strayed again to Xavier, who had settled against a wall near the food.

Unable to resist her curiosity, Vivian walked toward the man. His lip curled, surveying the mingling crowd. As she made her way through the party, Caspian gave Delilah a bow and moved to stand at Xavier's side. Vivian paused to linger at the food table, close enough to listen to their conversation.

"Come on, X," Caspian said. "Your aunt will be arriving any moment. You know she'll want to see you mingling, not standing about by yourself moping."

Xavier snorted. "Aunt Constance is perfectly well aware that I detest this business. The only woman here whose company I enjoy is your sister, and she's off-limits in my aunt's little experiment, thank goodness."

"Keep up, X. Ivey has put her hat in the ring as a potential spouse."

"Is that right? She didn't tell me."

"I'm not surprised. You're being terribly judgmental, even for you. Ivey is desperate to be a mother, for all she tries to hide it." Caspian clapped a hand on Xavier's shoulder. "But they've brought us thirty girls, enough for all of us if we take advantage of this head start Yarrow has given the Council. You know she isn't shipping out more until she's confirmed this first set has born us healthy, strong-boned babies."

Xavier grunted. "I saw you enjoying Delilah Bowen's company. A bit young, isn't she?"

Vivian looked up, startled, as they spoke of her sister, unable to hide her eavesdropping.

"She's the most beautiful girl I have ever beheld. And her sister is very pretty as well. Come with me. Let's become acquainted with her elder sister, Vivian. If our children were cousins, you'd be family in truth."

Xavier caught Vivian's eye. To his friend, he said coldly, "You know perfectly well she is not enough to tempt *me*. You'd better return to Delilah. You're wasting your time trying to change my mind." He abandoned Caspian to return to the bar.

Vivian's cheeks grew hot with anger and embarrassment. She pictured herself going up to Xavier at the bar and saying something devastatingly cutting and witty.

If only she could think of the right line.

The music ceased abruptly mid-song, and the murmur of voices hushed. The room's full attention turned to an older Martian woman who had stepped inside the hall. She moved with a brisk elegance, aided by a carved wooden cane, shaking hands with the Martians and exchanging greetings. Vivian recognized her on sight.

Secretary Constance Yarrow, leader of Arcadia.

The person responsible for bringing Vivian to Mars.

"Thank you, my dear friends," Constance called as she positioned herself to stand in the center of the banquet hall. Her dark wrinkled hands clutched her wooden cane. "And welcome to the Arcadia Dome, Red Mothers." The Martians around her tapped two fingers on each hand together in a light clap. "By the grace of the Intelligence, we have, at long last, formulated a solution to our generational problem. The Intelligence has generously decreed a sixty-day window to allow all Red Mothers the opportunity to select a suitable spouse and prepare to bear the future of Mars. Gentleman, ladies, and gentlefolk, over the next sixty days, please show the Red Mothers the famous hospitality of the Founding Families. On Presentation Day, we will debut the matches before the Council and all of Mars and hold the largest wedding ceremony Mars has ever seen."

Sixty days. Vivian's head spun. No one had bothered to warn her that she would only have two Earth months to choose her husband and the father of her children. How could she make such a monumental decision in sixty days?

She would have to try.

For the next hour, she determinedly spoke to nearly every man in attendance. She swallowed her personality and spoke softly and demurely. She listened and made agreeable noises until she wanted to scream.

Finally, when she could stand it no longer, she escaped to the bar. “White wine, please,” she said, trying to sound as if she knew what she was about. The only alcohol she’d ever tasted was Carolina moonshine.

Vivian took a sip and gagged.

The Earther bartender smiled at her reaction. “Too sweet, I know. The Martians like to make ice wine with grapes flash-frozen in the natural atmosphere. What I wouldn’t give for a dry South African Pinot gris.”

She nodded agreement as if she understood anything about wine and went to find a bare spot on the wall.

“You’re the first Red Mother to order a drink all afternoon,” an amused, posh voice commented.

Vivian turned her head to see Xavier Dorsey leaning against the wall, half-hidden in the shadow of a curtain. “Whereas you seem to have had several.”

Xavier swirled his half-full glass and raised one corner of his mouth. “Have you been watching me?”

“Only to understand why you’re here if you have no intention of meeting any of us.”

“I am in attendance to lodge a protest.” He fingered a silver button on his suit jacket lapel. “Why are you here?”

Hadn’t the headset told her this man wasn’t a match? Good. She could finally say what she really thought. “To get paid.”

Xavier barked a short laugh. “So mercenary. You express yourself with refreshing candor, Miss Bowen.”

“Even if I’m not enough to tempt you, Mr. Dorsey?”

His dark brown eyes held hers. "Oh, I'm very tempted, Miss Bowen," he murmured in a low voice that sent a shiver of heat through her. And then his tone turned harsh, like an abrupt plunge into icy cold water. "But not enough to participate in this despicable and dangerous experiment. Find someone else to bankroll your lifestyle." He gave her a short mocking bow and walked away.

Vivian sputtered at his retreating back. "Asshole," she muttered and tried to shake off the spark he'd ignited. An unsuitable match indeed.

But as she watched him walk away, her unease grew. *Dangerous? Where's the danger here?*

CHAPTER THREE

59 Sols to Presentation Day

"Y'all gotta come see this!" Camille's high-pitched voice pierced the walls of Vivian and Delilah's room.

Still in bed, her sister sat up. "What is it?"

Vivian put down the brittle paperback she'd brought with her from Sumter and stood from her position on the floor. "Probably nothing. You know how dramatic Camille can be."

In the dining room, the other women were gathered around a built-in console displaying a video. Against clips of yesterday's luncheon, an eager voice-over said, "The Founding Families came out in force to welcome the first Red Mothers to Mars. Secretary Yarrow opened the event wearing her signature Cartier diamonds and an exquisite gown of imported French silk designed by local rising star Po Quincy." Yarrow's brief speech to the luncheon crowd replayed on screen. Vivian's stomach clenched all over again when she heard Yarrow mention the sixty-day window.

"This reporter was shocked to see outspoken opponent of the Red Mothers initiative Counselor Xavier Dorsey in attendance, sporting a scandalous pin on his lapel."

The video turned to Xavier standing on the pathway outside the banquet hall with a Martian reporter. "You're looking especially dashing this afternoon, Counselor. The vest is quite becoming."

She tucked a lock of hair behind her ear and gave him a coy look. “Tell me, Mr. Dorsey, about the pin you’re wearing.”

First the bartender, now the reporter, Vivian thought. *What could they possibly see in him?*

Not that she cared.

“I wear a feather quill to symbolize my desire to write a new chapter in Arcadia’s history, free from the influence of AI.” His dark brows drew together. “The Intelligence may have conceived of the breakthrough in reproductive technology, but it’s not equipped to make decisions of ethics. I call upon my aunt, Secretary Yarrow, and the Council to halt the Red Mothers initiative immediately before further harm is done to these vulnerable women.”

Over more footage of the luncheon, the voiceover continued, “The Red Mothers hardly seemed vulnerable yesterday as they enjoyed their status as the guests of honor. The beautiful Earther women made their first appearance in Martian society dressed in a fashionable assortment of colorful gowns.”

The women on screen were unfamiliar, elegant socialites. Luz’s ruby-red lips made her normally closed expression seem mysterious. Delilah’s blond curls bounced as she laughed, dwarfed by the surrounding Martians who stood several heads taller. Camille’s smooth dark brown skin contrasted with her bright blue gown as she turned to reveal the dress’s low back. Vivian spotted her own pale face among the flashes of the women mingling in the crowd, delicate and ethereal. The Red Mothers on display were pampered, well-dressed, and desired, showing no trace of the desperate Earther refugees in jumpsuits who’d arrived on Mars only the day before.

“All eyes are now on the Red Mothers as the richest and most powerful descendants of the Founding Families vie for their hands in marriage. In the next sixty days, they will pick their spouses and prepare to bear the future hope of Mars. And as they do, you know you can count on *Arcadia Life* to keep you informed."

"We're famous," Camille's cousin Felicia exclaimed. "Imagine that!"

Leaning against the back wall, Luz drawled, "*Can* you be famous in a population of only fifty thousand people?"

"They have their own news here, don't they?" Camille retorted. "Why do you always shit over everything, Luz?"

"That outlet—" Luz pointed one finger at the now-black screen. "Is a gossip rag if I ever saw one."

"Girls." Delilah spun around the room, her white nightgown swirling around her. "We did enough bickering on the ship. Play nice. We're all in this together."

"If you insist." Camille gave her an indulgent smile. All the women doted on Delilah—the baby among them. And how could they not? Her optimism had made the tedious and claustrophobic nine-month voyage toward an unknown future bearable.

"I can't wait to be courted." Delilah giggled.

Vivian made a face of distaste. If yesterday was anything to go by, she wasn't going to enjoy anything about this experience.

"Come on, Viv." Delilah smirked. "You must have loved all those tall men dressed like they stepped off the cover of a Regency romance novel."

Vivian snorted. "Tall and well-dressed? Is that all it takes to impress you? You really haven't met any decent men." Not that Vivian had either. Except in her books.

"I've met Dad."

Vivian's chest tightened. Surely by now her parents had received their message that they'd safely landed on Mars. Why hadn't they sent their daughters a response? Vivian tried to push away her unease. She'd left. The Rinaldi brothers would have no cause to harass her family now that she was gone.

"None of us have met any decent men," Felicia said. "I think they make them especially mean in Louisiana."

"Preach," Camille murmured.

Another woman, Shiloh, barked a humorless laugh. "Then you've never been to California."

Delilah rested her head on Shiloh's shoulder. "We're on Mars, now. All the men are perfect gentlemen."

The outer door opened of its own accord, and a two-foot-tall metal box creeped in on skinny legs.

"What the hell is that?" Camille shrieked.

The box opened and an inner shelf raised with a whirring sound to place a collection of envelopes on the dining room table. With a final beep, it turned around and departed, closing the front door behind it with a spindly metal claw.

The women stared after the robot for a moment. Then Shiloh moved to pick up one of the envelopes. "Real paper. Can you believe it? This one's for you, Delilah."

Delilah eagerly ripped it open and scanned the contents. "Caspian Hayes wants to . . . What does 'promenade' mean?"

"Walk," Luz said. "Pretentiously."

"Caspian?" Vivian frowned. "He wants you for your looks. Yesterday, I heard him call you the most beautiful girl he ever saw."

"Did he? Well, I *am* the most beautiful girl he's ever seen. I think he's good-looking, too, in the strange Martian style. I guess we'll get used to it." She grasped Vivian's hand to pull her from the wall and spun her in a circle. "Who did you find yesterday, Viv? Xavier Dorsey was staring at you the whole lunch."

"With disgust."

"No, more like—" Delilah took on an exaggerated deep voice. "Vivian Bowen, I despise you, but I can't help myself! I want you. I need you." The women around them giggled, and Luz raised her eyebrows at Vivian.

Vivian snorted. "Absolutely not!"

"We'll see."

Vivian thought about how he'd toyed with her. Flirtatious one moment and rude the next. "I wouldn't pick him if he were the last person on this planet. He's an obnoxious, horrible man."

The other women were snatching up their own letters and passing them out. Shiloh shoved one into Vivian's hands.

"Caspian's coming!" Delilah exclaimed, brandishing a letter. "Here! In one hour. I have to get ready." She scampered from the room.

Vivian put her letter to the side unopened and went to the now-blank console. She toggled through options on the screen until she located her electronic mailbox.

Empty.

Her parents possessed no tech. They would need to pay for access or rely on the kindness of an aid worker. But her friend Evie owned a hard-won solar-powered comm. Sure, it was glitchy, but she should have gotten it to work by now.

The women around her were reading aloud their letters and laughing. Vivian picked hers up and tore it open. Ren. He'd written her a poem. Vivian refreshed her mailbox again.

When Delilah returned, clad in a lavender dress that sparkled against her alabaster skin, Vivian was still sitting at the console. "What's wrong?" her sister asked.

"Nothing."

Delilah leaned over Vivian's shoulder to check her own mailbox. Also empty. "They're fine, Viv. Dad's probably making a scrap metal trade right now. And you know Mom has an extra-large pot of brown stew bubbling away, ready to sell. They got on okay for thirty years before they met you—they don't need you mothering them."

"I don't mother them."

"You do. You have ever since we got to the camp."

"Well, somebody had to take care of them. And you."

When they'd first arrived at Sumter, her father had moved like a walking corpse. In all the time she'd grown up in their comfortable home by the ocean, he'd never let on how much debt he'd taken on to keep their lifestyle afloat, even as the rising sea level made it impossible to sell their house.

And then the storm hit.

Vivian cast around for a change of subject. "Did you get many letters?"

"So many. I'm *very* popular."

"I don't understand this place. Our role here is confusing."

Delilah playfully shoved Vivian's arm. "You're here to find a husband and have his tall Martian babies. And you know what I believe? We're going to both marry for love."

Vivian snorted. "In sixty days?"

"Yes! Is that so hard to believe?"

I'm not falling in love, Vivian thought. But to her sister, she only said, "Sweet baby sister, if any of us falls in love, it will be you."

"He's here, Delilah!" Shiloh shouted from the window.

Delilah fluffed her blond ringlets and moved to open the outer door. "Mr. Hayes." She wobbled an exaggerated curtsey.

"Ah, Miss Bowen," Caspian said from the doorway. "I trust you received my invitation?"

"I did. And I would love to *promenade* with you." She opened her eyes very wide and blinked up at him.

"Has anyone ever told you, Miss Bowen, that your eyes are the exact shade of blue of a Martian sunset?"

Delilah ducked her head. "No." And then she smiled. "But I've only been on Mars for two days. I haven't seen a sunset yet."

"We must remedy this. I shall take you to my terraforming facility outside the domes. There, the view is unobstructed."

"What's it like?"

"Like a miracle," Caspian whispered. "When the stars come out, they blanket the navy sky by the thousands, and the horizon is lit with glowing violet light."

"Wow," Delilah breathed.

Caspian's lips were parted as he gazed down upon her. Someone giggled, breaking the spell.

"Excellent," he said briskly. Touching a hand to his top hat, he murmured, "Ladies," and held open the door for Delilah.

Luz came to stand beside Vivian against the wall. "Everyone is acting so fucking stupid—like we don't know what can happen when one side has all the control. You'd think the girls would have learned something in the camps instead of falling happily into this fake-ass fairy tale."

Vivian couldn't help but feel a bit proud that Luz put her in a different category from her sister and the other younger women. She wanted the sophisticated, worldly Luz to see her as a peer, despite their age gap. "Delilah told me she wants to fall in love." She stepped into the kitchen and looked through the window above the sink where she could see Delilah and Caspian beginning their walk.

Luz followed her and leaned against the counter. "A lot of the girls do. I guess it makes sense to dream of a Cinderella story after escaping our shit lives on Earth. But I don't think real love is possible with such a power imbalance."

"Have you ever been in love?" Vivian asked. There was so much about Luz's past that she didn't know, even after nine months of friendship.

"No," Luz said bluntly. "I was once in love with the idea of a man, not the asshole he turned out to be. You can't know what someone's like until you're behind closed doors."

In the distance, Vivian could see Delilah's shining face upturned to Caspian's. His head bent attentively toward hers. "He seems kind. Or he puts on a good act."

To Vivian's surprise, Luz shivered. "Do you believe what Wim told us about the Intelligence? Could an AI be aware enough to know if a man was safe to be alone with?"

Vivian shrugged. "I have no idea."

"Wim told me the Intelligence tracks everyone on the dome."

Vivian looked up at the ceiling uneasily. "Is it watching us? Right now?"

"Yeah, I think so." Luz rubbed her arms. "I was doing okay, on the ship. But now that we're here . . . Viv, I'm fucking terrified to pick someone. I've never—I've never known a man who was kind. Not their true face." She touched her flawless, glowing skin, right below her left eye, and winced.

"I know." Vivian leaned her head against Luz's shoulder. "It'll be different here. You'll see."

Perhaps if she said it often enough, she would start to believe it.

CHAPTER FOUR

57 Sols to Presentation Day

"Who's first, ladies?" the doctor asked. Although she was clearly a Martian, she wore plain slacks, a T-shirt, and sneakers—so different from the formal old-fashioned clothing of the Martian oligarchs. A simple white lab coat didn't fully hide the silver augmentations covering her body.

Silence greeted the question. From her corner spot next to Luz in the packed clinic waiting room, Vivian watched Camille and her cousin Felicia exchange a darting look. Delilah examined her fingernails.

Vivian pushed herself off the wall. "I'll go."

There's nothing to be afraid of, Vivian told herself as she followed the doctor down the white-washed hallway. *This is the reason we're here.*

The small exam room held gleaming machines and a medical bed. Vivian swallowed.

"Sit down and lift your dress above your waist," the doctor instructed. Her eyes flicked, and a screen mounted to the wall flared to life. "Name?"

Face heating, Vivian pulled up her dress and leaned back against the bed. The vinyl stuck to her bare thighs. "Vivian Bowen."

"From the Carolina Republic in the American Federation?" The doctor's eyes moved rapidly as she stared into the middle of the room.

On the screen, Vivian saw her own name and vital statistics appear like magic. She shivered. "That's right."

"I'm Dr. Chavez." Her eyes focused on Vivian. One orb was artificial, like Wim's, although it seemed to do a better job staying in sync with her human one. "I trust that Reverend Adair explained what to expect today."

Vivian licked her lips. "Not in so many words." For all that he claimed to be their guide, Wim hadn't done enough to prepare Vivian for anything so far.

The doctor let out a short impatient huff. "Nothing too serious on this initial visit. Bloodwork and an ultrasound. It'll be less invasive than a pap smear." She opened a built-in drawer.

"A what?" Vivian asked.

Dr. Chavez lifted a syringe and frowned down at her. "A pap smear. You know, the cell collection process your OBGYN uses to test for cervical cancer."

Vivian clutched the edge of the medical bed, unable to look away from the needle. "What's an OBGYN?"

Dr. Chavez stared at her blankly. "Are they using a different term now on Earth? Your doctor who specializes in female reproductive health."

Vivian let out an involuntary snort of laughter. When had she ever had a doctor? Maybe a pediatrician, when her parents could still afford one. "Right, my doctor. Can we get this over with? I hate needles."

The doctor wrapped Vivian's arm in a rubbery blue ribbon and pushed the needle into her inner elbow. Vivian watched with sick fascination as the blood left her body.

Dr. Chavez placed the vial of red liquid directly into a small rectangular device in the corner of the room, and it began to whir. "Give that a few minutes."

"What are you looking for?"

"The level of follicle-stimulating hormone in your system."

Vivian didn't understand what that meant, but she wasn't sure how many more questions the strange doctor would tolerate.

Dr. Chavez pulled a small white oval object out of another drawer and coated it with clear gel. "This will be cold," she said abruptly and pressed the object against the side of Vivian's bare stomach. The screen mounted to the wall displayed a distorted gray image. "Good," Dr. Chavez said without glancing at the screen. "You have plenty of follicles." She removed the device and handed Vivian a paper towel. "Clean yourself off." She went to the instrument holding Vivian's bloodwork. The machine beeped, and the doctor removed the vial.

Vivian wiped the sticky substance from her belly, pulled down her dress, and sat up on the bed. "What do you see?"

"You're ready," Dr. Chavez told her. The screen with her data began populating with new information. *5.5 mIU/mL. 27.3 pmol.* "We'll begin treatment tonight, and in about two weeks your body will be prepared for the egg retrieval."

Vivian ignored the way her chest tightened. "Good—that's good."

Dr. Chavez handed her a clear package with a needle and a bag of vials. "Self-administer these follicle-stimulating and luteinizing hormones daily."

Vivian took the bag gingerly. "How?"

"In the stomach." She touched Vivian's lower belly. "Right here."

The bag shook in her hands. "For two weeks?" She could do this. She'd been brought to Mars to do this.

The needle looked very sharp.

"We're finished here. May the wisdom of the Intelligence guide you." The doctor brought her fist to her forehead in the same gesture Vivian had seen from Wim.

In the hall, Luz met her, coming out of another exam room. Her light expression was so unlike Luz that Vivian came to a halt.

"What is it?" Vivian asked.

"I'm ready to begin the treatment."

"Me too. Why do you look so damn cheerful about it?"

Luz grabbed her arm and murmured. "I'll tell you when we're out of here."

In the reception area, Vivian gave a thumbs-up to her sister seated with Camille and asked Luz, "Shouldn't we wait for everyone else?"

"I'm not spending my whole day in this tiny waiting room. Let's go."

They stepped unescorted onto the Martian street. The clinic was located in the central business district at the midpoint of the dome, surrounded by ten-story buildings that nearly scraped the top. The dome's translucent shimmer was so much higher and farther away compared to their compound located closer to the dome's sloped edge. Today, the sky was a warm butterscotch color.

The broad, gleaming street teemed with pedestrians clustered in groups of tall Martians and short Earthers. Two lanky Martian children ran past giggling, followed by their harried Earther parents. Inviting storefronts, cafés, and taverns framed the street, their facades bursting with planters of tall, colorful flowers. Above them, supported by arching rails, caterpillar trains glided at a sedate pace. Not a single groundcar was in sight.

Luz pulled Vivian along to follow behind a group of chattering Earthers in coveralls with bandanas covering their heads. "I've heard the Intelligence is less likely to perceive your words in a crowded street," she murmured in Vivian's ear.

"Why's that?" Vivian asked curiously.

"The way I understand it, the Intelligence is embedded into the dome itself and is able to observe everything happening—it can even perceive through ceilings and walls. Not to mention it has access to every electronic device in the dome."

Vivian shuddered. Why would the Martians willingly go along with living under constant surveillance?

"But what I've heard is that if you're surrounded by a lot of busy chatter, it might not be able to pick out your conversation."

"Alright. Start talking then."

"When the Arcadia rep came to New York, he didn't want to recruit me because I'm so old."

"Old! You aren't old."

"I'm thirty-two," Luz said in a low voice. "The ideal recruit for the Red Mothers initiative is eighteen to twenty-five."

"How'd you get in?"

Luz shrugged. "I fucked him. And he lied on the form for me. But ever since, I've been waiting for them to send me back, once they realized the truth."

"Could the doctor track your age?"

"If he could, he didn't mention it. My levels were all right."

"Red Mothers." A Martian man in a bright red uniform with a tricorn hat bowed to them. "The reverend has requested I escort you back home."

Vivian and Luz exchanged a glance. "So much for escaping," Luz muttered. "I guess the Intelligence *is* watching us."

In the train car, the man positioned himself across from them and folded his arms.

"Are you a cop?" Vivian asked him. Even from across the aisle, she could see the intricate detail work of the buttons of his scarlet tunic. He belonged in an oil painting, holding a rifle, not riding a solar-powered train car on Mars. The strange Martian clothing choices were still a mystery to Vivian.

He grunted. "A soldier. With the Arcadian militia. We keep the peace under the guidance of the Intelligence."

"Is there a lot of crime here?" Vivian asked.

"Of course not. The Intelligence's predictive algorithms prevent nearly all altercations." The soldier drummed his fingers on his knee. "But we may be called upon to defend our dome. By the grace of the Intelligence, Arcadia is the most well-resourced of all the Martian domes. What we have, we would die to protect."

Vivian frowned. "I thought the Intelligence was in all the Martian domes."

"The Intelligence is welcomed in every dome save one. But it is only in Arcadia that we worship the divine nature of the Intelligence." He raised one fist to the middle of his forehead and closed his eyes. "Under its guidance, Arcadia has flourished."

The other passengers within earshot raised fists to their foreheads. "We are grateful for the gifts of the Intelligence," they said in unison.

"That shit is creepy," Luz muttered in her ear.

"Save one?" Vivian prodded.

The soldier scowled. "I do not like to discuss the blasphemous Catena separatists."

"The Catena separatists? Who are they?"

"No one you need to worry about. The reverend will protect the Red Mothers from the threat they pose."

"Threat?" Vivian sat up straighter. "What threat?" She'd come to Mars to be done with threats to her safety.

The soldier pressed his lips together. "Forget I said anything." He turned his head to look out the window and folded his arms, clearly done indulging their curiosity.

Vivian shared an alarmed look with Luz.

Who were the Catena separatists?

And what did they want with the Red Mothers?

CHAPTER FIVE

55 Sols to Presentation Day

Vivian opened her eyes in the warm glow of the sun. She'd slept through the night for the first time since arriving on Mars. The extra forty minutes in a Martian day seemed to offer a chance to feel truly well-rested. Reaching her arms wide in her cozy bed, Vivian enjoyed the unfamiliar sensation of not being boxed in by any other bodies. Delilah was still asleep in the other bed, her legs curled into her stomach, facing the wall.

Before doing anything else, Vivian stopped by the dining room console to check her messages. Nothing. On the transport ship, they'd had almost no communication access. But it had now been five days since she'd landed and sent messages to her parents and Evie. She should have heard something by now.

In the bathroom, Vivian slipped off the soft, silken robe the artificial clothier had provided her, and stepped into the shower's warm cascade of water. She tried to let her worry for her parents and Evie run down the drain as she took the time to wash every inch of her body with a peppermint body wash dispensed from the wall and massage her scalp with a lavender shampoo. After nine months of sonic showers aboard the ship, she reveled in the sheer sensual joy of real hot water moving down her body.

After the shower, Vivian slipped the robe back on her clean skin and ducked her head under the built-in artificial styler. In a matter of minutes, the styler dried her long chestnut hair and gave it a soft curl. Vivian stepped back into her bedroom and dressed in a pale-yellow day dress with a sky-blue ribbon that gave her an unexpected wave of homesickness. The pinkish-red Martian sky, visible through the dome, served as a daily reminder that she was a stranger here.

She ran one hand through her silken hair and breathed in the scent of lavender, allowing herself a moment of pure indulgent bliss at the sensation of being clean, sweet smelling, and well dressed. Mars might still feel strange, but her new life came with benefits she was learning to appreciate.

Vivian turned to look at Delilah, who hadn't moved from her position curled on her side on the bed. Was her sister going to sleep all day?

"Delilah, wake up you sleepyhead." She snatched the covers off of Delilah's form.

Her sister moaned in response and grasped feebly for the blanket. Her pale face dripped with sweat.

Vivian's stomach plummeted. Sticking her head out the door, she shouted, "Luz! I need you." Without waiting for a response, she hurried back to kneel by her sister's bed. Vivian carefully tucked the blanket around Delilah's body and laid a hand against her brow. "You're hot."

"The room is spinning," Delilah whispered. "Viv, I feel strange."

Concealing her own terror, Vivian pushed the hair back from Delilah's clammy forehead and murmured, "Shh, shh."

Luz stuck her head in. "Shit. I'll make a call."

Vivian waited, holding Delilah's hand as her sister panted and whimpered in turn. Memories of the illnesses that had swept the camp passed through her mind. At the camp, if Delilah had been in this state, Vivian would be bracing herself for the possibility of her sister's death. Would it be different here?

Finally, Luz returned with Camille and Felicia beside her. Camille knelt in front of Delilah and pressed a cool cloth to her forehead. "My mom's a nurse. Or she was. Before." She turned over Delilah's arms and then pulled up her nightgown to expose her legs and belly. "No rash. Probably not measles." Delilah barely stirred, her eyes closed.

"We were vaccinated," Vivian whispered. "Before we got on the ship."

"For TB too?"

"I think so." Vivian swallowed. "How do we know what clinic we can afford here? Even if we pool all of our allowances from Wim, it won't be enough."

"Don't worry about that." Luz gestured to the door, where Caspian Hayes stood, chest heaving as if he'd run from the front gate. He crossed the room in two strides and crouched at Delilah's side.

Vivian moved out of his way and went to Luz in the doorway. "I thought you were calling Dr. Chavez!" she hissed. "Tell me you did not contact Caspian of all people?"

"Of course I did," Luz murmured in her ear. "You saw he owns a hospital, yes? We might as well allow some good to come of this. If he isn't as kind and thoughtful as he seems, better to find out now. And if he is, Delilah will have demonstrated she *needs* him. Men eat that shit up."

Caspian took Delilah's limp hand in his. "How long has she been this way?"

"She was fine yesterday evening," Vivian said. "Is it the fertility treatments? We've only been taking them a few days."

Caspian shook his head. "I'm not privy to the breakthrough in reproductive medicine the Intelligence has shared with Dr. Chavez, but I recognize these symptoms—a form of kinetosis caused when a new arrival has an incompatibility with Martian gravity." His normally affable expression was gone, replaced by a pale, pinched mouth and creased eyebrows. "You must allow me to treat Delilah in my hospital. At once."

Vivian hesitated. "We can't afford that."

Caspian jerked his head back. "Our hospital does not charge for its services."

Vivian had expected him to offer to cover the cost, not that there was no cost at all. At Sumter, any illness meant an agonizing scramble for sufficient funds for a medic visit and hours—or perhaps days—camped outside the clinic waiting to be seen.

"Please," Caspian continued. "Let me care for your sister. She will be safe at the hospital and well-treated. We need to leave. *Now.*"

Vivian exchanged a glance with the other women. "Fine. But I'm coming with you."

Caspian nodded in relief and hurried outside. Vivian watched him through the window speaking rapidly to one of his men. With astonishing speed, two Earther men entered their dormitory and moved Delilah onto a stretcher, and Luz helped Vivian scramble together an overnight duffel.

"Don't forget this." Camille pressed two bags of hormone treatments into her hand.

"I hardly think that matters now," Vivian objected.

"It matters to them."

Felicia nodded. "Don't let her miss a day, Viv. She wouldn't want to be behind."

"Fine." Vivian added the two bags to her duffel and rushed across the grounds to catch up with the stretcher.

Delilah gave a small moan and blinked open her eyes. Vivian grabbed her hand. "I'm here. Caspian is taking you to his hospital."

"Caspian?" Delilah struggled to sit up. "Vivian, no! I don't want him to see me like this."

Hearing her, Caspian raised a hand. The stretcher paused. He knelt in the ground cover and ran a thumb over Delilah's cheek. "Let me take care of you, Miss Bowen. Please."

A single tear dribbled out of the corner of Delilah's eye. "I wanted to be beautiful for you."

"You've never been more lovely." He nodded to the men, and they continued moving. Caspian stood, brushing dirt and thyme leaves from his trouser knees.

"Is that what you're looking for?" Vivian asked. "The most beautiful girl you've ever beheld? Isn't that what you told Xavier Dorsey at the luncheon?"

"I didn't realize my private conversation was overheard," Caspian said, a bit stiffly.

"She's more than that, you know."

"More than what?" Caspian began walking again, and Vivian hurried to keep pace with his long strides.

"Blond curls, long lashes, and eyes the color of a Martian sunset."

"I can see that, Miss Bowen. That is why I wish to know her better."

At the open gates of the compound, a small vehicle waited, flashing red and blue emergency lights. Delilah's stretcher was already loaded into the back, and Vivian and Caspian squeezed beside her. Vivian was close enough to him to notice that his trouser knees were stained with green, and she liked him better for it.

Pedestrians and the few groundcars scattered out of the way of the ambulance as it sped through the streets. In a matter of minutes, the car approached towering wrought iron gates that swung open at their arrival. They drove past a stately house with wide decorative columns perched on a sloping rocky hill and came to a sprawling utilitarian building topped with a red cross.

The doors to the back of the vehicle opened. Two intent medics lowered Delilah and her stretcher to the ground. Vivian exited the vehicle and watched the medics wheel Delilah through a set of double doors labeled *Hospital Staff Only.*

Vivian wanted to run after them and keep Delilah in sight. But instead, she stood, helpless and adrift, in front of the doors. Mars was supposed to be their new beginning, and now less than a week after arriving, her sister was already worse off than before they'd left.

"Miss Bowen?"

Vivian looked up into Caspian's grave eyes. She'd forgotten he was there.

"They'll do all they can for your sister. I pledge my word. Please, will you accept the hospitality of my home while we wait?"

Vivian cast one last look at the double doors and nodded reluctantly.

CHAPTER SIX

55 Sols to Presentation Day

Xavier Dorsey was there.

Vivian drew up short in the wide parlor of the Hayes Estate. The sun shone through the arched windows into an elegant, if oversized, sitting room with two opposing periwinkle sofas and a lush, patterned rug. Xavier glanced at Vivian indifferently before returning to his reader. Next to him on the sofa sat Caspian's sister Ivey, who immediately sprang to her feet.

"How is dear Delilah?" Ivey inquired.

"Too soon to tell." Caspian took a seat in a stiff-backed chair of faux wood next to the sofas. "I expect the doctors will need some time before they make a report to me. I've invited Miss Bowen to join us while we await news."

Xavier made a low noise that might have been a scoff, but no one else seemed to hear.

"We're happy to have you, Vivian," Ivey said. "May I call you Vivian?"

"Sure."

"Excellent." Ivey rubbed her hands together. "I was just persuading X to tear himself away from his dull Council briefs to play a game of Martian badminton. Join us, won't you? Two on two?"

Vivian hesitated. How could she enjoy herself while her sister lay in a hospital bed? "I don't think I can play in this awful dress."

"Come now, Miss Bowen," Xavier drawled without looking up. "You managed to con your way inside the house of a counselor within your first week on the planet. Surely you wish to explore the full estate. See if you can pocket the silver."

Vivian felt her face heat. She never should have told him she was on Mars for the money.

"Be nice, X," Ivey scolded. She took Vivian by the arm. "Come with me. We'll sort you out."

Vivian allowed herself to be led up the wide staircase into Ivey's rooms, clutching her duffel bag. At the doorway to the suite, Vivian froze, transfixed by the sight of the enormous bedroom with its tall four-poster bed, spacious sitting area, and en suite private bath. Like in the parlor, the furniture all appeared massive from her Earthborn point of view.

Her parents had once had an ensuite bath, Vivian remembered abruptly. At their waterfront home. Before the storm took it all.

Ivey stepped into her walk-in closet and returned a few minutes later wearing a white divided skirt that showed off her pale, lean legs and a sleeveless red shirt with a V-neck low enough to reveal the curve of her breasts. She held up a smaller red shirt and white skirt. "Look what I found at the back of the closet! I must have been fifteen when I fit into these. They should suit you rather well."

"Thank you." Vivian held up the short skirt with clenched fingers. "I'm not sure Wim would want me to wear this."

"Oh, Wim," Ivey said dismissively. "You cannot let that self-important bore control you."

"Do you not understand how this works?" Vivian snapped. "Right now, Wim has complete control over me."

Ivey let out a bark of laughter. "X warned me your meek appearance hid a spitfire."

Xavier had mentioned her to Ivey? They'd only conversed for two or three minutes. Had she made that much of an impression?

Unwillingly, she remembered the way his eyes had held hers when he'd said, *Oh, I'm very tempted, Miss Bowen.* He'd certainly made a lasting impression on *her.* With effort, Vivian shoved the memory away. Whatever attraction he might feel, he clearly despised her.

"What Wim won't admit, even to himself," Ivey continued, "Is that here, clothing is a game."

"A game?"

Ivey sat down on her raised bed, bringing her face to face with Vivian. "Don't you see we're all playacting? The Founding Families deliberately chose to adopt the elaborate clothing, headgear, and even the style of speech of Earth's British Regency era to establish ourselves as an aristocracy elevated above the rest of the society."

"Are you saying it isn't real?" No wonder this place had felt so strange since she arrived.

Ivey raised one elegant shoulder in a shrug. "We've made it real. Casp and X are totally bought in. Really, the whole Council believes sincerely in upholding our culture. It's in their interest, you see. Only the Founding Families can afford the elaborate lifestyle." Her lips turned up in a cynical smile. "And as long as the middle class is fervently trying to emulate our culture and fighting one another for our scraps, they won't turn to each other and ask why power, wealth, and even the ability to reproduce across generations is concentrated in the hands of the few."

Vivian stared at her in astonishment. "Why are you telling me this?"

"Casp is interested in your sister, and I'd like you to encourage Delilah to return his affection." Ivey's lips turned up. "I think the more you understand, the more you're likely to see the considerable benefits to your sister if she chooses to align herself with Hayes House."

Vivian thought of her sister blinking up at Caspian when he complimented her eye color. "I don't think Caspian needs any help from me on that front."

Ivey snorted. "I was watching your sister at the luncheon. Delilah is quite the flirt. I don't think she appreciates how serious Casp's intentions are." She leaned forward. "My brother is a good man, Vivian. He would be a kind and generous husband to your sister."

Vivian shrugged. Maybe Luz was right. What did Vivian know about how a man like Caspian would behave behind closed doors?

"On Mars, all resources are finite, even power. And you and your sister have considerable power at the moment." Ivey held up her hands to her sides, palms up, like two scales. "Thirty wombs. Several hundred contenders. Less than sixty days until Presentation Day. You should understand the leverage you possess."

"I'm not a fucking *womb*," Vivian snapped before she could stop herself.

Ivey seemed amused instead of offended by her outburst. She waved her long fingers. "You're a womb to Secretary Yarrow. One she is eager to fill with a designer fetus."

Vivian could think of nothing to say in response. After all, they'd brought her to Mars at great expense for that reason. Did she have the right to insist upon her own personhood when her only role in Martian society was to bear their children?

Ivey rose and went to the door. "Wear the ensemble or don't. It makes no difference to me except that it will impact the quality of your playing, and I'd like to boast of a win to my brother and X." She departed on long, bare legs, leaving Vivian alone.

Vivian stared at the outfit. The skirt was designed for a Martian body type and would end lower on her thigh than on Ivey's. But it would still be very short. She pictured wearing it in the camp. The group of men who always lingered outside the women's bathrooms would have hooted and whistled to see her with exposed legs. They would have tried to grab her, pinch her, maybe slap her bottom. Vivian's whole body shuddered.

Sumter was far away. A nine-month voyage. She had secured her escape and was determined not to squander her newfound freedom.

And so, Vivian joined the game of badminton with uncovered legs and arms, feeling horrifically self-conscious. Xavier stared at her for a long moment with his dark expressive eyes but didn't comment.

"Vivian," Ivey began as she served. "Have you heard we're planning a dance in the Red Mothers' honor here at the Hayes Estate?"

"A dance?" Xavier growled. "Ivey, you cannot be serious."

"You can go to bed before it begins, X," said Caspian as he returned Ivey's volley with ease. "Or crash at your cousin August's flat for the night. You know he's only there half the time. Or simply go home to Dorsey Estate. The ball is a settled thing. Constance Yarrow herself requested it of me."

Xavier scowled and hit the returning shuttlecock so hard that it bounced high in the light Martian gravity on the corner of Vivian's square and went out of bounds. "Do keep up, Miss Bowen," he jeered. "I heard Earther women were supposed to be athletic, but you look as if you couldn't hit a stationary target."

Vivian felt a surge of adrenaline course through her at his needling words. She was in no mood to tolerate it. Not here, free from Wim's judgmental gaze, with no potential husband around.

"How shocking!" cried Ivey. "X, you really are a beast today." She gave Vivian a wicked grin. "We absolutely must win now."

Vivian felt an unwilling answering smile tug up her lips. She hit the shuttlecock back to Xavier with all the force of her strong Earther limbs, and he scrambled to volley it back.

"Casp, do you truly want the press to be crawling all over your estate?" Xavier demanded. "You know how critical they can be."

"I don't know," Vivian put in. "The journalist in *Arcadia Today* seemed very impressed by your dashing appearance and scandalous feather quill pin. Almost fawning." She hit the shuttlecock, and Xavier missed the swing. It landed at his feet. Vivian smirked. "Point."

"You saw that, did you?" Xavier picked up the shuttlecock and strode to the net to return it to her. "They're always more interested in fashion than ideas. That's why I used the pin. But truth be told, I'm glad my dissent was covered at all. Even if it meant I had to stay at that interminable luncheon all afternoon."

Vivian reached up on tiptoes above the net to take the shuttlecock. "You seem to have found a way to pass the time," she said, thinking of the friendly bartender and the frequent refills.

"Indeed," he murmured as his hand brushed hers. His eyes flicked down for only a moment before returning to her face.

Vivian turned away to hide a blush, only to realize with chagrin that the skin on her exposed chest likely betrayed her.

"Give it here." Ivey took the shuttlecock. "My serve." She swung. "X, quit trifling with the poor girl. She doesn't need you to break her heart."

"That's not going to happen," Vivian sputtered.

Caspian made a sound of frustration as Xavier, once again, missed the volley. He tossed it back to Ivey.

"Glad to hear it," Xavier panted.

"Good." Vivian swung her racket, and it connected with a satisfying *thunk*.

"Indeed." The shuttlecock bounced at his feet.

"And that's the game," Caspian said in disgust. "Well done, ladies."

Ivey looked from Vivian to Xavier, pressing her lips together. "Let's retire for some refreshment. Vivian, you must try the lemonade. Our estate is known for it."

In the sunroom, a warm, contented glow enveloped Vivian as she accepted Caspian's glass of cold lemonade. Her muscles ached pleasantly from the unfamiliar exercise. She hadn't known her body was capable of such force and precision. Delilah was right—Martian gravity made her a superhero.

Delilah.

The thought of her sister was like a bucket of cold water over her head. She shouldn't be enjoying herself while Delilah lay in a hospital bed. Not to mention that she still hadn't heard from Evie or her parents.

"This is my favorite room in our home." Ivey came to stand next to Vivian as she stared blankly at the collection of succulents. "Our mother's family was from Arizona. Do you know it?"

"Only through the media. Barely anyone lives in Arizona anymore."

Ivey wrinkled her nose. "I can imagine why. From my mother's stories, it sounded like living in an oven. She left when she was seven, but it was enough time to develop a lifelong love of desert foliage."

Vivian carefully rubbed a hand along the lance-shaped leaves of a vibrant jade plant. "What's this?"

"Aloe vera. It has healing properties for skin irritations." Ivey broke off the tip of one leaf and offered it to Vivian. "The gel can be rubbed on skin to soothe it. My mother was very fond of it. She was forever burning herself attempting to do the household staff's jobs for them."

"Your mother—is she responsible for your perspective on Martian clothing?"

Ivey gave a tiny, surprised huff. "Oh well done, Vivian."

A Martian man in a liveried uniform entered the sunroom and cleared his throat. "Forgive me, Counselor Hayes, Miss Hayes. You're needed by the solicitor."

Ivey sighed. "Duty calls."

The moment Caspian and Ivey departed, Xavier put his reader aside. "I want you to take your sister and go home," he snapped. "Casp is to have no part in this. I won't allow it."

"What! Delilah is in the hospital. We aren't going anywhere."

"Spare me the theatrics, Miss Bowen." He leaned his long body toward her. "You've chosen to play a critical role in this despicable experiment."

"Chosen?" Vivian sputtered. "If you can't understand why, it was a choice without a choice, I cannot make you see."

"Please." Xavier crossed his arms over his chest. "It is a low trick indeed for your sister to pretend to be ill to gain Caspian's attention."

Hot anger coiled in Vivan's belly. "That's not true."

"No?" He regarded her with a scowl. She couldn't help but notice with her standing and him seated, their faces were at the same height. "She conveniently fell ill a few days after attracting his attention? When you knew full well that he owns the finest hospital in Arcadia? You must think Caspian is an easy mark."

Vivian took a step closer to him. "If you think it is *convenient* to be sick on a new planet with a strange culture and a contract to fulfill, you are out of your damn mind."

Xavier dropped his crossed arms. "I—she's truly ill?" The man had the nerve to look dismayed.

"She is." Vivian swallowed. "This kinetosis . . . Is it dangerous?"

Xavier's eyes shifted away. "It can be."

Vivian stared down at the broken piece of aloe vera still pinched between her fingers. Without her sister, Vivian wasn't sure she could go on.

"Miss Bowen," he said in a softer tone. "I spoke truly. The Hayes Community Hospital is the finest on all of Mars. Your sister is young and healthy. She will pull through."

Vivian covered her mouth in one hand. She would not cry in front of him. She wouldn't. "I have to go." She walked at a clipped pace out of the sunroom and down the grand hallway to the foyer. She was nearly to the front door when a call stopped her.

"Miss, where are you going?"

Vivian turned to confront an Earther woman in a brown dress with a white apron and cap. Taking a deep breath, she schooled her face to calm. She wasn't about to take her worry for her sister and anger with Xavier out on the Hayes household staff. "I'm going to the hospital to visit my sister. Am I being held here against my will?"

Trapped. Even here, she was trapped.

"Of course not, miss." The woman twisted her hands. "Only, perhaps you wish to change first?"

Vivian looked down at her short white skirt and sleeveless red top. She'd quickly become comfortable in the revealing clothing. "Is there a dress code for a sick bed here?"

"You are guests of the Hayes family, and you should reflect well on the estate."

"Right. Clothing is a game here."

"A game?" the woman asked.

"Never mind." Vivian ascended the stairs and found the morning's yellow dress. She looked at a wrought iron clock mounted to Ivey's wall and sighed.

From her small bag, she removed a needle and pulled off the packaging. She lifted up her borrowed shirt to expose her stomach, dotted with several bruises. Vivian found an unmarked spot of skin and, steeling herself for the prick of pain, pushed the needle into her stomach.

Two weeks. Only eleven more injections to go.

Goodness, she hated needles.

When Vivian had changed back into her dress, she thought of Camille's serious expression from that morning and tucked another sealed vial into her pocket before she crossed the street to Hayes Community Hospital.

When Vivian entered the hospital waiting room, heads swiveled to stare at her and an excited murmuring traveled through the room. Vivian's lacy yellow dress stood out against the drab outfits.

An older woman with an Earther build and a white old-fashioned nurse's hat looked up from studying a tablet. "You must be the sister."

Vivian licked her lips. "Is Delilah—could I—?"

"Your sister is very weak. Normally, I wouldn't allow you to see her in this state, but Counselor Hayes sent word. Come."

Vivian let herself be led through a corridor until, at last, she arrived at a private room. Delilah lay on a bed, eyes closed and breathing even.

"She's sleeping now, poor dear."

Vivian stood over her sister's bed, unsure if she should touch her. Had Delilah's skin always been so translucent? "Is she okay?"

The nurse frowned at the medical readouts. "Her fever has gone down. She's had a full blood transfusion, which can be hard on a body that's recently come out of nine months of zero-g." She looked up at Vivian and gave her a reassuring smile. "She'll be just fine, my dear. Just fine. You know, I went through the same thing when I arrived on Mars. And I went on to have three children."

Vivian let out a slow breath. "Thank you." From the pocket of her dress, she pulled out Delilah's syringe. "May I? I don't want her to miss a day of her hormone treatment cycle."

The nurse's eyes widened. "Was that granted by the Intelligence?"

"I suppose."

"We are grateful for the gifts of the Intelligence." She spread her hands in welcome. "Go ahead, dear."

Vivian lifted her sister's dress and whispered, "This will only hurt for a moment." She opened the wrapper and plunged the needle into her sister's stomach. Delilah whimpered slightly in her sleep.

When she looked up, the nurse's lips were parted eagerly, and her head was tilted forward. The woman caught herself and pressed a fist to her forehead. "What an honor you have given me tonight, my dear. I'm a witness to history."

Vivian disposed of the needle and pulled a chair to her sister's bed without meeting the nurse's eyes. She had no ambition to make history for these strange people and their weird god. She just wanted to protect her sister. "If it's alright with you, I'll sit beside her for a while."

"Of course, dear." The nurse hesitated. "I'm not sure I would have your courage. They say that in a single generation, you will break the cycle."

Vivian rubbed one shoulder. What was there to be courageous about? A few needles? "We aren't here to be brave. We're here because the alternative was worse."

"Believe me, I understand. Still, I'm grateful for your sacrifice. We're all grateful. Right now, Earthers living on Mars have no legacy. No future. It's a hard thing to see our children be unable to start families of their own. My sons—they'll be alright, I think. They joined the militia, which gives them purpose. But my daughter . . . She struggles. Left for the Catena dome, actually." She put a hand to her mouth. "I shouldn't have told you that. Please don't tell Counselor Hayes."

Vivian raised her head, curiosity piqued. "The separatist dome?"

The nurse blew out her breath. "I haven't seen her in five years."

"Oh, I'm sorry."

"Thank you, dear." She shook herself. "Ring if you need anything."

Veiled hints and unfamiliar politics—there was so much Vivian didn't understand about Mars. She watched the comforting sight of her sister's chest rise and fall. As long as Delilah made it through, nothing else mattered.

CHAPTER SEVEN

54 Sols to Presentation Day

The next morning, after a restless night sleeping in an enormous guest bed, Vivian came down the wide, open staircase to find Ivey seated at the dining room table while Caspian stood at a sideboard perusing the pastries.

"Ah, Vivian, there you are!" Caspian greeted her with a warm smile. "The doctors report that Delilah had an excellent night and will be ready to be released later today."

A wave of relief washed over Vivian, and she sat down abruptly next to Ivey. In the Martian-sized dining chair, her feet dangled above the ground like a young child.

"Bring her some eggs and bacon, Casp." Ivey took a sip of her coffee. "I find I can handle anything after a good night's sleep and a warm breakfast, don't you agree, Vivian?"

"I—I don't have a lot of experience with either." When Caspian placed a plate of food in front of her, Vivian realized she was ravenous.

Ivey poured her a cup of coffee. "You're on Mars now, my dear. Everyone in the dome has enough to eat. It's a point of pride."

"I have meetings." Caspian took a bite of a flaky roll and walked toward the door. "Vivian, I'll find you later when Delilah is ready."

"Thank you." Vivian moistened her lips. "You've been so kind." Perhaps she *should* push Delilah to pick Caspian. After a day watching Caspian and Xavier side-by-side, Vivian could clearly see Caspian's merits as a husband.

Vivian had just finished the last of her eggs when she looked up to the sound of heavy footfalls. "Walk with me." On the opposite end of the dining table, Xavier loomed over her.

"Goodness, X, do you have to be such a brute?" Ivey said with some amusement. "You may refuse him, my dear."

Vivian was about to do just that when Xavier cleared his throat and said in a softer tone, "Miss Vivian Bowen, would you honor me with a promenade in the gardens?"

Ivey tapped two fingers on each hand together. "Much better." Leaning toward Vivian, she murmured, "He can be taught after all."

Keeping her voice neutral to hide her curiosity, Vivian said, "Alright." She put down her coffee cup and rose to her feet.

The two stepped out the dining room's glass side doors into the gardens. Pruned lemon trees framed a redstone path winding through the grounds. The tiny chartreuse fruit made for a cheery backdrop to their uncomfortably silent walk.

"You spoke of a choice that was no choice," Xavier said abruptly. "Explain."

Vivian looked out at the manicured landscape. At first glance, it seemed lush. Purple flowers of varied heights flowed in garden beds in front of pointy green shrubs. But there was a curious absence of life. The garden had no wind or birdsong. Even in the barren dirt fields of Sumter, squirrels and mice found a home. When she'd left, the only thing she'd expected to miss was her parents and friends. She hadn't reckoned she'd miss Earth itself.

"Arcadia made us a good offer," Vivian said. "Do you know about our backgrounds?"

Xavier nodded. "My aunt recruited all of you from American refugee camps."

"She did. Do you understand what that means?"

"Of course I understand. I've read all about it." Xavier paused, rubbing his temples. In a softer tone, he said, "Forgive me. I don't understand. Not like someone who's lived it. Tell me. Please."

Vivian raised her head and looked at the rosy sky. "I remember the smell. For months on the transport ship, I'd wake up in the middle of the night gagging on the memory of unwashed bodies crammed together. It wasn't so bad when we first arrived after Pippa, but every year there was a new storm, and new families would arrive. And they wouldn't let us leave—not without a sponsor or a work permit. But there was no work and nowhere to go. And only each other to take out our frustration upon. Until the Arcadia reps came." She rubbed her throat reflexively and didn't mention Max Rinaldi. What if her parents had tried to send a message to her in the dormitory while she was gone? She shouldn't linger in this lovely aristocratic dreamworld.

"No matter what the conditions, my aunt does not have the right to take advantage of your situation to use you as a vessel for breeding genetically enhanced Martian babies."

"A vessel. Yes, that's one way to put it." A womb. A vessel. Either way, a tool to be exploited.

Xavier frowned down at her. "Do you even understand the contract you signed? The risks you've agreed to?"

Vivian shrugged. The Arcadia representative had put the electronic contract in front of her and verbally explained the arrangement. She hadn't read it. What would have been the point? It wasn't as if she'd had room to negotiate. "A first payment when we select a partner." Enough to buy her parents' escape. "I must have at least three babies. There's a bonus for more. I understand the terms."

"A partner." Xavier snorted. "The marriage terms in the contract you signed offer you no protection. You have no rights to your spouse's property or wealth. If you divorce, you lose custody of your children. In the event of a disagreement on a decision about your children's medical care or education, the Martian partner's will takes precedence. It's obscene."

"I won't get divorced." Vivian tried to push away his words. "Why would I want to walk away from stability and protection?"

"My Earther mother thought similarly. My father put a prenuptial agreement in front of her, and she signed it without negotiating. And then she was trapped. Martian oligarchs have been playing this game with Earther women for a hundred and fifty years. Now, my aunt has found a way to institutionalize it."

"What—what happened to your mother?"

"She died," he said shortly.

"I'm sorry," Vivian offered.

Xavier shook his head. "It was a long time ago." He let out a breath. "Do you understand how painful carrying these genetically modified fetuses will be? The in-utero calcium treatments will wreak havoc on your body. And they plan to put you through it three times. It's no wonder they had to recruit desperate women off-world from a failed state. No Earther woman already comfortable here on Mars would subject herself to the pain and potential for lifelong side effects."

Vivian shook her head. He was exaggerating. He must be. But the nurse's words came back to her. *I'm grateful for your sacrifice.* With a bravado she didn't feel, Vivian said, "I've known hunger pangs and stitches without anesthesia. I can handle pain."

"You think that now, but what if you change your mind? What if your first pregnancy has complications, and it's unsafe to continue?"

They had reached a fork in the walkway, and Xavier turned to the left decisively.

"They've said they'll make an exception if our life is in danger." Vivian wasn't sure why she was defending the arrangement. She'd only agreed to it as a way to escape. But it was better here, wasn't it? She'd gained weight on the ship and more since they'd landed. Her skin was brighter. She had more energy. She'd even slept through the night.

"An exception determined how?" Xavier frowned down at her. "And by whom?"

Vivian crossed her arms. "I'm not playing games with you. If you know, tell me."

"By my aunt. And the Intelligence, of course. I'm no longer certain who works for whom. Do you think the Intelligence's risk tolerance will match your own? Does it even understand the concept of pain? It's programmed to make decisions based on what's best for the long-term interests of the dome." Xavier let out a breath. "Believe me, Miss Bowen, the Intelligence cares nothing for the quality of life of one Earther woman."

"I'm not expecting the institutions on Mars to care about me when the American government was actively causing me harm. You can't imagine what our lives were like."

"I know what life was like for my Black American ancestors. They left to found a world not plagued by a legacy of racism. I have no wish to replicate Earth's suffering on my planet."

"I'm not suffering!" Vivian protested. She had never met a more exasperating man. "I have enough to eat. A comfortable bed and nice clothing."

"Is that enough, Miss Bowen?" Xavier looked intently at her with his dark brown eyes. "Does it take so little to make you happy?"

"Happy?" Vivian sputtered. "I'm not expecting to be *happy.*"

Xavier gave her a little bow. "You should expect more." He walked away, leaving her speechless alone on the path.

Upon her return to the house, Vivian banged open the side door. "I hate him. I've never met a bigger asshole."

At the dining room table, Ivey looked up from her reader and regarded Vivian with amusement. "I've always been fond of X. I enjoy his candor. I may even persuade him to marry me if I cannot hook an Earther woman."

"Marry him!" Vivian plopped down on the cushion of an ornately carved enormous dining chair. "That sounds horrible."

Ivey gave an amused snort.

"If you want to marry him, why are you trying to wed a Red Mother?"

Ivey poured Vivian a fresh cup of coffee in a delicate mug embossed with teal flowers. "I want a child. Children. Look at this beautiful home, so lonely except for Casp and me."

Vivian took a sip of coffee and tried to let the warm liquid soothe her frustration. "Why not have your own?"

Ivey laughed bitterly. "I must have a word with Reverend Adair. Can it be that he hasn't explained the full situation to you?"

"I've only been here a week." Vivian swallowed around a sudden lump in her throat, frustrated by her lack of knowledge. "There's still so much I don't understand."

"I can't have children," Ivey said. "No native-born Martian woman has successfully carried a child to term. My Martian foremothers tried, for many years, in many different ways. Nothing worked. Eventually, we stopped trying and now every Martian with a uterus receives a permanent contraceptive implant by age sixteen." She pointed to the bare skin of her inner arm. "The Founding Families found a way to make their households the best option for Earther women to marry into. They looked to a beloved aristocratic era in Earther history for inspiration and set up Houses and walled estates and elaborate costumes to make their lifestyle attractive."

"So that's why your mother was an Earther?" *And Xavier's?*

"Vivian, my dear, *everyone's* mother is an Earther. But my mother had no business making the attempt to have children. She was born on Earth, yes, but she spent her adolescence in Martian gravity." A tiny sigh escaped Ivey's lips. "She managed to carry Casp and me. We were both premature and underweight, but we survived. Before and after us, she had many, many miscarriages.

The last one killed her." Ivey looked down at her coffee cup and swallowed. "Casp and I apportioned half our estate to run the hospital in her honor."

"I'm sorry," Vivian whispered. She had known, of course, that Martian women struggled to bear children. It was the reason for the gene modifications and in-utero treatments, after all. But she hadn't realized it was impossible. She felt a sudden sympathy for Secretary Yarrow. She had found a way to save her people. Of course she would make any decision, no matter the ethics, to create this chance for Mars.

Ivey waved one long hand in dismissal. "It was a long time ago."

Vivian hesitated, then ventured, "Can I . . . Can I ask you about the Intelligence? Xavier said it was indifferent to individual human life."

"X is hardly an unbiased source on the nature of the Intelligence."

"But do you think he's right?" Vivian persisted.

Ivey gave a shrug of her elegant shoulders. "I've no idea. I believe that without the Intelligence, we would not have the same quality of life. For nearly two hundred years, it has guided us to a life of abundance on a cold, deadly planet where the standard of living could easily be one of subsistence. But I am not qualified to gauge the Intelligence's priorities. I've never spoken directly to it. Few of us have."

"But Wim does?"

Ivey's forehead wrinkled in a frown. "Reverend Adair has modified a large portion of his body in order to commune directly with the Intelligence. The option is available to all Martians, although only a few of the most devoted have chosen to pursue such an extreme path. Can you imagine willingly consenting to the removal of an eyeball?" She shuddered. "I think not."

"Is that the only way to communicate with the Intelligence?" Vivian asked.

"For most of us. I've heard a rumor that the Secretary uses a device that gives the Intelligence a physical form she can converse with directly and bypass the reverend and his ilk. But I've never seen such a device."

She'd learned more about the history and culture of Mars in her brief time with Ivey than she had in a full week in Wim's company. More questions bubbled to Vivian's lips, but she cut them off when Caspian rapped twice on the door frame. "I've just heard word that Delilah is ready for release. Join me, Vivian?"

"Of course." Vivian gulped the last of her coffee and rose with alacrity. "Thank you," she said to Ivey. "For everything. I hope I can call you a friend."

Ivey looked up sharply. Had Vivian violated another Martian custom? Were Martians and Earthers not often friends? But then Ivey inclined her head. "Friends, then."

At the door, Caspian grabbed his top hat from the stand in the front hall and bowed her out of the house.

Vivian thought she'd become accustomed to the stares that had accompanied yesterday's hospital visit, but the attention was so much greater walking at Caspian's side. He nodded comfortably at everyone they passed and strode confidently through the hospital halls without an escort. *As if he owned the place*, Vivian realized with some amusement.

Delilah was sitting up when they entered, the color restored to her cheeks. A wave of relief passed over Vivian. "How are you feeling, baby sis?"

"Just fine," Delilah said with a tired smile. She looked up at Caspian and blushed. "Mr. Hayes."

Caspian swept off his top hat and bowed deeply to her. "Miss Bowen, I am so very glad you are recovered. You gave us all quite a scare."

Delilah stared down at her hands as they twisted the blanket.

Vivian recognized the signs of exhaustion in her normally gregarious sister. “Ready to go? I bet without you to referee, Camille and Luz are about to murder each other.”

“You’re both welcome to stay an extra day,” Caspian said. “It would be my honor to host you in my home.”

Delilah looked pleadingly at Vivian.

“Thanks, but we should be getting back,” Vivian said to Caspian. She was desperate to check her messages again and see if she’d heard from her parents or Evie.

Caspian’s face fell, but he recovered gallantly. “Of course, you must be missing your friends. I will arrange transportation at once. Please, allow me to extend my hospitality until the car is ready.”

Delilah’s eyes widened when Caspian escorted them to the gates of the Hayes House and grew even rounder when they stepped into the bright, wide atrium.

“Xavier! Ivey!” Caspian bellowed. “Come wish our guests well before they are on their way.”

Ivey emerged with good grace and lightly embraced Delilah. “I am so glad you are feeling better.” To Vivian, she said, “I very much enjoyed getting to know you,” and touched the top of her hand.

Xavier took longer to arrive and, when he did, his nose was buried in his reader. “Safe travels,” he said without even looking at her.

Vivian exchanged a glance with Ivey. Honestly, the man was infuriating. And then the groundcar was there, and Vivian and Delilah were whisked away from the estate.

CHAPTER EIGHT

54 Sols to Presentation Day

"You're home!" Shiloh exclaimed when Vivian opened the dormitory door. "We've been so worried."

Camille pushed past Shiloh to fling her arms around Delilah. Vivian watched her sister's face soften as she hugged her friend.

Luz met Vivian's eyes over the crowd of women. "You received a message. From Earth."

Evie or her parents? Vivian couldn't wait another minute to find out.

"When?" she demanded as she pulled her sister out of Camille's embrace and practically dragged her into the dining room.

"Only one or two hours ago, no longer." Luz's face was grave. She'd known how desperate Vivian had been to hear from her parents.

Vivian sat down on the console chair, and her sister brought another chair over from a table in the dining room. With a shaking hand, Vivian located the message. She recognized the woman who appeared on screen as Miranda, a Sumter aid worker who'd snuck them extra food and books.

"Vivian," Miranda said urgently. "Evie's dead." Vivian's stomach dropped to the floor. Beside her, Delilah hissed. Vivian reached out and gripped her sister's hand tightly. "She tried to continue your work with the children's food supply, and they killed her. Beatrice took in her little boy. I'm sorry." Miranda bit her lip. "Your parents asked me to record a message and send it to you, but I couldn't let you think everything was all right. The truth is, they are in danger. Terrible danger. I thought you should know."

The video cut to her parents, standing side by side near the aid shelter where Miranda worked. "We're rolling," came Miranda's voice.

"Vivian, Delilah," her mother began. "Thank you for telling us you arrived safely."

"We're doing just fine here," her father cut in. "Everything's a-okay." He gave two thumbs up.

"We love you, girls," her mother continued. Vivian studied her face for clues. Tufts of gray hair stood out from her mother's head, and the lines on her leathery face seemed deeper. "You must be having a wonderful time on your adventures."

Her father put one arm around his mother's shoulders. "Don't spend one more minute thinking about us. We're fit as a fiddle over here." He looked away from the camera. "That's a wrap, Miranda."

"Don't you want to tell them about—"

"No!" both her parents said in unison.

"Okay then."

The screen went dark.

"The Rinaldi brothers." Delilah rubbed a trembling hand over her face. "There's no other explanation."

"Why did she try to continue our work after everything that happened?" The eggs and cultured bacon Vivian had eaten for breakfast at the Hayes' dining table sloshed in her stomach. "We have to do something."

"We all left people behind," Felicia objected behind her. Vivian turned in her chair to see all the women gathered in the large dining room. "What are you going to do about it from here?"

"Who killed your friend?" someone asked.

"Camp men." Vivian swallowed. "The Rinaldi brothers. We were creating a stockpile of nonperishable food, to make sure the kids never went hungry during the lean times, and they didn't like it. Said it interfered with their business."

"Vivian was brilliant," Delilah added. "She convinced all the younger women in the camp to pool our resources together. There was a whole distribution system and the most detailed security plan."

Vivian swiped at her eyes. "If my plan was so brilliant, how were we overpowered so easily?"

"Because men will always be stronger than women," Shiloh said bitterly. "Did you know I earned a black belt in karate when I was a kid? Didn't do shit for me at the camp. Not when it counted."

"My momma said that when she got off second shift at the hospital, she'd walk to her car carrying mace in one hand and her keys pushed through her fingers in the other," Camille added. "But by the time we got to the camp, she didn't have mace or keys to give me."

"Trust me, it wouldn't have helped," Shiloh told her. "Anyway, it's easier if you don't fight back. Fewer bruises. Higher chance you'll survive."

Luz made a sound low in her throat, but Vivian couldn't tell if it was an agreement or denial. Vivian had been lucky, in some ways, compared to many of these women. She'd never been raped. But it would have only been a matter of time if she'd stayed. A choice between proactively giving into Max Rinaldi's pressure in the hopes that he would treat her gently or waiting for him or another man to take her by force.

Vivian rubbed her bare arms with her hands. Evie was dead. If she'd stayed, maybe she would be dead too. *Are Mom and Dad next?*

She thought about what Xavier had said. Constance Yarrow hadn't been able to recruit local Earthborn women to bear the genetically modified children. They needed to find women in more desperate circumstances. And she was grateful, absurdly grateful, to be here in safety. Surrounded by her friends. Well-fed. Rested. Delilah, healthy and sparkling with life, by her side.

But Evie was dead.

"There's nothing we can do today," Delilah said to Vivian. "We need to complete the egg retrieval cycle before we can select a spouse. But we'll get them out, Viv. They just need to hold on for a few more weeks." Then, she leaned forward with a wicked glint in her eyes and whispered conspiratorially, "Let's get out of here."

Without waiting for a response, Delilah rose and walked in the direction of their bedroom. Vivian caught up with her just as she slipped into the room. Delilah pulled her hat from a hook on the wall and adjusted it in the mirror.

"What are you doing?" Vivian was so tired. She hadn't slept well at Hayes House, and now the combination of adrenaline, fear, and grief was too much to bear. All she wanted was to curl up in her bed and cry until she fell asleep. "You're weak."

"I'm perfectly healthy. I've done nothing but rest for two days straight." Delilah's bottom lip stuck out in a playful pout. "Mom and Dad think we're on an adventure. So, let's go on one."

"Stop it!" Vivian snapped. "Don't do this right now. Evie's *dead.* Let yourself feel that. Let yourself mourn." She knew this mood of her sister's. She'd seen it many times at the camp. When things got hard, Delilah disassociated.

Delilah's face changed to a blank mask. "I can't think about that right now. I'm going out, with or without you."

Vivian knelt to put on her shoes. "I'll come."

Her sister gave her a dazzling smile. “We’re going to have so much fun.” She grabbed Vivian’s arm and pulled her out the side door without any of the women spotting them.

Delilah hummed as she walked, swishing her skirts. Vivian had to hurry to keep pace with her sister’s energetic strides, even as her thoughts whirled.

How old was Evie’s boy now? He couldn’t have even turned three. Too young to remember his mother. Vivian had left them behind, knowing how dangerous Max and his brothers could be. If she’d stayed, she could have bought protection for Evie with her body. She could have moved into Max’s tent. Let him do all the vulgar things he’d described in graphic detail during her last weeks in the camp. And Evie would still be alive.

And where would Delilah be? In the next tent over with one of Max’s men?

Vivian stopped and bent over, fighting a wave of nausea. She’d had no good choices. And, in the end, she’d picked Delilah over Evie.

“Come on, Viv.” Delilah pulled her upright. “We’re almost at the front.”

In a few more steps, they were at the tall, gated entrance. It had no door handle. Vivian shoved the gate with her shoulder, but it remained solid and unyielding. She drew a shaky breath. “When I left the gates in Caspian’s company, we had no trouble.”

Delilah shrugged. “Come on. I know another way.” She grabbed Vivian’s hand and led her along the high wall. “Time for Plan B.” She gestured triumphantly to a tall tree near the wall. “There!”

“Delilah, I don’t know . . .” The spindly tree stretched above the wall. What if Delilah tumbled down from a high branch and broke her leg? She’d never convince Xavier they hadn’t been manipulating Caspian if they ended back at the hospital before the day was done. “Wim must have a good reason for confining us to the compound. Let’s walk around the grounds instead.”

"An adventure," Delilah insisted. She knotted her skirt around her waist and pulled herself onto a low branch.

Vivian watched her clamber up the tree with ease and blew out her breath. She couldn't let her reckless baby sister wander the streets of Mars alone. Reluctantly, she secured her skirt and lifted herself onto the tree. The climb was easy—much easier than it would've been on Earth. Her strong Earther limbs scaled the tree in moments, and soon she'd joined Delilah at the top of the wall with a triumphant grin.

The ground was ten feet below with nothing to break a fall.

"This is a bad idea, Delilah." Vivian squinted down at the paved ground.

"Don't be such a wimp," Delilah said and launched herself off the wall.

Vivian let out an involuntary gasp as her sister fell ten feet to the ground. Delilah scrambled up and gestured to her. "One-third the gravity of Earth. Come on."

Scrunching up her eyelids, Vivian jumped.

She sailed through the air at an oddly low speed before landing with a jarring bump, crouched on her feet. *Superheroes.* Vivian let the unfamiliar feeling of power wash over her as she rose from her crouch.

Delilah laughed, a bit wildly, and shoved Vivian's hat back onto her head. "Let's go."

As they walked on the wide, open streets of Mars, Vivian's heart grew unexpectedly lighter. They'd escaped—for at least a little while. Delilah was right. There was nothing she could do for her parents right now. Today, she could enjoy a taste of freedom.

The only ground vehicle in sight inched forward slowly, yielding to pedestrians. Trains rumbled overhead. Almost everyone, it seemed, was walking to their destination at a leisurely pace, pausing to greet one another or stopping altogether for a spontaneous conversation.

A mix of willowy Marsborn children and their solid Earthborn peers played with a ball against one wall. The Earther children must have just arrived, to look so stocky, Vivian mused, thinking of Ivey's description of her mother's childhood. As they grew in the Martian gravity, their bones would lengthen and weaken.

Vivian was conscious of her new lens for looking at the society. Now, she could see the quality of Delilah and her clothing set them apart—their dresses more colorful, their hats wider, and their ribbons shinier. Yet most Martian women wore a humbler version of their ensembles. And the men sported drabber versions of Caspian's and Xavier's wardrobes. Everyone on the Arcadian street, regardless of gender, age, occupation, or rank, wore a hat.

A game, Vivian thought. Had Ivey told her the truth about the purpose of fashion in Martian society?

A Martian soldier in a bright red uniform swept his tricorn hat off his head and bowed to them. Delilah giggled after he departed. "Come on," she said, guiding them in the soldier's direction.

After a short walk down the sparkling clean Arcadian streets, they arrived at a soldiers' barracks. Martian men, women, and people of indeterminate gender milled around, some wearing full scarlet uniforms and others in shirtsleeves. The lack of any real weather under the domes made Vivian question the purpose of the heavy embroidered red coats. Every fashion choice on Mars, it seemed, came with its own hierarchy.

Don't they have somewhere to be? Vivian remembered the soldier who'd escorted Luz and her home. She didn't understand the point of a standing militia on a Martian dome. *What are they defending against?*

"Who's this, then?" a Martian soldier asked the sisters, tipping his tricorn hat in their direction. Curly auburn hair framed a startlingly handsome face with pale skin and vivid blue eyes. Delilah batted her eyelashes at him as she introduced herself. The soldier greeted her politely before turning his attention to Vivian. "I must have your name, you exquisite creature."

Her stomach fluttered. "Vivian Bowen. We just arrived from Earth."

The soldier took her hand and raised it to his mouth. His lips were dry and warm. "Silas Gatlin."

She was used to feeling wary around strange men, but there was something about the Martians that put her at ease. With their refined manners and alien features, they were so different from the men at Sumter. She'd never had her hand kissed before, and she found she rather liked it.

The hum of conversation and laughter around them suddenly stilled. Without dropping her hand, Silas looked up sharply, his sapphire eyes alert.

"It's Counselor Dorsey!" Vivian heard one of the soldiers hiss.

Vivian turned her head to see Xavier's regal form striding down the sidewalk. Although she had only bade farewell to him that morning, she found she could not look away.

Xavier seemed determined not to look at her, casting his eyes in all directions until suddenly caught by the sight of the stranger. Vivian was astonished to see Silas turn red and Xavier's face shutter. Silas, after a few moments, released Vivian's hand to touch his hat—a salutation that Xavier just deigned to return. Without a word or gesture to Vivian, Xavier stalked in the direction of a taller building that Vivian assumed was a military headquarters from the number of flags posted atop it.

Delilah had not noticed the exchange and was soon diverted by a hat stall. With a wide smile, she went to the merchant to try on his accessories, and a group of friendly soldiers soon surrounded her, eager to offer their opinions.

Silas cocked his head to one side. "Are the rumors true?"

"What rumors?" Vivian asked.

"A young woman newly arrived from Earth with a striking face and an elegant dress. You are, I think, a Red Mother."

Vivian smiled. "I am."

"The oligarchs do not deserve you." He turned his head, for a moment, in the direction of the headquarters building.

She shrugged. "I have a contract to fulfill."

He eyed her playfully. "Vivian, Vivian, you'll break my heart. If you are already spoken for, tell me now and put me out of my misery."

Vivian found herself quite taken by his roguish grin. Perhaps she was disassociating too, but it felt nice to have a man's attention who wasn't evaluating her for her ability to bear him children. "I haven't chosen a husband yet, if that's what you're asking."

"Excellent. I wish to invite you to drink with me at this fine establishment."

Vivian followed his gesture to a rounded hut in the shadow of the barracks. She turned and looked back at Delilah. Her sister was laughing, still surrounded by soldiers. Vivian caught her eye, and Delilah made a shooing gesture.

If she'd still been in the camp, she would never have agreed. But she wasn't at Sumter anymore. She was safe here. Safe in a way Evie never would be. Sometime in the next fifty-four days, she'd need to pick a husband interested in her for her ability to have his children. Just this once, couldn't she enjoy the attention of a handsome man who had no other agenda?

Vivian smiled at Silas. "I accept."

He offered her his arm with a courtly bow, and Vivian took it with amusement. The Martian airs of grandeur were quite over the top. She let herself pretend, for this moment, that he was courting her in earnest. For herself.

Inside the dark tavern, Silas pulled her into a corner and tapped out an order on the surface of the table. "Tell me, lovely Vivian, how do you find Mars so far?"

Vivian stared around at her surroundings. She'd never been inside a bar before. Soldiers gathered in groups of twos and threes, chattering and laughing. Vivian relaxed into the back of her comfortable padded chair. "The people are so friendly and welcoming. Well, most of them."

Silas rubbed his lips. "And who might be mistreating you, my darling Vivian?"

"Counselor Dorsey," said Vivian, glad of the chance to complain about Xavier. "I've just spent two days in the same house with him, and I think he's an insufferable jerk."

Silas smiled to himself. "X, you never change." He raised his hands in the air in an expression of surrender. "I can't give an opinion. I've known him too long and too well to be an impartial judge."

Vivian sat up straighter. "You know him?" That explained their strange reaction upon seeing one another. She wished to know everything this handsome stranger could tell her about the irritating man. "I can't stand him."

"I'm glad to hear it." Silas took their drinks from a robotic server. "Martian society is blinded by his fortune and frightened by his power on the Council and sees him only as he chooses to be seen." He handed her a glass of dark red liquid, his scraped knuckles brushing her hand. "We grew up together. My mother was the house manager of Dorsey Estate." He gave her a tight smile. "His father was one of the best men I've ever known. When he died, he intended to provide for me amply, and his wishes were disregarded by his son. A man of honor could not have doubted his father's intention, but X chose to ignore his own father's wishes and refused to honor my inheritance. The fact is, we are very different sort of men, and he hates me for it."

Vivian took a sip of her wine to hide her perplexity. "But why would he be so cruel?"

"Jealousy," Silas answered promptly. "His father treated me as if I were his own son. X is not one to tolerate any competition."

"He really is terrible."

"Hear, hear." Silas raised his glass. "But I did not bring you here to talk of my childhood. Tell me, how are you finding the attention of being a Red Mother?"

Vivian looked down at her drink. She thought of her parents, still trapped in the camp. Of the tiny bruises dotting her stomach. Of the Earther nurse telling her she would break the cycle. "In the last week, everyone has been kind to us."

"And yet?"

You should expect more. Vivian pushed Xavier's words away. What did *more* mean to someone like him? He'd never known what it felt like to survive on one meal a day or dodge handsy guards. He didn't know what it was like to hear about a friend's death millions of miles away and be helpless to do anything about it.

"And yet, nothing," Vivian said firmly. "I'm fine."

"Why be satisfied with mere contentment?" Silas moved his chair closer to hers. His words sounded so much like Xavier. Well, he'd said they'd grown up together. "Has anyone ever told you how beautiful you are?"

Vivian ducked her head. "My sister is the beautiful one."

"You—" He cupped her cheek with one hand. "Are exquisite. Like a porcelain doll."

He was so different from the men at Sumter. No crude gestures or dirty jokes. His eyes on her face, not leering at her body. She should pull away. He wasn't on the list. But instead, she leaned in when his rough fingers traveled down her neck, shivering in pleasure. No one had ever touched her like this before. Like she was something precious.

"You have porcelain dolls on Mars?" she managed to ask.

Silas chuckled. "We do, actually. Ivory skin and bouncing brown curls." He took one lock of her hair and tugged gently on it.

Vivian stared into his vivid blue eyes. What pre-recorded commentary might Wim make about Silas? "I should go." She forced herself to pull back. "I don't want to leave my sister for too long."

"May I visit you, Vivian?"

A thrill went through her at the idea of seeing him again under Wim's nose. "In the dormitory? It's locked on both sides."

Silas took her hand and kissed it again. "For you, I'll find a way."

CHAPTER NINE

53 Sols to Presentation Day

Wim was furious. "What's this I heard about the Bowen sisters running around with the soldiers yesterday?" he demanded the next morning.

The other women murmured in surprise as they came to gather together in the dining room. Vivian winced. She ought to have known they would be caught. After all, the Intelligence's eyes were everywhere. Always watching.

The table she'd sat at with Silas had an electronic ordering screen. Hadn't Luz said the Intelligence could tap into any electronics? It must have been able to clearly listen to every word of their conversation. The idea made Vivian's skin crawl.

"We're grown women," said Delilah, crossing her arms and lifting her chin. "We can go where we choose."

A shadow crossed over Wim's face. "You are here at the pleasure of the Intelligence. I feel I must remind you, Delilah Bowen, that there are no Arcadian soldiers on the Intelligence's list of approved spouses. And furthermore, the contract you signed asserts the Red Mothers won't indulge in sexual congress until you've selected a co-parent and been successfully impregnated with an augmented embryo."

Delilah made a face. "Sexual congress?"

Luz put a restraining hand on Delilah's arm. "We understand the terms of our contract, Reverend Adair. My friends were only familiarizing themselves with Martian society."

"I hope so," Wim said in a mollified tone. "Nevertheless, I have been remiss in your orientation to your purpose here and the reasoning behind the Intelligence's expectations." He gestured expansively. "I've asked Dr. Chavez to meet with us to explain things properly. Let's go."

"I can't believe you snuck out," Camille said to Vivian and Delilah as they walked across the compound. "That's so badass."

"We met the cutest soldier." Delilah giggled. "Too bad he's not approved."

Vivian felt her face growing warm, and she stumbled over her long skirts. Luz grabbed her arm. "Careful, Viv baby."

Wim led them to a squat, utilitarian building on the opposite side of the compound. They entered a room set up like a classroom, with rows of chairs facing a screen.

The Martian doctor who had examined Vivian a few days prior was waiting for them, staring into nothing with a vacant look. Vivian remembered what Ivey had told her about how the augmentations allowed some Martians to communicate directly with the Intelligence. After a moment, the doctor blinked and looked around the room more sharply. "Sit down, ladies. For those of you who don't know me, I'm Dr. Chavez, the chief researcher for the Red Mothers initiative. Under the guidance of the Intelligence, my team has developed remarkable innovations in embryo development. Reverend Adair has asked me to explain the basic science behind our research."

The doctor made no discernible gesture, but, suddenly, the screen in front of them displayed an image of an ovum. "After we harvest your eggs, they will be treated in our lab to maximize their health and the odds of a successful pregnancy. When you choose a spouse, they will provide a DNA sample that we will inject into lab-grown sperm cells." The image on the screen changed to a single sperm cell. "We will immediately prepare the genetically enhanced embryo, and it will be ready for transfer in about a day. We anticipate a 95-percent success rate."

Vivian stared at the new image of an embryo, lumpy with dividing cells. She could hardly imagine selecting a husband and within days being impregnated with a genetically enhanced version of their child.

"The children you bear who are born female will grow to be adults with pelvic bones strong enough to carry their own healthy children to term. And the children born male will carry on the DNA that will allow their own female children to have successful pregnancies. In a single generation, the reproduction challenges Mars has experienced since its founding will be resolved. As Red Mothers, you truly will be the mothers of the future of Mars."

Vivian swallowed around a sudden lump in her throat. *The future of Mars.* She wasn't a vessel or an incubator. This role she had accepted mattered. They would be ending generations of failed reproduction.

In the hushed silence, Delilah asked, "So no sexual congress?" The women surrounding her snickered.

"What about side effects?" Vivian called over the giggles. "Will the pregnancies be painful?"

"No sex," Dr. Chavez said, frowning at Delilah. She didn't spare a glance for Vivian, as if she hadn't heard her question. "Not until we are certain the embryo has attached to the uterine wall. Our hormone treatments make you extra fertile, and we wish to avoid being forced to terminate a natural pregnancy and set our timeline back."

"Excuse me." Luz raised her hand in an uncharacteristically deferential motion. "Can you explain why sex is a required part of our contract if the fertilization occurs in a laboratory?"

Dr. Chavez exchanged a glance with Wim. "The Intelligence has analyzed data from several millennia of marriage and child rearing and has determined that an optimal experience—especially when having multiple children—is achieved when the parents have developed intimacy through a physical relationship." She spread her hands. "But I am a geneticist, not a psychiatrist. This isn't my area of expertise."

Wim cleared his throat. "We shall defer to the infinite wisdom of the Intelligence."

Dr. Chavez put a fist to her forehead and bowed her head. "We are grateful for the gifts of the Intelligence." She turned back to the women and continued as if there had been no interruption. And, despite herself, Vivian realized she was getting used to the bizarre AI worship on Arcadia. "The sexual relationship with your spouse will require thoughtful communication. You have, of course, received a basic background on the parameters of sex between an Earther woman and a Martian partner?"

Around her, the women nodded. Vivian exchanged a glance with Delilah. "We must have missed it when Delilah was sick."

Camille snorted. "You sure did. Did you know we can crush a Martian's pelvis in the bedroom? I can't wait to try it out."

The women tittered nervously. Dr. Chavez held up one hand. "This is no laughing matter, ladies." An image of two skeletons simulating sex appeared on the screen. Dr. Chavez pointed to the bottom skeleton. "An Earthborn woman-on-top position is the most dangerous for a Marsborn partner. She can fracture their pelvic bone if she moves too vigorously on them."

Vivian could feel her face turn red as Dr. Chavez moved through a series of skeleton images explaining the optimal sexual positions for an Earther woman with a variety of Martian partners of all genders. "Consent. Communication. These are core Martian values for a reason. No safe sexual relationship between a Martian and an Earther may occur without them."

Vivian shivered. What did consent mean under these circumstances?

"Thank you, Dr. Chavez." Wim stood from his perch at the back of the classroom. "You have been most helpful. Now that we understand the importance of keeping chaste until we select partners, it's time to turn to other business. Counselor Caspian Hayes and his sister Miss Ivey are hosting a dance in four days' time. It's an excellent opportunity for all of you to refocus your attention on obtaining a partner. The Intelligence is eager to see all of you successfully matched prior to Presentation Day."

CHAPTER TEN

49 Sols to Presentation Day

The night of the dance, Caspian sent sleek black vehicles for the women that pulled up to the open gates in an elegant line. Vivian, Delilah, and Luz carefully found seats in one groundcar with several of the other women, mindful not to wrinkle the fine new formal dresses the artificial clothier had selected for each of them.

"I've never attended a ball before," one of the women said. "It's like something out of a fairy tale."

"You mean a story that ends with a woman surrendering her independence to hitch her life to a man she just met?" Luz muttered.

Camille glared at Luz. "You don't have to be here."

"Actually, I do. It's in our contract."

Camille flicked her hand dismissively at Luz and turned to Delilah. "I hope Theo is coming. Did I tell you he wants to take me to see live music? He said there's a few Earthers from New Orleans that formed a jazz band. I haven't seen jazz in forever." She bumped her friend on the shoulder. "You're thinking about seeing Caspian again, aren't you?"

Delilah giggled. "If he isn't too busy hosting to dance with me."

"He saved your life!" Camille responded. "He'll make the time for you. I guarantee it."

Looking out the window of the groundcar, Vivian allowed herself a moment of indulgent fantasy. What if Silas was on the guest list? He'd been raised at Dorsey Estate after all. Perhaps he knew the Hayes family. He'd ask her to dance the moment he laid eyes on her and encircle her in his arms while Xavier watched with a scowl. She would dearly like to confront Xavier on Silas's account. She pictured the clever retorts she'd throw at Xavier while Silas looked on approvingly.

Luz touched her arm. "We're here." Her friend looked especially lovely in a dress of burnished orange that brought out her deep brown eyes and golden skin. Her straight brown hair was swept into a high sleek bun on the top of her head, accented by a sparkling comb. Luz's stoic face reflected none of the other women's cheeriness.

Ambient lighting bathed the manor, and the strains of string music echoed. The women mounted the steps and entered the great hall. Emerald vines adorned the spiral staircase cascading down into the spacious entryway.

In the foyer, they were met by Wim. He seemed to startle when he looked at her, then his head tilted as if he were listening to something far away. Wim bowed stiffly in her direction. "At the advice of the Intelligence, I take this opportunity of soliciting you, Miss Vivian, for your first dance."

Vivian frowned. Why would he pay her attention, especially after her recent unsanctioned adventure? After a nudge from Luz, she cleared her throat and said, "I'm honored."

Wim placed his hand lightly under hers and led her into the great room.

The walls of the room sparkled with glowing violet lighting. Tiered platters of food lined the edges of the room and discreet Earther servers moved through the crowd with trays of coupe glasses filled with pale sparkling wine. Martian couples circled elegantly to the classical music played by a six-piece orchestra mounted on a low dais. Without giving her a moment to catch her bearings, Wim took her directly onto the dance floor.

The dance was mortifying. Wim was both awkward and solemn, often moving wrong without being aware of it. He spoke to her very little and seemed intent upon following the steps. She was relieved when he released her.

Finally free, Vivian found Luz and Delilah standing near one of the refreshment tables. "Did you not enjoy Reverend Adair's undivided attention?" Luz teased.

"I think he bruised my toe with those awful little boots." She looked sharply at her sister. "Why aren't you on the dance floor?"

"Oh . . ." Delilah twisted her hands. "I'm just . . ." She looked across the room, and Vivian followed her gaze to where Caspian circled, shaking hands with his Martian guests and laughing jovially. Perhaps her sister cared about Caspian's attention after all. "Have you tried the pastries, Viv?"

Vivian had just popped the pastry in her mouth when she sensed a tall, looming presence behind her. "Miss Bowen," said Xavier. "I would like to claim the next dance, if you'll have me."

She gaped up at him, still chewing her pastry. Luz spoke for her. "Vivian would love nothing more."

Xavier nodded seriously. "I will find you when the next song begins." He walked away again immediately.

"Oh, for goodness' sake," Delilah growled. "I can't wait for him to come to me." She marched determinedly away in Caspian's direction.

Vivian glared at Luz. "I did tell you I hate the man, didn't I?"

Luz smirked. "Hate is such a strong word. Don't let your little crush on that soldier distract you. Xavier is on the approved list."

"He isn't approved," Vivian protested. "Wim said so himself. Besides, he has no interest in this bizarre courtship ritual we're being marched through."

"For someone with no interest in finding a wife, he's found excuses to put himself in your path a lot since we arrived."

Vivian was spared having to form a response by Xavier's return. He held a hand out to her, and she took it in silence.

The Martian style of dancing involved joining the man's left hand and the woman's right in a feather-light clasp. On the opposite side, the man kept his hand below the woman's arm, and she rested her hand on his shoulder. When the women had practiced the dance forms in their dormitory, Vivian had been relieved by the distance and formality of the formation.

Xavier looked down on her with no expression as he turned her in confident, precise movements around the dance floor. His hand held hers in a firmer grip than was customary between Martians and Earthers. Elsewhere on the dance floor, Vivian could see Delilah and Caspian spinning and talking earnestly. Her sister's cheeks were flushed, and her eyes sparkled.

When she could stand the silence no longer, Vivian asked, "Do you dance a lot?"

"No."

After another excruciating pause, she addressed him a second time with, "It's your turn to say something now, Mr. Dorsey. Reverend Adair has stuffed us full of Martian ballroom etiquette. I talked about the dance, and you ought to talk about something equally boring. I don't know—the size of the room or the number of couples."

He looked down at her with a smirk. "Do you talk by rule then, while you are dancing?"

"I've never been to a dance before tonight. We didn't have balls in a refugee camp."

"Of course," Xavier said soberly. "Forgive the impertinent question." He said nothing for a time and then forced out, "Did you and your sister enjoy exploring the barracks?"

"We did." Unable to resist the temptation, she added, "When you saw us there the other day, we were making a new friend."

Xavier scowled. "Silas Gatlin is very skilled at making friends. He's not as good at retaining them."

"He told me he lost your friendship. And an inheritance too."

Xavier's face returned to its polite neutral mask. "Let's talk of other matters."

"We've had no luck finding a topic so far," Vivian shot back. "I can't imagine what we are going to talk about next."

"What do you think of books?" he asked, smiling slightly.

"Books—" To conceal her delight at being asked such a question, Vivian said. "I'm sure we don't read the same things." He read dry Council briefings. She wasn't about to discuss her favorite crumbling paperback romances from the camps. And she doubted he would be a lover of Earther nineteenth-century women's literature.

"I am sorry you think so, but if that's the case we can compare our different opinions."

She cringed at the memory of Max Rinaldi mocking her reading choice, and said, "No, I can't talk about books while thinking about dancing." She cast around for a change of subject. "I didn't expect to see you here tonight. Didn't Caspian tell you that you could skip the dance and go to bed?"

Xavier scowled. "I did not expect to be here, either. My opinion of this whole affair is unchanged."

"Then why did you come?"

"I find, Miss Bowen, that I am quite unable to stay away from you." He gripped her hand tighter.

Vivian flushed and said nothing.

When the dance ended, Xavier bowed to her and parted in silence. Vivian stared after him in confusion. He seemed so cold to her one moment and drawn to her the next. Why bother attending the ball if he had no intention of marrying a Red Mother? And why dance with her and then barely speak to her?

Wim again claimed a dance with her. He held her stiffly in his arms with clammy fingers, and the way his artificial eye roamed in all directions made her shudder. "I am so pleased the Intelligence has brought us together."

"Yes." Out of the corner of her eye, she saw Xavier bow to Caspian and Delilah. He took Delilah's hand and led her onto the dance floor.

"The other Red Mothers admire you, Miss Bowen. It would hearten everyone to see you be the first settled with an optimized match."

They'd certainly admired her unauthorized trip to the soldier's barracks. Is that what Wim meant? Did the Intelligence not approve of the taste of freedom she'd found or that she'd told the other women about it?

"What's it like to speak directly to the Intelligence?" she asked.

Wim jerked his head back, as if surprised by the question. "An honor."

"Is it really the exact same AI that was created nearly two hundred years ago by the tech billionaires that founded Mars?"

"It has improved itself with time, but, yes, it is an immortal being."

"Wouldn't it get, I don't know, a little stale? Outdated? Why don't you upgrade to a newer model?"

"Upgrade! My dear Miss Bowen, the Intelligence is a nearly perfect creation."

Vivian couldn't think of what to say to this ridiculous statement, so she remained quiet.

When the dance finished, Wim offered to take her for another. When Vivian declined, he stayed stuck to her side, his sweaty hands stroking a silver augmentation embedded in his bald skull as he spoke to her in a never-ending monotone. Vivian watched

Xavier escort Delilah back to Caspian. Delilah sparkled at all the attention, and Vivian felt a pang watching her sister turn her full charm onto Xavier.

A pang of what? Vivian shoved the concern away.

Wim, meanwhile, chattered away about how pleased the Intelligence would be at the success of the ball. Vivian listened with half an ear, making the occasional noise of interest.

"Vivian, darling," Ivey's voice interrupted Wim's speech. "I am so pleased you could return to my humble home." She turned her cynical smile upon Wim. "I hope you don't mind me stealing away our Vivian, Reverend."

Wim frowned at her. "Miss Bowen has no interest in a female partner, Miss Hayes."

"I know. Such a tragedy for me." She turned to Vivian and gestured lazily with one hand. "Vivian, have you seen the art on loan to the Hayes Estate for this occasion?"

Vivian allowed Ivey to lead her away out of the ballroom and down the quiet hall.

"You seemed in dire need of rescue," Ivey murmured to her. "And I do think you'll appreciate the gallery."

In the wide hall of Hayes House, a series of paintings were mounted on easels. Couples strolled down the gallery, and Vivian caught the eye of Camille arm-in-arm with a handsome Martian with ebony skin and a deep purple cravat.

"Ivey!" The man gestured to one of the framed paintings. "Tell me where the devil you acquired this piece."

Ivey's smile turned genuine. "Theo, have you met Miss Vivian Bowen? Vivian, let me introduce you to Counselor Carpenter, one of the foremost patrons of the arts in Arcadia."

Vivian spread her skirts in a curtsey.

"How do you do?" Theo said abruptly. "Ivey, this is Catenian work, is it not? How in blazes did you manage to get a hold of it?"

Vivian turned curiously to look at the painting. The large canvas depicted a lush garden with a riot of colorful tropical plants—under a pink Martian sky.

"On loan from Chancellor Hawk in an attempt to win my brother's favor," Ivey replied. "They want Caspian's terraforming tech. You know his team has made impressive advancements in the last few years."

Theo snorted. "If Catena wanted our tech, it shouldn't have cut itself off from Arcadia quite so thoroughly."

Camille let go of Theo's arm and leaned closer to the green, orange, and yellow brush strokes. "It looks like home. Is this possible on Mars?" she asked in wonder.

"No," Ivey and Theo said together.

Ivey pinched the bridge of her nose. "My brother's terraforming project is developing techniques to create a greenhouse effect to warm the atmosphere of Mars," she explained to Vivian and Camille. "It doesn't literally mean the planet will turn into a green jungle. But they have grandiose dreams on Catena, and their new leader wants our research and technology."

"Caspian isn't fool enough to consider it, is he?" Theo demanded. "He knows the Intelligence would never allow it."

Ivey waved a hand airily. "Caspian is happy to take Catena's art and string River Hawk along with vague promises. Don't fret, Theo dear. This isn't a Council matter yet."

Theo frowned and seemed inclined to object until Camille fit her small hand to his bicep. "Another dance, Mr. Carpenter?"

He looked down at her, and his features smoothed. "Of course, my lady." He inclined his head to Ivey and Vivian and allowed himself to be dragged away.

"Oh, she's good." Ivey's eyes narrowed at the couple's retreating forms. "I can never get Theo to let a subject go, no matter how much I bat my eyes."

"They've bonded over jazz," Vivian told her.

"And you, Vivian, how are you fairing?"

Vivian shrugged evasively. "Fine."

Ivey regarded her gently. "X isn't going to make you an offer. I hope you realize that."

Vivian's stomach lurched. "But he might make you one?"

"Perhaps. In time."

"I do have some dignity, you know. I'm not going to pine over a man who isn't interested in me."

"I never said he wasn't interested in you. But he will never marry you."

Vivian tried to ignore the somersaults in her belly. "Show me around the gallery, will you?" As they perused the space, she tried to allow the paintings to replace thoughts of Xavier's parting words.

I find, Miss Bowen, that I am quite unable to stay away from you.

CHAPTER ELEVEN

48 Sols to Presentation Day

The morning after the ball, when Vivian and Luz stepped out of the dormitory for a walk, they stopped immediately upon seeing Shiloh and Felicia on the front lawn.

"Keep your feet under your shoulders, like this." Shiloh adjusted Felicia's hips. "You need a strong stance first. Your punch's power will come from your legs and knees."

"What are you doing?" Vivian asked.

"Shi's teaching me a few moves." Felicia tucked one hand against her chin and made a fist.

"No, no, keep your thumb outside your fist." Shiloh moved Felicia's fingers.

Vivian and Luz exchanged a glance. "Could you show us too?" Luz asked.

"Sure, babes. Stand right here."

Vivian felt a little silly learning the right way to punch in an emerald silk dress, but it was fun to see what her body could do. Sometime between the nutritious liquid diet of the nine-month voyage and two weeks of solid food on Mars, her ribs had disappeared from view under her skin. Her arms were still thin, but she no longer felt like she was about to break in two.

Now, standing on the lawn learning how to stabilize her legs to give her punch power, she wondered if her body was capable of building muscle. She wanted to be strong. From the number of women who'd come out to join them, diligently following Shiloh's confident instructions, her friends seemed to want the same thing.

"Look, the mail's here," one woman said after they'd been practicing for a while. The now-common sight of the spindly artificial mail carriers trundled into view.

"Four at once?" Another remarked. "That might be a new record."

"Can we do this again another time, Shi?" Camille asked. "I want you to teach me how to flip someone holding me from behind, like in the movies."

"We'll work up to that," Shiloh promised with a grin.

The women adjusted their hair and skirts as they walked back inside the house, energetically discussing punching techniques. In the dining room, mail and packages were piled on the table in a large heap.

Delilah picked up a silver box with her name on top and opened it. "Oooh. Look at this!" The box contained a row of charcoal pencils and a spiral sketchbook. "I told Caspian when we walked through the gallery that I wanted to learn to draw. He's so thoughtful."

Vivian thought of Ivey's words in her bedroom. Should she try persuading Delilah to choose Caspian? But her sister was already sifting through her other letters and gifts, exclaiming over each one. Ivey was right—Delilah wasn't taking Caspian's interest seriously.

She's only eighteen. Why shouldn't she be enjoying all the attention? At least for a little while longer.

"Vivian, this one's for you." Camille thrust a brown paper package in her hands. On the top, *Miss Vivian Bowen* was written in an elegant hand. Several of the women gathered curiously around Vivian as she opened it to find a sleek gray reader. An enclosed handwritten note fluttered to the ground. Vivian bent to retrieve the small square of heavy cream paper.

Expect more. —X

"A reader?" Delilah exclaimed. "Someone must be getting to know you well, Viv."

Vivian frowned at the gift. Why would Xavier send her a reader? She swiped it open to find a book preloaded: *An Introduction to Martian Law* by Dr. Ayesha Wilson, with foreword by Counselor Xavier Dorsey.

The arrogance of the man, to assume she would want to read his writing!

Luz leaned over her shoulder. "Do you think you'll be able to understand that?" she asked gently.

Did Xavier give her the gift in mockery after she'd evaded his questions on books the night before? Did he seek to draw attention to her poor education in order to remind her that she was unworthy of entering into Martian society?

She would prove him wrong.

Vivian lifted her chin in stubborn determination and opened the book of law to the first chapter, skipping the introduction. "I will learn."

The text *was* difficult. It assumed a basic knowledge of Martian history that Vivian didn't possess. The complex vocabulary and syntax were beyond the measly education she'd pieced together from the limited Sumter public readers and donated paper textbooks. As she read, she needed to pause every few sentences to use the reader to look up a word or concept on the nexus.

But the book was a revelation.

In the small courtyard adjacent to the dormitory, Vivian learned about the first permanent Martian settlers, before the creation of the Intelligence. They'd been scientists and explorers, comfortable with considerable risk and hardship for themselves. At the same time, they were self-aware enough to understand what was needed to develop a sustainable, multigenerational system on an inhospitable planet. They decided early in the settlement's history to establish the Martian entitlement to a basic standard of living, with meticulous optimal requirements for water, air, temperature, and food. They called these requirements the Martian Fundamental Rights.

Vivian traced the detailed chart the first Martians had published on nutrition standards and swallowed a lump in her throat.

Calorie minimums based on sex, height, origin planet, and occupation.

An optimal mix of proteins, fats, and carbohydrates.

Appropriate levels of vitamins and minerals.

Vivian knew firsthand the unpleasant consequences of not consuming adequate protein. And she'd seen the hollow-eyed children at the camp during lean months. It's why Vivian had joined forces with Evie and other women in the camp to pool their resources to collect a stockpile of nonperishables.

Until Max Rinaldi had intervened.

Vivian traced the surface of the reader as she learned about the concept of Martian Collective Sovereignty. All Martians had fundamental rights over their own bodies and the right and expectation to contribute to the collective well-being of the community. Martians contributed to the self-reliance of Mars, independent from Earth, and had a responsibility to aid with producing adequate nutrition on-planet.

She'd never known anything like it.

No one had ever given her a chance to produce anything herself. She and her family had been entirely reliant on the meager handouts of an increasingly broken government. She thought of her father, who would have welcomed the opportunity to return to a factory and earn a living instead of being trapped in the camp without any chance to find work. Her heart squeezed as she pictured her parents' uncertain future. Despite reaching out every day, she and Delilah had heard nothing further from them since Miranda's message.

A shadow covered her reader, and she looked up in surprise to see Wim hovering above her. "Vivian, excellent, I was hoping to have a word with you."

"Is all the food in our kitchen produced in this dome?" Vivian asked him.

Wim blinked. "I believe so."

"Could I see it?"

"You wish to see the greenhouse farms?"

"And the cultured meat labs. And the water treatment plants." Vivian wanted, powerfully and suddenly, to visualize Martian Collective Sovereignty in action. She didn't know, she realized, if tomatoes grew on trees or bushes. Or the ingredients in a loaf of bread.

"I'm sure your partner would be happy to arrange a tour." Wim sat beside her on the courtyard bench. "Which brings me to the reason I'm here."

Vivian put down her reader and fixed a polite, attentive smile onto her face. Whatever it was, she wished he'd be quick about it so she could return to her book.

"Yesterday, at the dance, the Intelligence informed me it had singled you out as the companion of my future life," Wim declared. "But before I run away with my feelings, perhaps I should state my reasons for marrying."

All thoughts of collective sovereignty fled Vivian's mind. She suppressed a hysterical laugh. *Wim? Run away with his feelings?* Her laughter faded into dread when she realized he was deadly serious.

Wim continued, "My reasons for marrying are, first, I think it is right as a servant of the Intelligence to set the example of its great vision for Mars's future." He put a ringed hand on his chest. "Secondly, I am convinced it will add very greatly to my happiness. And thirdly, which perhaps I ought to have mentioned earlier, that it is the advice and recommendation of the very noble lady whom I have the honor of calling patroness." He stared dreamily into the distance as Vivian beat back the panic in her chest. "Secretary Yarrow has declared I must be among the first to wed. As the servant of the Intelligence, it is my duty." He turned his attention back to her. "And now nothing remains for me but to assure you of my affection."

Vivian held out one hand, as if to try to stop his words. "No. Thank you, but this is my choice, isn't it? My answer is no."

"Decline!" Wim scoffed. "I have heard that it is usual with Earther women to reject the man they secretly mean to accept. And that sometimes the refusal is repeated a second or even a third time. I will, therefore, not be discouraged."

For a moment, Vivian was so angry by this idea that she was unable to speak. "You can't really believe such nonsense," she finally sputtered. "I mean it. No. You couldn't make me happy, and I'd bet I'm the last woman on this planet who would make you happy."

Wait . . .

She hadn't meant to bring happiness into the decision-making. Her parents were in danger. She couldn't afford to care about her own happiness.

"The Intelligence believes we could make each other happy."

Vivian couldn't help herself from bursting out, "Then the Intelligence is wrong!" She grabbed her reader and rose to depart.

Wim sprang to his feet, towering over her. "The Intelligence is incapable of making a mistake. When I speak to you next on this subject I expect a more favorable answer. I will refrain from accusing you of cruelty because I know it to be the established custom of your culture to reject a man on the first application."

Was he listening to her at all? She couldn't accept this man. She couldn't. "You aren't making sense," she said weakly.

Could he force her to accept? Was the commitment to allow the women to choose their own partners merely lip service?

"You must give me leave to flatter myself, my dear, that your rejection is merely words. I'm not of the highest echelons of Martian society, true, but I'm Secretary Yarrow's most trusted advisor and have a direct line to the Intelligence. It doesn't appear to me that my offer is unworthy."

Vivian trembled in frustration and an uneasy fear. "Thank you again, but I can't accept. Good day, Wim." She hurried away without another word.

CHAPTER TWELVE

47 Sols to Presentation Day

Vivian spent the rest of the day and a sleepless night tense and agitated. How could the Intelligence match two people so ill-suited for each other? Over and over in her mind, she replayed Xavier's words from their walk at the Hayes Estate. *The Intelligence cares nothing for the quality of life of one Earther woman.*

What had Miranda meant when she'd warned that her parents were in danger? Were the Rinaldi brothers trying to shake them down for cash or valuables? Surely, surely, they wouldn't kill her mild-mannered parents, who'd never made trouble for anyone.

If her parents were murdered, Vivian would spend the rest of her life knowing she could have accepted Wim and prevented their deaths. She would have to live with that knowledge forever.

When Wim returned the next day, he wouldn't meet her eyes. Instead, he turned his attention to Luz, who listened patiently to him. Vivian was relieved and grateful to her friend for providing a buffer. Luz led Wim out to the courtyard, where he spoke with a furrowed brow, droning in an endless monologue.

She couldn't have accepted him, she told herself. She would have been miserable. For years.

Vivian touched the spot at her throat where Max Rinaldi's shank had pierced her skin. Had he killed Evie with that weapon? Or had he simply used his stronger muscles to overpower her and choked the life from her with nothing but his bare hands? Evie had been thin from years of malnutrition. Frail. Like Vivian before she'd left for Mars.

She remembered what Shiloh had said. *It's easier if you don't fight back.* With the blade at her throat and Max Rinaldi's bulky, well-fed body pressed against hers, she'd been rigid with terror. It hadn't even occurred to her to attempt to fight. If she'd tried, she'd be dead.

Like Evie.

A knock at the front door startled Vivian out of her dark thoughts. Vivian opened it to find Silas, dressed in a full soldier's uniform, his hat pressed to his chest. He gave her a slow, lazy smile that made Vivian's heart speed up. This is what she needed. A handsome gentleman soldier to distract her. Someone not on Wim's approved list.

"How did you get over the walls?" she hissed, stifling an unexpected girlish giggle and pulling him inside. "You shouldn't be here."

"Called in a few favors." He reached out a hand to cup her cheek. "Vivian, I can't get you out of my mind. I had to see you again."

Vivian leaned into his touch. Silas had come to see her for the pleasure of her company, not for the child she could carry. Under his admiring gaze, she felt young and carefree. More like Delilah than herself. What would it be like to be as vivacious as her sister? To believe falling in love was possible?

"Wim Adair is in the courtyard," she said. "We can't let him spot you. Come on." Vivian led Silas to the only private space available—her bedroom—and shut the door firmly behind her.

Silas's sapphire eyes sparkled as he looked around the small space. "How very spartan. This room nearly resembles our barracks. I was under the impression Yarrow was treating the Red Mothers like people of importance."

"I'm not sure Secretary Yarrow and the Intelligence see us as people at all," Vivian said bitterly. "Just bodies to be dressed up and paraded around until we're impregnated. I think the Intelligence gave us a shared dorm to encourage us to choose a partner faster."

Silas closed the curtain on her window. "Will it work?"

"Hardly." Vivian stretched out her arms to enjoy the feeling of openness. "Living in safety with my sister and a fully stocked kitchen? This house is paradise."

How could she say such a thing when her parents still lived in their one-room tent in Sumter? Vivian abruptly put her hands down.

Silas picked up one of the charcoal sketches Delilah had left scattered on the bedside table and examined it with a little smile. "There are those of us who believe that the Intelligence should not have such a prominent role in our society."

Vivian glanced at the ceiling. "Should you say that out loud? Aren't you worried the Intelligence will overhear you?" Was the Intelligence watching them right now? She gave an involuntary shudder.

Silas shrugged and returned the drawing to the table. "Why should I care what the Intelligence hears? We do not yet live in a society that blocks all speech." His eyes glittered. "I believe the Intelligence is stifling our ability to live as free, independent Martians. The AI was designed by the First Families to protect their offspring by any means necessary, and it cares nothing for the rest of us not born into privilege."

His attitude toward the Intelligence was so much like Xavier's. What would Xavier think of his boyhood rival in her bedroom? She pictured his rich dark eyes smoldering with jealousy. A tempting image. She smiled flirtatiously up at Silas. "You're quite the radical, aren't you?"

Silas grunted. "Some may think so. But you must already see what it feels like to move within the Martian oligarchy without being part of it. I know they must treat you with condescension and disrespect, the way they've always treated me. And the Intelligence refuses to share this new reproductive tech. Why should the Founding Families be the only ones able to populate Mars? Why should they be the only ones with access to the Red Mothers?"

"Access? You're here with me now, aren't you?"

"You know what I mean. The ability to have our own enhanced children." Silas walked closer to her. "Is it true the partner you select will share your bed?"

"True enough."

"What a waste. Those stuffy aristocrats will have no idea how to please you."

"And you do?"

Silas ran a single finger along the line of her jaw. "I do."

She could believe it. He was handsome enough to have his pick of lovers. She thought, suddenly, of Xavier at the luncheon on her second day on Mars, leaning toward the bartender in that tight-fitting brocade vest. Silas wasn't the only one who was good-looking enough to attract anyone he wanted.

"Wim warned us to refrain from—from sexual congress." Vivian ducked her head, torn between curiosity and shyness. Should she tell him to leave? No. This might be her only chance to be with someone outside of Wim's approved list. Someone who wasn't interested in her for her womb.

"Did he indeed?" Silas's voice had gone low. His large hand wrapped around the back of her neck, and his thumb came to rest on the faint scar at her throat.

Vivian looked up at him. She was forever looking up at Martian men. Silas's eyes were a mischievous azure blue, and his lips looked warm and inviting. He bent his head low and kissed her.

At twenty-two, Vivian had never allowed herself to be alone with a man before.

She'd never been kissed.

Until now.

Silas's hand gripped the back of her neck as he explored her mouth with his tongue, barely giving Vivian a chance to breathe. Her head was bent fully backward to accommodate their height difference. This was how it was supposed to feel, Vivian assured herself. She wasn't trapped. As an experiment, Vivian tried to pull away slightly, and Silas tugged her closer against him.

She could get away, if she tried. She could. This was nothing like being pressed against Max Rinaldi. She was stronger than Silas. Her bones were denser. Hadn't Wim warned her on her first day on Mars that she could crush Martian finger bones with her bare hand?

I'm not trapped.

Silas guided her down onto her bed and moved his lips down her throat to the swell of her breasts. With one hand, he reached up her skirt.

Her skirt.

Vivian's head spun. Everything was happening so fast.

Don't let yourself be alone with a man, her mother had told her the day they'd arrived at Sumter. *If you get pregnant in here, you will never get out.*

The Martians may receive contraceptive implants as teenagers, but no one had offered one to Vivian. Why would they? She was to be a Red Mother and bear the future hope of Mars.

His hand was between her legs now, probing with long, calloused fingers. "You aren't wet yet," he muttered, his face tensing, and spit into one hand. "We'll have to do something about that." He shoved two fingers deep inside her, and Vivian winced.

Was she supposed to be wet? All she could think about was keeping still. Waiting for it to be over. Remembering shaking under Max Rinaldi's blade as his big hand cupped her hips to press her bottom tighter against him.

The door burst open. "Viv baby, I need to talk to you." Vivian looked up to see Luz standing still in the doorway, her face frozen in shock. "Who the hell are you?"

"A thousand pardons," Silas said, leaping to his feet and adjusting his trousers.

Vivian's hands were shaking as she sat up and smoothed down her dress.

"You need to leave," Luz ordered. "Now."

Silas bowed to them both and grabbed his hat. "Vivian, I— I'll come back another time."

Vivian looked up to meet his beautiful blue eyes. Did she want to see him again? Why had she been so cold and disconnected? She'd wanted him too, hadn't she? At least until it had actually happened.

"No, you won't." Luz's mouth was pinched as she spoke. "Vivian isn't going to fuck up her future for you. Leave."

Silas gave Vivian one last look and fled from the room.

"It was nothing—"

Luz held up one hand. "We're at peak fertility—that's what Dr. Chavez said. You were really going to throw everything away to fuck some pretty Martian soldier? You're smarter than this, Viv."

Vivian winced. "We weren't going to have sex. I was curious, that's all." She touched the back of her neck, where Silas had bent it at an odd angle. What would have happened if Luz hadn't interrupted them? Would she have found the words to tell him to stop? And would he have listened?

Her hands were still shaking. Could she have gotten pregnant today? After all the care she'd taken. *Stupid.* She had just wanted, for a moment, to forget about the fate bearing down upon her. To just be a young woman spending time with a charming, handsome man. Why had she assumed Martian men were different from the men at Sumter? *Stupid, stupid, stupid.*

The door opened again, and Delilah walked in. Vivian felt some relief to be spared Luz's lecture until she caught sight of her sister's tear-streaked face. "What's happened? Is it Mom and Dad?"

Her nightmare had come to pass. She'd been too selfish to save them. She should have accepted Wim's offer when she had the chance.

"Caspian sent me a letter." Delilah brandished a sheet of paper the same cream color as the brief note that had accompanied Vivian's reader. "He and Ivey have left Arcadia with Xavier and are on their way to visit the far domes. He says that Xavier wants to see his sister who is studying music in another dome."

"Fucking Xavier," Vivian muttered, relieved for the chance to replace her muddled mix of emotions with pure anger. "He found an excuse to take Caspian away from you. He only needs to keep you apart for six weeks." *And maybe he needed to find an excuse to keep himself away*, a treacherous part of her mind wondered. She pushed the thought away.

"I didn't—Vivian, I . . . I didn't think I cared. I have so many suitors." She sank down beside Vivian on her bed. "Why does it hurt so much for one to leave me?"

Vivian tucked a lock of hair behind her sister's ear. "I'm sorry."

"I should have told him that he was the one I wanted. I should have made him feel special. I thought—" Delilah hiccupped. "I thought he'd be waiting for me when I was ready."

Still standing, Luz crossed her arms. "You both need to cut the crap. Pick someone. Anyone. Do it as soon as our eggs are harvested. There's no reason to draw this out."

"I haven't seen you pick anyone," Delilah shot back. She wiped her eyes with the back of her hand.

Luz had an odd look on her face as she replied, "Watch me."

CHAPTER THIRTEEN

43 Sols to Presentation Day

"What are you doing?" From her elevated position on the wheeled medical bed, Vivian peered down to watch the top of Dr. Chavez's close-cropped brown hair bent over Vivian's hand.

"Placing an IV to administer propofol. To put you to sleep." She rubbed the skin on Vivian's hand and, without warning, pressed a needle into the blue vein.

Vivan closed her eyes against the pinch of sharp pain. "And then?"

"I'll perform a transvaginal ultrasound aspiration," Dr. Chavez replied crisply. She didn't seem to care that the words were like a foreign language to Vivian.

"Could you explain it to me?"

Dr. Chavez sighed. "Alright. I'll insert a needle into an ultrasound device to find follicles. The needle passes through the vaginal wall and into the follicle to retrieve the egg. I'll then collect the egg with suction."

"Oh." Vivian weighed her next question for a moment. But she had to know. "How large is the needle?"

With one gloved hand, the doctor held up a needle wrapped in sterile packaging. It was very, very long.

"Can I ask you something?"

Dr. Chavez grunted.

"What are the side effects of the treatment?"

The doctor paused before saying, "We'll have to find out, won't we? You will be the first patients to receive the in-utero calcium treatments."

"I heard—I heard they will be painful. And perhaps lifelong."

"Have you been speaking to Counselor Dorsey?"

Vivian saw no reason to deny her source. "Yes."

Dr. Chavez let out a slow breath. "An excess of calcium can lead to nausea, vomiting, muscle and bone weakness, kidney stones, and confusion, among other things. We don't know what impact the in utero treatments will have on your bodies yet."

"Kidney stones," Vivian repeated. "My dad passed a kidney stone once. I've never seen him in so much agony."

Dr. Chavez turned toward the screen and didn't meet her eyes. "Martian painkillers are potent and fast-acting."

"Counselor Dorsey told me that you couldn't recruit Earther women who'd already immigrated to Mars to the Red Mother's program."

"Counselor Dorsey talks too much."

"Is it true?"

The doctor shrugged. "The population of single, eligible Earther women already living on Mars is rather small." She met Vivian's eyes again. "I took the Hippocratic Oath. I won't let you suffer needlessly. We will use every tool at our disposal to minimize your discomfort and pain. Now can we get on with it? I'm doing fifteen of these procedures today." Without waiting for an answer, she depressed the valve attached to Vivian's hand.

Vivian had only a moment to experience a tingling in her face before her world went dark.

Sometime later, Vivian blinked open her eyes to the bright glare of fluorescent overhead lighting. She turned her head to see Luz staring blearily at her.

Vivian craned her neck to see she was still dressed in a hospital gown, lying on the same medical bed. A bandage covered her hand. She could sense, as if from behind a curtain, that her lower abdomen ached.

"We're supposed to stay here and rest," Luz told her weakly, gesturing around the large room to several other women still sleeping in the other cots. "A car will come by eventually to take us home."

A screen took up half of one wall, a video playing on low volume. "Is that the secretary?" Vivian's voice came out as a whisper.

"Looks like it." Luz pressed a button on her bed and the sound became audible.

A male Martian journalist wearing a pinstripe blue suit sat across from Constance Yarrow in a wood-paneled office. "Today is a momentous day in Martian history. The Red Women at this very moment are donating their eggs to the Intelligence. What would you like to say to them?"

Secretary Yarrow had never bothered to visit the dormitory or even speak to the women, but now, she looked directly into the camera. "Red Mothers, you are giving your very body to provide for us. You are the mothers of the future. The bridge that will take us into a glorious new era where Martians can finally populate this planet. The Intelligence"—she touched her fist to her forehead briefly—"has asked me to pass a message along to you. Red Mothers, we will remember your bravery and sacrifice for all of Martian history. Your names will be spoken and remembered."

The anesthesia was wearing off in earnest now, and Vivian could feel a painful pressure on her pelvis. Her hand stung. Her skin smelled like dried sweat. She didn't feel very brave.

The program shifted to footage of a crowd gathered on the street outside the clinic. They held signs of support and wore large hibiscus flowers attached to their hats.

One young Martian woman with tears streaming down her face clutched a sign in front of her chest that read *THANK YOU FOR YOUR SERVICE* in large block letters. "You know what it's like to want children desperately and know that a baby would kill you," she said to a journalist. "When I see an Earther mother, with her little Martian baby, I just want to hold that sweet little baby and never let them go. But I was that baby. We were all that baby. That baby will grow up to be just like the rest of us—we're all essentially sterile."

"Is there anything you'd like to say to the Red Mothers?"

"I want them to know that when I'm walking down the street a few decades from now and see a beautiful, tall Martian woman with a round belly, I'll ask her for her mother's name. I'll speak her mother's name and remember it. I'll remember her sacrifice."

The *Arcadian Life* coverage went on like that for a while. Vivian watched the interviews numbly as her abdomen pulsed with dull pain. The rows of cots grew, until all thirty of the women were crammed side-to-side in the large space, staring at the footage of grateful Martians.

Finally, hours later, they were told their driver had arrived, and the first wave of women could dress and depart. Vivian pulled a dress on with shaking hands, every movement sending pangs through her lower stomach.

She remembered how she'd blithely told Xavier she had a high pain tolerance. What a foolish thing to say. It was easy to forget about the impact of pain once it was gone, but now that it was back, she found herself reliving every memory of pain from Sumter. How much worse would the next step be? Nine months trapped inside a prison of her own body as Dr. Chavez injected her with treatments designed for the health of the fetus, not her own health.

When Vivian stepped onto the street, a bright flash caught her by surprise. A camera. "Vivian Bowen, how does it feel?"

Vivian's stomach cramped so sharply she doubled over. The journalist didn't miss a beat. "Look at the sacrifice the Red Mothers have taken for our planet. Look how Miss Bowen moves stoically through the pain. The Intelligence chose wisely when it selected such a brave young woman to be a Red Mother."

Luz gripped her arm and pulled her upright. "Come on, Viv baby. One foot in front of the other."

Looking up through a haze of pain, Vivian could see the onlookers locking arms, forming a path from the clinic's door to the groundcar. Their signs lay forgotten at their feet. They were singing, Vivian realized. An old Earther hymn that made Vivian think of the church basements, acoustic guitars, and red Kool-Aid of her childhood in the Carolinas.

Amazing grace, how sweet the sound,

That saved a wretch, like me.

Luz was staring at the onlookers, her pinched face softening with wonder. Vivian gripped her friend's hand and tried to anchor herself on Luz's expression. If Luz could find purpose out of this unpleasant day, so could she.

I once was lost, but now am found,

Was blind, but now I see.

"Shit, I think they actually mean it," Luz whispered. "They think we're here to save them."

"Can we get a move on?" the driver demanded, holding open the groundcar door. "I've gotta make five trips to bring all you girls home."

Vivian tugged on Luz's hand, and they made their way to the quiet groundcar. As they pulled away, Vivian's eyes met the woman she'd seen on the TV show, the one who'd cried. The woman pressed a hand to her chest and mouthed, "Thank you."

CHAPTER FOURTEEN

38 Sols to Presentation Day

"More wine, Miss Bowen?" offered the Martian man seated next to her.

Vivian blinked at him. "Oh, no thank you." The glass of pale sparkling wine she'd sipped while awaiting her breakfast was plenty. She tried to focus on the conversation happening around her.

In the days since her recovery from the egg retrieval procedure, Vivian's social calendar had filled up, and three men had settled into a friendly rivalry as they courted her. Vivian sensed from their easy banter that they had spoken to one another about their intentions, but they certainly hadn't consulted her.

At least they'd brought her outside the four walls of the compound. The open-air restaurant terrace overlooked a sculpted park with twisting redstone paths leading through a landscaping of inky-blue jagged volcanic rocks and ornamental grasses dotted with vibrant flowers. Vivian watched a young Earther man weaving unobtrusively through the Martian couples and groups as he pruned the path. No one else seemed to notice him. Vivian wondered what had brought him to Mars and what sacrifices he'd made to pay for his ticket.

The three Martians hadn't noticed her distraction. Ren, the man who enjoyed poetry that she'd met during the first luncheon, was lecturing on some topic while the other two nodded vigorously.

"You must understand, Vivian dear, my Martian foreparents were among the first to establish a base on the planet," Ren told her. "Their wise choices have allowed our family to be one of the wealthiest and most powerful in the dome. They had the good sense to sell their property in Tokyo before the sea level rose too high. After Typhoon Michi, they were able to sponsor much of our extended family to flee to Mars. Populating the planet with their genetically enhanced descendants would honor their legacy."

"Then Mars has always been a home for refugees," Vivian offered tentatively in response.

"I would like to think so." Ren gave her a bashful smile. He was good looking, Vivian decided. Objectively. He had straight black hair that brushed his shoulders, a neatly trimmed beard, and kind eyes.

One of the other men leaned across her. "If the Nakamura family wishes to retain their wealth, you should tell your uncle to stop pouring good money after bad into the lanthanum mines. Everyone knows they are about to bust."

Ren turned away from Vivian to argue about mining investments, and she returned to making the occasional noise of interest. The Earther man on the path ducked his head and scrambled out of the way of two Martian women's swishing skirts.

In the next five weeks, she would need to select a partner. She thought of Silas's mouth on her breast and tried to picture one of her three dining companions in the same position. Putting her fork down, she stared at her cooling cultured sausage. She didn't think she could eat another bite.

The day before, she'd gotten a brief text-only message from Miranda, the camp aid worker. She'd helped treat a burn on

Vivian's mother's neck. A cooking accident, her mother had explained. Only the regular, circular pattern looked more like a cigarette burn.

She needed to get her parents out. Could she pick one of these men today? Would they think she was too forward? Too transactional?

Their genetically modified eggs were ready for fertilization, Wim had announced yesterday. The Intelligence had recommended implantation as soon as possible, not waiting for the official wedding ceremony on Presentation Day. The day after they selected their partner, the embryo would be implanted. The very next day.

I can wait a little longer, she thought with a wave of guilt.

At the conclusion of their breakfast, Ren offered her his arm. "Please allow me the honor of escorting you home, Miss Bowen." Vivian took his proffered arm and stepped down the winding redstone path to the street. "Give me a moment to summon my driver." Ren strode toward a nearby café where the driver must have been waiting.

"Vivian." She looked up to see Silas leaning in the shadow of a door frame. "I hoped I'd catch you alone."

Vivian tensed. "How did you know I was here?" *Was he following me?* A few weeks ago, she might have found his interest exciting, but now all she wanted was for him to go away.

"Word travels," he said with an air of put-upon casualness. "I miss you, Vivian. I was hoping we could find a chance to be alone together again."

"I . . ." Vivian looked around for Ren, but he was nowhere in sight. "I'm not sure that's a good idea." The memory of giggling and pulling Silas into her bedroom seemed far away, as if it had been some other woman.

"Why? Because the Council is forcing you to do their bidding? I could help you. You could come with me, away from here."

"What! I can't simply melt away. The dome is only seven square miles."

Silas waved a hand. "I have connections. You could start over, Vivian. We could start a life together somewhere else."

"A life together?" Vivian repeated incredulously. He didn't seem to care about her own expectations for her life. But then again, who did?

Xavier cares, her treacherous mind thought.

"The groundcar will just be a moment," Ren said as he strode back to her side.

Vivian turned away from Silas, and, when she glanced back, he was gone.

When Ren returned Vivian to the compound, she escaped to the garden. She put aside her fascinating and dense Martian textbook and loaded an Earther historical romance novel onto her new reader. Anything to forget the real world that morning. On the screen, the dashing duke declared himself to the beautiful debutante. He pulled her against him, crushing her to his chest as he kissed her fervently. The heroine wanted the embrace. She was caught up in the moment.

There had been no birth control during this period of history either, Vivian thought glumly, but the debutante was not afraid of getting pregnant prematurely. *She* was not having flashbacks to her mother's childhood lectures during a moment of passion.

Something is wrong with me.

"Vivian, I am glad to have found you." Wim stood over her. He gave her a little bow, his red robes flapping around his ankles. "We are all liable to error." He cleared his throat. "I certainly meant well. My only objective was to honor the wishes of the Intelligence and my patron, Secretary Yarrow. I should have listened to you when you first declined my proposal. If my behavior was inappropriate, I beg your pardon."

Wim, apologize? It was so unexpected that Vivian could do nothing but stare at him in astonishment. Finally, she cleared her throat. “Thank you, Wim. I accept your apology.”

“Good, good.” He fingered one of the augmentations on his skull nervously. “I wanted to be the first to tell you the happy news that I have made an offer to Luz that she deems acceptable. The Intelligence has sanctioned our arrangement.”

Vivian opened her mouth and closed it several times before managing, “What?”

“I am most grateful to you for refusing me.” He gave another little Martian bow and departed.

Vivian set down her reader and went to find Luz, who was calmly preparing dinner in the shared kitchen. “You’re marrying Wim?” Vivian exclaimed. “Luz, that’s impossible! He’s rude and condescending and thinks too highly of himself.”

Luz snorted and continued chopping a carrot. “I’m aware.”

“I don’t understand.”

“You will. Viv, you and I, we’re the same. We aren’t starry-eyed romantics like Delilah or Camille. This is about safety and security. Period.”

Vivian nodded in reluctant agreement. If the experience with Silas taught her anything, it was that being swept up in a moment of passion wasn’t going to happen for her. But if security was all she cared about, why had she turned Wim down?

“You know I don’t have time to waste to fulfill my part of the contract.” Luz put the knife down and turned to look at Vivian. “And Wim—” She faltered. “He knew things. The Intelligence told him. About . . . what’s happened to me. My life before. There’s so much I haven’t told you. Oh, Viv baby, I’ve seen some ugly shit.” Luz briskly wiped a tear from her cheek. “You can’t know what a gift it is to have someone know and understand without having to go through the horror of retelling.”

Ashamed of her quick judgment, Vivian placed her hand on Luz's arm and squeezed.

Luz put her own hand on top of Vivian's. "Wim told me he's asexual. He—" Her hand tightened. "He said—he said he spoke with the Intelligence and in our situation there's a high probability of successful co-parenting without us needing a sexual relationship."

At least her friend wouldn't need to discover what other body augmentations lay beneath Wim's robes. "Is that really what you want? A life without sex? Without love? Without intimacy?"

Luz's mouth quirked. "Viv, he doesn't experience sexual attraction. He's still capable of love. Not that *I'm* capable. I know I talk a good game, but, I swear, a life without sex is my ultimate fantasy. And who knows? Intimacy may come, in time."

Vivian's eyes filled with tears. "I'm happy for you. I really am. It's only that I'll miss you."

CHAPTER FIFTEEN

23 Sols to Presentation Day

Change came for Luz bewilderingly quickly. The next morning, her meager possessions were packed, and she bade the Bowen sisters farewell with tight hugs, leaving for her new life on the far side of the dome.

"I don't understand why they're making you go now," Delilah complained. "Shouldn't you wait until you're married on Presentation Day?"

Luz's lips turned up. "You know why. They want these fancy-ass embryos implanted as soon as possible." She touched Delilah's shoulder. "Have you found someone else now that Caspian is gone?"

Delilah pasted on a bright smile that Vivian knew was fake. "I have so many suitors I think I'll form a harem. I can hardly decide between picking the most beautiful, richest, or most powerful."

Luz wrapped her arms around Vivian and murmured in her ear, "Good luck with her, Viv."

Vivian snorted. "She'll be okay."

"Visit me?" Luz asked. "Once I'm settled in."

"I'll try." Vivian embraced Luz one more time and tried to push down her overwhelming sense of dread. *The next time I see her, she'll be pregnant.*

And so, thirty women became twenty-nine. Then twenty-five. Then seventeen. Finally, it was Delilah's turn.

Vivian spent another evening party at the same banquet hall trapped behind the same high walls. She was hiding in a corner hoping to escape a third dance from a persistent suitor when Delilah shared the news, coming up to her arm-in-arm with the Martian woman who had treated Vivian with such disdain at her first luncheon.

"Sister, let me introduce you to Mitzi King, my future wife," Delilah proclaimed rather proudly.

Vivian opened her mouth in shock. *Mitzi King? Really?* But even as she thought it, her chest eased with a traitorous sense of relief. Delilah was going first. Her parents would be alright.

"Delighted," Mitzi drawled without letting go of Delilah's arm. "Have you found a partner then?"

Vivian pressed her lips together. "Not yet."

Mitzi looked down her angular nose at Vivian. "Ticktock, as it were. Delilah is fortunate I was still available."

"*You* are the one that is fortunate," Delilah replied with a smile.

The woman barked a laugh. "I do adore your sass. Come home with me tonight." She leaned into Delilah's ear and whispered something too low for Vivian to hear.

"But—I thought—aren't we to wait until the embryo is successfully implanted?" Vivian sputtered, twisting her hands in front of her.

"Come now, Miss Bowen, that directive is for the men. Delilah is in no danger of conceiving an unmodified fetus with *me*." She swatted Delilah on the bottom, and Delilah giggled.

Vivian grabbed Delilah's arm. "I need a moment with my sister," she snapped as she dragged Delilah away. Out of Mitzi's earshot, she said, "You can't be serious. That woman will eat you alive."

Delilah smirked. "She promised to eat me for hours."

"This isn't a joke, Delilah! This is the rest of your life. What about Caspian?"

"He's gone. I'm not making the same mistake again. I'm not letting someone else leave me because I couldn't make up my mind. At least Mitzi is interesting." She gestured across the room to where Mitzi stood, sipping a cocktail and watching Delilah with heat in her eyes. "Look at how much she wants me. It's sexy."

Vivian's stomach churned. Soon it would be her turn to go to bed with one of her suitors. Would it be like it had been with Silas? Would she turn stiff and cold, enduring until her partner finished? Was she too broken for anything else? "I don't think I can do this."

"You can." Delilah wrapped her sister in a sudden fierce hug. "You brought me to this beautiful place with parties and sketchbooks and ballgowns. For the first time, I think I could be truly happy."

This place is a cage, Vivian thought. But she couldn't say that to Delilah. Her sister's happiness made everything worth it. She'd always believed that.

Then why did she feel close to vomiting?

Vivian rested her chin on her sister's shoulder. "I'm glad."

"Viv, you'll find someone you're compatible with. I know it."

Vivian drew back. "I'm not sure. Luz told me it's not possible to know what someone's like behind closed doors."

"I love Luz dearly, but she really is a tough old bitch. She's turned you into such a cynic."

"Maybe." Vivian blew out her breath. "But I think I am going to take Luz up on her invitation to visit her new home for a few days. I can't attend these endless parties in this walled estate with the same dull people for the next three weeks. I may as well get a chance to see more of Mars before I pick a husband."

"Seeing Luz will be good for you." Delilah hugged her sister one more time and then gave her a smirk. "The next time you see me, I'll be . . ." She stuck out her belly and proclaimed in her best Wim impression, "A Red Mother, carrying the future hope of Mars."

CHAPTER SIXTEEN

21 Sols to Presentation Day

When Vivian arrived at Luz's new home, she held her friend as if it had been years, not weeks since they had last parted. "How are you feeling?" Vivian asked anxiously, thinking of Dr. Chavez casually rattling off potential side effects.

Luz made a throwaway gesture. "Just some nausea. Nothing I can't handle. Come inside and let me show you around." With only five rooms, Wim's home would be considered modest by the standards of the Martian aristocracy, but Vivian found it charming. She liked the simple, practical furniture with none of the pretense of Hayes House. From the window, Vivian glimpsed the grandeur of the Yarrow family house shining down on them from its elevated perch atop a crater.

After giving her a tour, Luz sat her down in the living room across from Wim and returned with a tray with three glasses and a pitcher filled with a bright green drink. As she poured, Luz warned, "I'm still perfecting the recipe. I overdid it on the lime juice."

"This is excellent, my dear," Wim told her cheerfully. "It would never occur to me to drink a vegetable. Your creativity astounds me. What do you call this?"

"It's just a cucumber agua fresca." Luz gave a pleased little smile at the compliment. "I grew up on them. In Harlem, we'd add a spicy rim of tajin, but I'm not sure yet how to re-create the chamoy sauce." She tapped a finger on her glass. "I think I want to try tracking down dried hibiscus flowers, if they exist here."

"We saw people wearing hibiscus flowers on their hats," Vivian said. "Outside the clinic. Do you remember?"

Luz's expression lit up. "That's right."

"A rim of spice? Ingenious!" Wim exclaimed. "If you have need of hibiscus flowers, then that is what you shall have, my darling."

Luz regarded him fondly and sipped her agua fresca. Vivian, for her part, was completely baffled. Where had her jaded friend gone?

"I am so pleased, Vivian my dear, that you have come to visit," Wim continued. "I admit I have been remiss in my duties since I welcomed Luz into my humble home. But the Red Mothers are thriving in my absence. Secretary Yarrow has been most pleased by the pace of partner selection. Most pleased. My lady has always concerned herself with results."

"Secretary Yarrow is a very sensible woman," replied Luz.

Vivian raised her eyebrows at Luz, who lifted a corner of her mouth in response.

"Very true, my dear, that is exactly what I say. She is the sort of woman whom one cannot regard with too much deference." Wim made a sudden gesture at his artificial eye. "Ah . . . it is Secretary Yarrow now. She is inviting us to dine with her this evening. Who could have imagined we would receive an invitation so immediately after your arrival, Vivian? Such an honor. Let us make haste."

Vivian wasn't sure she wanted to have dinner with the formidable Constance Yarrow, but she'd known it was a possibility. She took a moment to change into the elegant lilac dress she'd brought with her just in case.

"How are you? For real?" Vivian asked in an undertone as they followed Wim up the steep redstone path to where Yarrow House perched on the top of a low crater.

"Wonderful." Luz squeezed her arm. "I have a home again. A kitchen! Wim found me a steamer pot—he went to three stores to track one down—and I made my abuela's pork tamales. Took me all day. I made the chili ancho sauce and everything."

"I miss your cooking," Vivian confessed. "I'm glad you can continue here."

"All my life, I've had to hustle. And now . . . I have time. My most important job is growing this baby. And—I can't believe I'm saying this—I'm looking forward to being a mother."

"And Wim?" Vivian couldn't help wrinkling her nose.

"I know what you think of him, Viv baby. And you were right to turn down his offer. But I find being with him restful."

"Restful? He never shuts up."

Luz snorted. "He says what he means. He doesn't play mind games. And he isn't trying to trick or force his way into my bed. Works for me."

"I suppose," Vivian agreed doubtfully.

The walk was brief, and they had no opportunity to converse further. Up close, Vivian could see the U-shaped great house had a copper facade. An elegant inner courtyard held an expansive redstone plaza and an opulent bubbling fountain with a fish spouting water into the sky. They were greeted at the double doors by a stoic Earther man in an old-fashioned butler uniform who bowed them into the spacious dining room.

Xavier Dorsey was there.

Again.

How did the man keep showing up when she least expected him?

Next to him sat a younger man with the same deep brown skin and a much more pleasant expression. The man sprang to his feet and bowed over her and Luz's hands. "It's an honor to meet two of the esteemed Red Mothers. I'm August Yarrow, the nephew and heir of the much-admired Secretary Constance Yarrow."

"I'm pleased to meet you," Vivian said to August. She raised her eyebrows coolly at Xavier. "Mr. Dorsey, I wasn't expecting to see you again so soon. I thought you'd traveled to the far domes."

Xavier rose. "There and back. I had the honor of escorting my younger sister Zuri home to Dorsey House."

Poor Delilah. She'd been certain Caspian would be kept away through Presentation Day. If she'd known otherwise, perhaps she wouldn't have settled for such an inadequate substitute.

Vivian turned her attention back to August. "Why haven't we seen you at any of our events?"

August glanced at his cousin. "I have not yet found the time."

At the head of the grand faux-wood table, still seated, Secretary Yarrow harrumphed. "And yet, you have found the time to play soldier with the militia, haven't you?"

August's eyebrows drew together. "The security of our dome is of the utmost importance. The Catena separatists have become increasingly provocative since the election, and we need to ensure our forces are prepared to defend our dome."

"I have Catena handled. Securing the Yarrow bloodline"—she pointed a finger at Xavier—"and the Dorsey bloodline are of the utmost importance. Above all else." Secretary Yarrow turned to Vivian, asking her, "And have you made any progress in selecting a spouse, Vivian Bowen?"

Vivian glanced at Xavier and suppressed a note of hysterical laughter. "I haven't found a man who holds my interest."

"You do give your opinion very decidedly, don't you, Miss Bowen?"

Xavier pressed his lips together in what Vivian could only surmise was disapproval.

"Madam, your final guest has arrived," the butler announced from the doorway. "Chancellor River," he declared with a bow.

Constance rose at last and moved slowly to the arched doorway with her carved wooden cane in time to greet a handsome young

Martian with bronze skin and sharply cut cheekbones wearing a high-necked, floor-length black tunic with silver buttons down the front.

Beside her, Vivian heard Xavier mutter, "She invited them *here*. Whatever for?"

August replied in an undertone, "And with no warning." His hands at his sides clenched into fists.

"Chancellor, I trust you are acquainted with my nephews and the reverend? Let me introduce you to two of our Red Mothers, Miss Luz Flores and Miss Vivian Bowen. Ladies, this is Chancellor River Hawk, newly elected leader of the Catena dome."

Luz and Vivian exchanged a curious glance and gave their best Martian curtsies.

River smiled. "A pleasure. Constance graciously invited me to dinner when she learned how much I wished to speak with the Red Mothers."

Constance barked a short laugh. "After you begged and bullied me, you mean to say." To Luz and Vivian, she said, "I have learned in our short time together that River can be most persuasive when they set their mind to it."

River tilted their head, and their short curly hair flopped on their forehead. "I hope I can always count on you, Constance, to speak the unvarnished truth as you see it."

"Shall we dine?" August asked diplomatically and offered his arm to Vivian.

River swept into the room unescorted, their tunic flaring at the waist to reveal slim black pants. When everyone was seated on the brocade dining chairs, River looked between Luz and Vivian. "What do you think of Arcadia so far?"

"It's quite pleasant, thank you," Luz murmured.

Vivian had spent so much time seated at dull meals with potential partners, making polite, restrained conversation. She found she had no taste for it this evening. Batting her eyes at River, she cooed, "Martian society is the height of fashion. I can hardly keep up with the social schedule and the style of dress."

River gave her a toothy grin. "I think you'll find, Vivian, if you ever have the chance to visit the Catena dome, that Martian society comes in many forms. Not all of us believe in spending our limited resources on frivolity."

"I thought your people wanted as little to do with Earthers as possible," Xavier objected.

"We wish to limit our dealings with *Earth*. Earthers are always welcome in Catena if they share our vision of Mars's future. And the addition of two Red Mothers would be a great asset to our cause."

"None of that." From her seat at the head of the table, Constance pointed a long finger at River. "Play nice, Chancellor." She looked between Luz and Vivian. "You would find Catena dirty and poorly run after spending time in the greatest dome on Mars."

River's eyes glinted, but they didn't respond to the jab.

August leaned forward from his position at the right hand of his aunt and poured Vivian a glass of dark red wine. "Are you interested in fashion, then, Miss Bowen?" he asked in a clear attempt to change the subject.

Vivian was perfectly willing to go along with him. What did she care for political posturing on topics she barely understood? "Oh yes." She winked at Luz, seated across the table. "We ladies are obsessed with Martian hat couture."

Seated next to her on her right, Xavier murmured, "I have not known you long, Miss Bowen, but I believe I am correct in saying that you sometimes enjoy professing opinions that are in fact not your own. I would venture to say you care nothing for hats."

Vivian let out an involuntary snort of laughter. "Careful. If you tell my secrets, I may tell yours."

"I'm not afraid of you," he said with a smile. It was a genuine smile, so unlike his usual smirk. Vivian found she could not look away. An Earther servant moved between them, setting a salad down in front of her with young greens, radishes, and dill fronds.

Across the table, Luz watched her with an unreadable expression, looking between Vivian and Xavier with two fingers pressed to her lips.

"How did your first appearance before the Arcadian Council go today, Chancellor?" August asked.

"Nothing can match the thrill of speaking as a democratically elected leader with the full support of my people behind me. You should try it."

Xavier scowled. "Democracy devolves into violent populist demagoguery. There is no place for such a dangerous, unstable system of government on the domes of Mars."

Constance waived a hand. "It isn't River's fault they were born into a democracy. Chancellor, I am most pleased you have opted to resume diplomacy between our domes after so long without relations."

"And I would be more pleased if you would agree to share your technology." River tilted their wineglass toward Vivian and then toward Luz. "And your resources."

Vivian glanced down to see Xavier's nails digging into his palm underneath the table.

"The Intelligence has advised against the sharing of technology with Catena when you insist on devoting so much of your limited resources to terraforming," Wim put in, leaning past Luz to glare at River.

"I have no interest in the derivative ideas generated by a machine."

Vivian covered her face with her napkin to hide her grin.

"My lady!" Wim exclaimed. "I fear I must protest this blasphemy."

"Don't provoke him," Constance told River. "Remember you're a guest in my home."

"Not to mention the Council agreed today to send you fifty thousand gallons of water at considerable expense," Xavier murmured.

"My people are so grateful." River pressed a hand to their heart.

"Your people despise us," Xavier retorted.

"I am sure their feelings would change if you shared your reproductive technology."

Xavier took a sip of his wine and said mildly, "The decision is not mine to make."

Vivian had intended to stay out of the contentious conversation, but she couldn't help asking, "You need water? Are your treatment plants not enough?"

River shrugged. "We had a temporary shortage."

"I trust, Chancellor, you will use our generosity as an opportunity to rethink the ratio of resources Catena pours into terraforming. You must invest in the fundamentals first." Xavier's serious expression made Vivian think of her textbook. If Catena had been neglecting water treatment, it would be a breach of Martian Fundamental Rights. Not to mention incredibly dangerous on a desert planet.

"Thank you for your concern, but I assure you that I have the matter under control." River turned to Luz and Vivian. "My parents named me River because they believed I would see rivers on Mars in my lifetime."

All the other Martians at the table wore varying expressions of exasperation at the statement.

"How lovely," Vivian exclaimed. "Isn't that a lovely idea, Mr. Dorsey?" She bit her lip to keep from grinning at Xavier's stuffed expression.

"Terraforming Mars is a fool's errand," Xavier said stiffly.

"The Intelligence quite agrees," Wim announced.

"How nice it must be, Mr. Dorsey, to have the Intelligence on your side," Vivian said.

As August made another attempt to steer the conversation onto neutral ground, Xavier turned to her and murmured in a voice pitched below the conversation, "I know what you're doing."

"And what's that?"

"You're trying to provoke me."

"Is it working?"

Xavier made a sound low in his throat. "You have no idea."

"Good."

As their next course arrived, Vivian found herself aware of Xavier's body seated beside her. The deep rumble of his voice. The way his long, elegant fingers held his wine glass.

She nearly forgot she despised him.

CHAPTER SEVENTEEN

20 Sols to Presentation Day

In the morning, Luz and Wim departed early for an obstetrics appointment with Dr. Chavez. "I'll be back soon," Luz whispered in Vivian's ear. "I can't wait to hear your opinion of last night's dinner. Privately."

Vivian grinned. "You're on." The night had ended amicably enough, but Vivian could tell none of the Martians had been sorry to see River depart.

As soon as the couple had left for the doctor, Vivian grabbed a hat and walked out the door. She intended to make the most of her time at the Yarrow Estate after spending so many days isolated within the walls of the dormitory. The vast, craggy grounds boasted a manicured garden, a badminton court, decorative greenhouses, and numerous modest staff homes. Walking without a destination, Vivian heard a faint clanging sound. Curious, she followed the sound up the path to the elevated inner courtyard of Yarrow House.

On the redstone patio, Xavier and August were locked in an altercation. Vivian froze. The two men had seemed so close the night before. What could have changed?

August laughed and brought his sword—*his sword?*—down hard on Xavier's bicep, causing Xavier to drop his sword reflexively.

Vivian let out an involuntary gasp, looking for the well of blood that was sure to follow.

August stepped back and held up his blade. "Too easy. Where are you this morning, X? Your mind's not on the bout. Mooning over a certain lady?"

Xavier bent to retrieve his sword and scowled, rubbing the unmarred sleeve of his arm. "I am doing no such thing." He raised his sword arm. "Again."

This time, Xavier attacked his cousin with a high, chopping motion, pushing August back farther and farther, closer to Vivian, who stood still and unobserved against the wall. August parried the thrusts, and the two locked in a flashing dance of steel. With a hard blow, August disarmed Xavier and knocked him to the ground. He pressed the sword tip, blunted with a rubber stopper, to Xavier's throat.

"Your technique is terrible today, X. The lady is available, you know. And it would keep our aunt off *my* back for a spell. Quit being stubborn. Do you yield?"

What lady? They'd mentioned no one at dinner last night. She wondered if they were speaking of Ivey, who had made no secret of her interest in pursuing Xavier.

Not that it made any difference to her.

Xavier grabbed the sword edge in both hands and twisted it out of August's grip. In one sweeping motion of his leg, he knocked his cousin off his feet.

"Ow," August complained, sitting up and rubbing his head. "Not fair. You wouldn't perform that move with a sharpened sword."

"I don't play fair." Xavier reached one hand out and helped August to his feet.

August's eyes widened in surprise upon seeing Vivian standing nearby. "Ah, Miss Bowen, good day. I'm pleased to have a witness to X's unsportsmanlike behavior."

"I've never seen a sword fight before." Vivian rubbed her arms.

"I'm sure it won't be your last," August replied. "Swords are the weapon of choice on Mars."

"Why swords?" *More Regency playacting?*

"You don't know?" August pointed upward. "The integrity of the domes could fail in a gunfight, and we'd all be dead in a matter of moments. We don't make guns on Arcadia."

Vivian frowned. "Guns can be smuggled."

"The Intelligence enforces the prohibition." Xavier retrieved his fallen sword and pulled a handkerchief from his pocket to clean it. "One of the few good things it's ever done."

August turned his back to Xavier and quickly put a fist to his forehead. Xavier, rubbing a spot on his sword, didn't appear to notice.

"Would you care to try it, Miss Bowen?" Xavier asked.

"*Me?*" Vivian exclaimed. "Wouldn't I hurt you?"

Xavier gave a scornful laugh. "If you managed to land a blow. I'll take my chances."

August's brows drew together. "I don't know about this, X. Fencing between Earthers and Martians is dangerous."

Xavier tossed her a sword, and it sailed slowly through the Martian gravity. Vivian, to her surprise, easily caught it. She smiled and threw her ribboned hat to the side to land on the ground next to the fountain.

"Feet perpendicular, like this. Raise your sword arm. Higher. Keep your elbow clear of your body."

Vivian obeyed, feeling absurd and hampered by her restrictive skirts.

Xavier's eyes were bright when he looked at her. "Good. We'll do a straight thrust. Come forward toward me with a lunge." Vivian leaned her right foot forward and thrust her sword out clumsily. Xavier easily parried. "Again."

Learning fencing was a bit like learning Martian dancing. She moved through the choreographed steps that Xavier showed her.

Their bodies stayed at a distance, a sword's length away, but Vivian found herself completely focused on the moment in front of her. The backdrop of Yarrow House and August's quiet observation faded away.

And then, suddenly, she made it inside Xavier's guard, pressing the tip of her blunted sword into his chest. He let out a grunt and grinned down at her. With one long arm, he reached for her sword hand and lifted it to move the sword off his chest. His hand was warm. "Very nice. You'll leave a bruise I won't soon forget."

Vivian stepped back. "I'm sorry! Mr. Yarrow was right. We're unevenly matched."

Xavier held her hand a moment longer. "I like that we're unevenly matched." He pulled her fingers from the sword handle.

August cleared his throat. "X, we should go. The family governance meeting is starting soon."

Xavier bowed to her. "Miss Bowen. May I—may I call upon you later at the reverend's home?"

"I suppose," Vivian agreed. What more did they have to discuss? She remembered, suddenly, Xavier was the reason Delilah had abandoned hope for a love match in favor of the loathsome Mitzi King.

Xavier nodded seriously and clapped his hand on his cousin's shoulder. "Let's make this quick, shall we?"

Vivian walked slowly back to the house, replaying the thrilling moment when she'd stepped inside Xavier's guard. What would it be like to learn to defend herself with steel?

In the house, Luz had not yet returned. Vivian poured herself a cup of coffee and curled up on a comfortable chair to read. She opened to *Chapter Thirty-Three: After Survival: The Next Generation of Martian Collective Sovereignty*. She was puzzling over the fascinating history of the Martian water purification system when a series of sharp taps startled her.

Vivian put down her reader and opened the door. "Mr. Dorsey!" She reflexively stepped back to let him into the room and looked involuntarily to her reader, the law text still visible. "I wasn't expecting you so soon."

Xavier had changed clothing since she'd seen him on the fencing grounds, but his cravat was askew, and he had not brought a hat. Vivian had never seen him look so disheveled. He didn't speak but only paced the room, looking anywhere but her. Vivian took the opportunity to return to her seat and discreetly close her reader so he wouldn't see his textbook on the screen. What was wrong with him?

"I—I—"

"Yes?" Vivian prompted.

Xavier ran a hand over his short black hair, still not meeting her eyes.

"Spit it out, would you? I've never known you to be at a loss for words."

This sparked a glare, and then he burst out, "In vain, I have struggled, but I cannot suppress my feelings. Miss Bowen—Vivian, you must allow me to tell you how ardently I admire and love you."

Vivian stared up at him blankly, her mouth opening in astonishment. "You what?"

"You are brazen and opinionated, and you do everything you can to vex me. I've tried not to love you. I don't want to love you. I love you against my will and my reason." He finally seemed to run out of words and sat down heavily on the couch opposite her.

"Is that all?"

Xavier covered his face in his hands and said in a muffled voice, "That is all."

Vivian suppressed an absurd desire to laugh. "You don't seem happy about your feelings."

"No."

"And how do you expect me to respond when I know you took Caspian away from my sister?"

Xavier removed his hands from his face to give her a condescending smile that caused anger to rise in her chest. "I do not deny that I did everything in my power to separate my friend from this despicable act of human bondage."

"Delilah wanted Caspian," Vivian said in frustration. "She would've chosen him. They could have had a love match. It's not up to you to make decisions for my sister."

"Your sister clearly did not esteem Caspian above her other suitors. Why shouldn't she be content with another? My only goal was to persuade Casp away from this path."

"It is not only Delilah I'm thinking about. Silas Gatlin told me everything."

"You take an eager interest in that man's concerns," growled Xavier.

"Of course I do! You caused his misfortune."

"Misfortune!" scoffed Xavier. "Yes, his misfortunes have been great indeed."

"He was owed an inheritance from your father. And because you were jealous, you stopped him from inheriting. What kind of man treats someone who was raised beside him so badly?"

"Ha!" Xavier walked with quick steps across the room to stand in front of her. "And this is your opinion of me? I thank you for explaining it so fully."

Vivian sprang to her feet. Her heart was hammering in her chest. "From the very beginning—from the first moment I met you, you have been arrogant and conceited. You don't care about the feelings of others. You are the last man in the world—this world or any other—that I could ever love."

Xavier's eyes were blazing. He closed the last foot of distance between them and bent his head toward her upturned face.

Vivian wondered for one thrilling moment if he planned to kiss her and how she would respond if he did.

"You have said quite enough. I understand your feelings perfectly and am now only ashamed of what my own feelings have been." He straightened and walked away from her. "Forgive me for having taken up so much of your time and accept my best wishes for your health and happiness." The door vibrated in its frame as he slammed it on his way out.

Vivian sat down abruptly. Xavier, in love with *her*? Absurd. How many times had he made it clear he wanted nothing to do with her? And how had he expected her to react to his brash confession? What arrogance! To assume she would fall into his arms after everything he had done to Delilah. And to Silas.

Vivian's breath quickened. She pictured the way his eyes had narrowed, how close his face had been to her own. What if he had kissed her? She was stronger than a Martian. She could have easily pushed him away. What if she had kissed him back? It would serve him right if she had. She would have bit his lower lip. Pulled at his shirt collar. Anything to get a reaction from him.

The door opened, and Vivian jerked her head up. Had Xavier returned? She didn't think she could get through another argument with him without acting on her rash impulses.

"Vivian!" Wim said urgently from the doorway. He was swaying under Luz's weight as she folded against him. "Help me!"

Vivian was at their side in two strides. She pulled Luz away from Wim and helped her to the couch. Luz lay down with her head on Vivian's lap and let out a whimper.

"What's wrong with her?" Vivian asked Wim.

His face was stark white. "She was perfectly fine on the train ride home. It was not until we rose to exit that she informed me that she felt dizzy. And then she vomited on the walk from the station." Wim's hand clutched his bald head, his middle finger tapping on one of the augmentations on his skull.

"Don't just stand there gaping like an idiot," Vivian snapped. "Bring her some water."

After Wim had left the room, Luz blinked up at Vivian. "Be nice to him, Viv baby. For me."

Wim's hand shook as he returned with a glass of water and brought it to Luz's lips. Luz lifted her head slightly to swallow and then leaned back down onto Vivian.

"Is this kinetosis again?" Vivian asked Wim. "Like Delilah?"

Wim shook his head, lips pressed together. Two red splashes of color had formed on his bleached face.

"Do you know something?" Vivian demanded.

"I—the Intelligence does. Nausea and vomiting are an anticipated side effect of the in utero calcium treatments. This is . . . expected."

"Expected." Vivian felt her own stomach roil. "Is that what you saw Dr. Chavez for today? The first calcium treatment?"

Wim wasn't looking at them. He stared, with both his real and artificial eye, into a corner of the room, his head cocked for long minutes. Vivian watched his face contort and forced her hand to remain steady as she stroked Luz's hair. "I can't!" he suddenly growled, and then bent to his knees, his fist pressed against his forehead. He leaned forward, touching his fist to the ground, and in a barely audible whisper said, "Forgive me, Intelligence. I am weak."

Luz sat up slowly and picked up the water glass from where Wim had left it under the couch. She gulped the water with her eyes never leaving Wim's prone form. And then, she rose shakily to her feet and crossed the room. She knelt at Wim's side and touched the bare skin of his head. He turned into her, wrapping his arms around her body, shuddering.

"I'm to be your husband," he whispered in a muffled voice into her chest. "It's my duty to keep you safe from harm."

"Baby, this one isn't in your control."

"It should be. I speak with the Intelligence's own voice."

Vivian pulled her knees into her chest and watched the two of them uncomfortably. They seemed to have forgotten she was there.

"And what does our AI overlord say now?" Luz asked wryly.

"The Intelligence counsels patience and an eye toward the end goal. It assures us this is all part of the plan."

"Mm-hmm."

"I didn't know." Wim's voice was soft.

She snorted. "Yes, you did."

"No, I mean, I didn't know what it would feel like to watch you suffer. I've never much cared about the suffering of others before."

"Charming," Luz drawled, but she was smiling.

Wim pulled back, wiping tears from his cheeks. "You did ask me for the truth. Always."

"Alright, then here's some hard truth. I'm pregnant with a child designed for an alien planet's gravity, and these nine months are going to be hell a lot of the time. But I'm here because I chose to be. And I'm glad I chose you."

The moment was too intimate for Vivian to stay a second longer. As quietly as she could, she rose and made her way to her guest room. She wondered when Delilah's first calcium treatment would be. And hers—she couldn't put it off much longer. Would the nausea come upon all of them so quickly or would their symptoms vary?

She would not soon forget the look of anguish on Wim's face as he argued with the Intelligence. It was the scenario Xavier wished to avoid, she realized suddenly. *I've tried not to love you. I don't want to love you. I love you against my will and my reason.* Who would be willing to subject the person they loved to such treatment?

Not Xavier.

She needed to forget all about him. He would never be her partner.

CHAPTER EIGHTEEN

20 Sols to Presentation Day

Later that afternoon, after she'd seen Luz put to bed for a nap, Vivian slipped out to further her exploration of the well-manicured grounds of Secretary Yarrow's estate.

Near the great house, she was drawn to a one-room ornamental greenhouse. The air inside was richly humid and heavy with large tropical plants. The lush, colorful garden gave her a powerful wave of homesickness for the hot Carolina summers of her childhood. Then, she stopped short.

Xavier.

Again.

Seated at a wrought-iron bistro table, he held a pen hovering over a stack of cream-colored papers written in a close hand. "Ah." He glanced down at the paper, and his lips pinched.

"I can go," Vivian offered.

"No, wait, please. I have just finished writing you a letter."

"A letter?" Vivian raised her eyebrows, curious despite herself.

He gave a helpless little gesture at the paper. Vivian lifted the top sheet up and read aloud, "*Miss Bowen, I fear I expressed myself most inappropriately. I can only say that I was quite overcome with emotion and unable to think clearly. While I have no intention of bringing you pain or humbling myself, I do ask that you read this letter so that I may better explain myself.*" She met his eyes, and her mouth lifted in one corner. "No intention of humbling yourself?"

"I . . ."

"You've never unbent at all, have you?" She returned to the letter. "*You have accused me of two very different offenses. The first is that I took Caspian away from your sister, and the other, that I ruined the prosperity and prospects of Silas Gatlin.*" She met his eyes again and couldn't hold back a smirk. "You've listed my accusations so clearly. I do like a man who can listen."

Xavier covered his mouth with one large hand.

Vivian sat down across from him at the table and continued, "*At the evening of the ball at the Hayes Estate—where I had the honor of dancing with you—I watched Caspian and your sister together. Caspian, I saw, was falling in love with Delilah. But your sister, while polite and kind, was not, I judged, in love. She had many suitors to choose from and did not single out Caspian in her affections. If she agreed to an arrangement with Caspian, she would do so out of a sense of duty, and my dearest friend would be perpetuating a system of injustice against everything we value as Martians. If you are correct here, then I must have been in error. Your superior knowledge of your sister must make the latter probable.*" Vivian stopped again. "How kind of you, Mr. Dorsey, to give me superior knowledge of my own sister. That must have been difficult for you."

Xavier seemed unable to contain his own smile. "This may be the most humiliating moment of my life."

Delight bubbled up in her chest at his willingness to let her poke fun at him. Had she realized he was capable of putting aside his pride?

"Good," she shot back. "You've earned it." She continued reading. "*My abhorrence for the Red Mothers initiative is well-known. I will not apologize for convincing my friend to avoid participation. On this subject I have no other apology to offer. If I have wounded your sister's feelings, it was unknowingly done.*" She tapped the letter. "This is a terrible apology. One of the worst I've ever seen." She reached across the table and picked up the next page. "How is this letter only half over? What more could you possibly have to say?"

Xavier barked a laugh and made a gesture for her to continue.

Vivian read on, "*With respect to that other, more serious accusation, of having injured Silas, I can only refute it by explaining in full his connection with my family. Silas is the son of the house manager of Dorsey Estate, and we were raised together as boys. When my father died, he left a considerable sum of money for Silas.*" Vivian looked up at him. "I know this part. Silas told me everything."

"I assure you, Miss Bowen, you do not know the whole story."

"Fine." Vivian returned to the letter. "*After having gambled away the windfall, Silas came to me and begged for additional funds. I foolishly agreed. He then asked me again, and again, as his debts increased, until, finally, I refused to comply. I must now mention a circumstance that I would wish to forget myself, and which nothing less than the present circumstances would make me tell any human being. Having said this much, I feel no doubt of your discretion. Please do me the courtesy of burning this letter after you read it.*"

Vivian sat up straighter, intrigued despite herself. "Are you about to trust me with a juicy secret, Mr. Dorsey? How unexpected."

Xavier raised his eyebrows. "I suppose I am."

"I can hardly wait." She continued, "*My sister, who is ten years younger than me, was fifteen when Silas began to show an interest in her. Zuri remembered Silas fondly from when she was a child and believed herself in love. She had not yet received a contraceptive implant, and Silas—*"

She paused for a moment.

"Silas impregnated her. He persuaded her to attempt to carry the fetus and to hide the pregnancy from all around her. Zuri sought no healthcare until she suddenly began hemorrhaging and needed an emergency abortion. She nearly died, and she still experiences chronic pain from her ordeal."

Vivian had to put down the letter. She closed her eyes and pressed one hand to her face. The living nightmare of Sumter. A woman bleeding out, begging for help at the clinic. Turned away. If Zuri had been in the camp, she would have died.

"Oh," she finally whispered. "I'm sorry for making light. I shouldn't have done that."

"You didn't know," Xavier murmured.

"I'll stop. I shouldn't have mocked you."

"Please, Miss Bowen. Continue."

With trembling fingers, Vivian resumed reading: *"Silas's chief interest was undoubtedly my sister's fortune, but I cannot help believing that he also wished to take revenge on me. If he had caused the death of my sister, his revenge would have been complete indeed."* Vivian cleared her throat. *"You were correct when you accused me of being unhappy with my own feelings of love toward you. I can only say that I've been used badly in the past and regard love as a danger to my sanity. I should have done you the courtesy of keeping my feelings to myself, since I have no intention of participating in the immoral project you have been contracted to see through. You can be assured that I will no longer express such sentiments to you. You have asked me to stay away from you, and I will respect and obey your wishes. Sincerely, Xavier Dorsey."*

Vivian clutched the letter tightly with both hands. The lightness she'd felt only moments before had dissipated, leaving only the familiar feeling of dread as she faced her future.

"So there you have it," Xavier said, rising to his feet. "I find, often, I am unable to express myself fully with speech. I trust in this letter I have explained myself in full."

Vivian re-read the last line again. *Had* she asked him to stay away from her? Did she want him to keep his distance?

"I will ensure the next time our paths cross is after Presentation Day. I am doing you no favors hanging around like a besotted fool while you are working to fulfill your contract."

"I—alright." What else could she say? He'd made her no offer at all when he'd confessed his love, and he clearly had no expectation of her returning the sentiment. She'd known from the very beginning he was an unsuitable match, hadn't she? And he was right—she had a contract to fulfill. She would endure three difficult pregnancies on behalf of another man, and Xavier's moral code would remain unbroken.

"Goodbye, Vivian."

She shivered upon hearing her name from his lips for only the second time. "Goodbye, Xavier."

CHAPTER NINETEEN

18 Sols to Presentation Day

When Vivian arrived home, she stopped short in front of the dormitory. Delilah paced around the grounds, her violet skirts swirling around her feet.

"Are you alright?" Vivian asked. "Is it the baby?"

"Baby?" Delilah snorted. "The blastocyst is fine."

"What is it then?" Vivian touched Delilah's shoulder to stop her frantic pacing.

Delilah gave her a brief smile that did not reach her eyes. "A message has arrived from Earth."

Vivian dug her nails into her palm. "What message?"

"I haven't watched it yet. I was waiting for you."

Inside, Delilah tapped the shared console off the kitchen, and her parents' smiling faces appeared on the screen. A tightness in Vivian's chest eased.

"Girls, we have received news from Arcadia that Delilah has found a partner," her father began. His thin voice carried an unfamiliar upbeat and energetic tone. "Congratulations, darling. I hope that she gives you a lifetime of love and happiness."

Their mother leaned in. "We wish you a marriage as blessed as ours has been."

Delilah huffed a humorless laugh. "Love and happiness. Does she honestly think that's what this is about?"

Vivian turned worried eyes on her sister. All Delilah had wanted was to fall in love. Were things with Mitzi really that bad?

"Arcadia has sent us a payment," her father continued. "Enough for us to rent a trailer outside of Greenwood. Delilah, my girl, you got us out."

"Girls, we can't thank you enough for your courage. We had to use most of the money to buy permits to leave the camp, and the trailer is only paid for a month. Those nice Arcadia reps explained we'll receive another lump payment in a few weeks when Vivian selects her partner. That should hold us over for a while." She wiped a tear from her eye. "Everyone is so friendly here. And there's a bus only half a mile down the road to take us into town. That's where we are right now. We're recording this at the post office."

"Your mother's trying to convince me to get a dog," her father put in.

"Oh! Our time is about to be up. We love you both so much."

"Girls, I hope you know how much we appreciate you and—" Her father's voice cut off as the recording ended.

Her parents were safe. Vivian let out a slow breath. The awful weight she'd carried since she'd left Sumter was suddenly lifted.

Delilah rose abruptly to her feet. "I need to get out of here."

"I'll come with you. Delilah, we should celebrate! A dog? Can you imagine?"

Delilah's face flicked in a smile that came and went. "Alright, come on."

"Where are we going?"

"The barracks," Delilah answered promptly.

"I don't know if I want to see the soldiers again," Vivian said, thinking of Xavier's revelations.

"Suit yourself. I'll go alone." She walked toward the door without looking back.

Vivian scrambled to catch up with her as her sister hurried through the grounds. "Delilah, what's wrong? Talk to me."

"I'm fine." Delilah walked rapidly to the wall and found the low tree they had used before.

"You can walk freely out of the compound, can't you? Now that you're partnered?"

Delilah made a face. "Mitzi gets a report every time I use my ID. No, thank you." She reached for the tree branch.

"Should you be climbing trees?"

"I've been pregnant for one week. Don't be such a spoilsport," Delilah grumbled and lifted herself easily onto the branches.

At the top, Vivian winced as she watched Delilah jump off the wall, but she climbed to her feet without issue. They easily located the barracks, and Delilah soon struck up a conversation with her old acquaintances, giving the soldiers a bright smile Vivian knew was forced.

In the distance, the door to the militia tavern opened, and Silas stepped out, his handsome face alight as he turned behind him to speak to his companion. Vivian blinked. Was that River Hawk? Surely not.

"What do you think, Viv?" Delilah called.

Vivian turned to see her sister twirling in a tricorn hat. "You should enlist."

"Look who's here," a voice murmured beside her, and Vivian glanced up into Silas's vibrant green eyes. She looked behind him for his companion, but there was no one in sight. "I heard you had the displeasure of dining with Xavier Dorsey at Secretary Yarrow's home."

"Word travels fast." Without giving him the satisfaction of a smile, she continued, "I think Xavier improves the more one gets to know him."

"Really?" Silas looked dismayed. "Has he learned some manners? For I doubt he has improved in character."

"Oh, no!" Vivian ducked her head. "In character, I think he's unchanged." Now, she knew Xavier to be passionate in his ideals, unyielding in his convictions, and loyal to his friends. To Silas, she simply said, "I only mean that I understand him better, now that I've spent more time with him."

Silas curled his lip. "You, who so well know my feelings toward X, will understand how happy I am to hear that he is wise enough to assume even the appearance of what is right. I only fear that he was only behaving himself in front of his aunt, whose good opinion and judgment he values highly."

Vivian thought of Xavier's grin as he sat across from her in the greenhouse, allowing her to mock him with good humor, and answered Silas only by a slight inclination of the head. Now that she understood his true nature, she was in no mood to engage with him. This man caused a fifteen-year-old to nearly die from a dangerous pregnancy. For him to act as if he was the wronged party made her ill.

Delilah returned to her side. "Silas, great to see you again."

Silas turned his full charismatic attention on her sister. "The pleasure is all mine. Congratulations on your good fortune. Mitzi King is a lucky woman indeed."

"Please make sure you tell her the next time you see her." Delilah gave Silas a coy smile. "Mitzi could use a reminder."

Vivian frowned at her sister. What was going on with Delilah?

"You deserve to have all the affection in the world showered upon you," Silas murmured. He took Delilah's hand in his and kissed her palm.

He'd used a similar move on her, Vivian realized. And she'd been foolish enough to fall for it.

Delilah cocked her head. "I do, don't I?" She pulled her sketchbook out of a skirt pocket. "Would you let me draw you, Mr. Gatlin? You have such an interesting face."

Silas bowed to her, his eyes glinting. "It would be my honor."

Delilah kept her gaze on Silas as she said, "Viv, I've heard the largest law library is just up the road. Silas, did you know my sister is practically a law student?"

"Oh, excellent. Vivian, you must view the original version of the Charter of the Planet Mars." He pulled Delilah's free hand through his arm.

Vivian caught herself. "The original version?"

"Turn left at the headquarters," Silas said helpfully. "You can't miss it."

Vivian followed his gesture with interest.

"Go on," Delilah urged, her gaze returning to Silas. "I'll join you when I've finished my sketch. I don't have many opportunities to draw the male form these days."

Vivian hesitated. "I don't know, Delilah. We should stay together." Xavier's letter had clearly been intended for Vivian's eyes only, but perhaps she could at least give Delilah a warning not to trust Silas.

"I'm fine," Delilah snapped.

Vivian looked at the street that led to the library and back at her sister. How much trouble could Delilah get into with Silas if Vivian left her for a few minutes? Especially if she was just practicing her drawing. Delilah had chosen a partner. And she was already pregnant.

"Viv, stop mothering me and go."

Vivian knew there was no arguing with her baby sister when she used that tone. "Fine."

Lifting her skirts, she followed the directions and soon came to a three-story building. She stopped short when she saw the name *Dorsey Law Library* embossed above the door. Xavier had promised he'd keep away from her, but everywhere she turned were reminders of his presence.

Vivian pushed the door open and entered a hushed, low-ceilinged room. Martians sat in study, turning the pages of paper books with gloved hands or hunched over consoles typing furiously.

"May I help you?" an older Martian woman asked her from her seat behind a reference desk.

"I . . ." Vivian looked around. She was the only Earther in sight. "I was hoping I could view the original Charter of the Planet Mars."

The woman's stern face broke out into a friendly smile. "Come on then." She led the way up two flights of stairs to a room packed with artifacts encased in glass. "Here is the Phillip Dorsey Museum of Martian Law. We don't get a lot of interest in these dusty old relics, but House Dorsey believes in the importance of preserving our history. The current Counselor Dorsey is especially passionate about upholding the values Mars was founded upon."

Vivian walked to the center wall to view a long, rectangular page of cream-colored paper posted behind glass. The text was crisp and legible with no signs of decay. *Article I: All Martians are entitled to the fundamental rights of water, food, air, and energy.* Vivian reached out a hand, hovering over the glass above another. *Article VI: No one shall be held in slavery or servitude; slavery and the slave trade shall be prohibited in all their forms.*

America used to revere documents like this, kept behind glass. Back when it was the United States of America, not a fractured group of semi-independent regions barely agreeing to govern as a loose federation. But here on Mars, the ideas behind these documents were real. Or they should be. Her finger strayed to the word "servitude."

Were the Red Mothers in servitude?

No, of course not. She knew the basics of the history of American slavery, at least as much as her censored education allowed.

Her experience was nothing compared to those horrors. But was Xavier right? Was the Red Mothers initiative an echo of earlier forms of bondage throughout Earth's history?

"Are you interested in law, dear?" the reference librarian asked.

"I think I am," Vivian said slowly.

"I love hearing that. Please, let me show you everything."

CHAPTER TWENTY

15 Sols to Presentation Day

"And here is our lettuce farm."

Vivian stared at the heads of lettuce stretching in rows down the long greenhouse. She remembered the first time she'd eaten Martian lettuce, devouring chicken pita sandwiches with Luz. This was the place where that lettuce had grown.

Standing at her side, Ren glanced at the clock above the back wall and stifled a yawn. "Very nice."

Never mind him, Vivian thought. She moved through the rows of vivid green, breathing in the humid, earthy air so different from the rest of the dome.

Their Earther tour guide, Alvin, gestured her to look below the trays of lettuce heads to the filtration system. "Mars has spent two hundred years developing the most efficient approach to growing food." His voice held the barest hint of a familiar drawl that made Vivian almost taste the salty sea air of her childhood. "Hydroponics results in larger, faster yields with less water than soil gardening. The system recycles water efficiently by using a pump that pulls water from the reservoir into a tray and then slowly drains through the porous substrate, back into the reservoir."

She crouched down to examine the pump. "Like a Martian shower?"

Alvin's eyes lit up at her interest. "That's right. Only, the water circulates over the course of days, not seconds."

Ren remained some distance away, arms crossed and tapping his foot. When Vivian caught his eye from across the greenhouse, he dropped his hands to his sides, as if to hide his impatience. He was trying. Vivian should give him some credit. After all, he'd agreed to escort her here even though he clearly didn't care about food production. Ren was a decent man. A decent choice.

Her parents needed to pay rent on a trailer in three weeks.

Vivian touched her chest involuntarily to Xavier's letter hidden in her clothing and felt the comforting crinkle of the real paper. He'd asked her to burn it, but she couldn't muster the strength to do so. *I love you against my will and my reason.* She rubbed one shoulder and tried to push away the memory of Xavier's glowering brown eyes, inches from her own. And that smile that had slipped out when she'd teased him about his written apology. He wasn't an option for her. She had to be practical.

An Earther woman in gray coveralls entered the greenhouse. "Counselor Nakamura, sir? The plant manager would like a word, if you are amenable."

"Certainly," Ren agreed, a note of relief in his voice. "Vivian, I won't be long. Please do not hold the tour on my account."

Alvin stared after him. "Never thought Counselor Nakamura had any interest in food production. His family is more focused on the mining industry. Does he mean to invest?"

"I . . . I couldn't comment on Ren's investment decisions," Vivian said diplomatically. "But he's here today because I asked him to bring me."

Alvin jerked up his chin. "Whatever for? I assure you, Mars will feed your future children quite well."

"I needed to understand. How is the government here able to feed everyone on the dome? Aren't there lean times?"

"Why would there be?" He shrugged. "There's no weather or seasons under the domes. Few pests. When there's the occasional mold or disease outbreak, we isolate it and stamp it out."

Vivian looked around the productive greenhouse with sudden frustration. "Then why can't we do the same in America?"

"You know, when I first arrived, I asked myself that question every day." Alvin ran his hand through his graying blond hair and grimaced. "Now? I think the answer is simple. Political will. In Arcadia, providing for the basic needs of everyone is baked into the foundations of the government. In America, not so much."

"How long have you been here?"

"Oh, nearly nine years now. I left when my university closed in Savannah."

Vivian swallowed. "After Pippa?"

"That's right. I was a professor of English Literature. Not a practical bone in my body. But I scraped together all my savings to buy a ticket here and learned, for the first time, how to make a living using my hands." He rubbed the back of his neck. "I gotta tell you, I'm mighty jealous of your position."

"Of me?" Vivian exclaimed. "Why?"

"I'm stronger than a native-born Martian and that makes me valuable on the job market. But my biological assets have only given me the means to rent a one-bedroom apartment. Yours will give you access to a walled estate." His lips turned up in a cynical smile. "I hear the Nakamura Estate is stunning. They even have a koi pond. Can you imagine the expense?"

"The Yarrow Estate has a fountain," Vivian offered. "The spray is taller than a Martian's head."

He shook his head. "And here I am bending over backward to conserve every drop of water in this place as if it were a sacred calling." He glanced at the clock. "Come on, let's continue the tour."

As they moved through the rest of the tour, Vivian reflected on Alvin's words. *Did* she have the better deal? Maybe, but in that moment, she'd trade almost anything to swap out her current future for a tiny apartment and a manual labor job.

But she wouldn't trade her parents' security.

Ren met her on the street outside the greenhouse. Vivian looked around their surroundings, fascinated by how different this neighborhood felt from the others she'd been to. The street facade consisted of a row of gray buildings with wide garage doors and a line of small trucks. The streets were nearly empty of pedestrians. "What other industry is in the district?" she asked Ren. She saw a sign on the building across the wide street and began walking toward it to get a better look.

"All sorts." Ren caught up to her in a few strides. "Water treatment, air purification, solar cell manufacturing—all the elements for ensuring life is sustained on Mars. The industrial district is the backbone of Arcadia."

"Martian Collective Sovereignty," Vivian murmured.

Ren looked taken aback. "Indeed."

"When I was in the law library the other day, I saw the original Charter of the Planet Mars. Is it true that all Martians must support the essential services, or is that just the idealism of the founders?"

"It's true." Ren's face remained befuddled, but he answered her readily enough. "In a 687-day Martian year, all native-born Martians must volunteer a combined fifty days at the facilities for the production of water, food, air, and energy."

"Even you?"

"Well . . . my contributions may be more advisory in nature."

"Of course," Vivian said with some disappointment. Even on Mars, it seemed the wealthy found ways to avoid getting their hands dirty. She had reached the sign, lettered in bold on the top of the large door. "Oh—the water treatment plant. I'd love to go inside."

"Mm-hmm."

Vivian bit her lip to hide a smile at his carefully neutral expression. "Another day, I mean. When I met Chancellor Hawk, I was surprised to hear them say that there was a water shortage on Catena. Arcadia doesn't seem to have any problems with water."

"You met Chancellor Hawk? First the law library and then meeting a foreign politician. You have certainly been getting around, Vivian." Ren seemed a bit bewildered by the conversation, as if Vivian was not staying in the box he'd put her in. A rebellious part of her enjoyed shocking him . . . but, no, she didn't want to drive him away. He was her best option.

"I was with Reverend Adair at the time," she explained.

"Oh . . . I suppose that's alright then." He took a breath and offered her his arm. "Would you care for a stroll around the district, my lady?"

Vivian let her smile show. He might have a sense of humor after all. "I would love that."

Roaming the industrial district felt like her textbook coming to life. Every industry she'd read about was represented, each building maximizing the limited square footage by reaching multiple stories into the air. After a walk of a good twenty minutes, they reached a structure labeled *Terraforming Research Facility.*

In the doorway, Caspian Hayes stepped through, putting a top hat upon his head as he ducked out. He stopped short upon seeing them. "Counselor Nakamura, Miss Bowen, what a pleasant surprise." He touched a hand to his hat.

"Counselor Hayes, how do you do?" Ren asked stiffly, and Vivian remembered witnessing the disdainful way he and Mitzi King had spoken about Xavier and the Hayes siblings on her second day on Mars. "Vivian and I were just touring the industrial district. It seems she has an interest in Martian Collective Sovereignty."

"Do you?" Caspian's eyes brightened. "I've been trying to convince the Council to expand the definition to include terraforming. Unfortunately, without success. The Council does not regard an effort that will benefit our descendants, and not ourselves, as essential to the well-being of all Martians."

"Surely," Ren snarled. "Witnessing River Hawk debase themselves in front of the Council to beg us for water is a cautionary tale. We cannot take our staples for granted."

Vivian wondered what Xavier would say if he were a part of the conversation. Even if Ren and Xavier were political rivals, she suspected Xavier would agree with him on this. She should ask him the next time she saw him.

Her stomach clenched. There wouldn't be a next time. Xavier had promised as much.

"I come from a place," she ventured, "where the government doesn't care about the basic needs of its citizens. I hope that the Council will always make sure our needs are met."

"Well said," Ren told her approvingly and patted her hand on his arm.

Caspian shrugged good-naturedly. "Point taken. How is your sister, Miss Bowen?"

"Very well," Vivian replied automatically. "She has chosen Mitzi King as her partner and is nearing two weeks into her pregnancy."

"I heard," Caspian said with a good cheer that rang false.

"She was sorry to see you take yourself out of the running," Vivian told him, wanting to wipe the false bravado off his expression.

She was rewarded by seeing Caspian's face fall. "So was I," he murmured. "Very sorry indeed. I—" He looked at Ren and then back to Vivian. "Ivey and I both decided that as much as we hope for a continuation of the Hayes line, this approach was not for us. I wish—" He broke off without finishing.

"You mean you let Dorsey do your thinking for you," Ren snapped.

Caspian jutted out his chin. "I'm my own man. X simply made a compelling case. The sacrifice asked of the Red Mothers is too great." He bowed to Vivian. "Forgive me, Miss Bowen. This does not seem to be a fit matter to discuss in front of you."

A snort of laughter escaped Vivian before she could suppress it. *Yes, why discuss a procedure that directly impacts my own health in front of me?*

Under her fingers, Vivian could feel the tension vibrating off of Ren as he said, "I would think, Counselor, that as a fervent supporter of terraforming, you of all people would understand. Are we not taking an action today that will directly benefit our descendants? And we're doing it in a much shorter timeline than converting the planet's atmosphere. It's a sacrifice necessary for our long-term survival that our generation must bear."

"*You* are not the one making the sacrifice." A red flush stained Caspian's pale face as he looked pointedly at Vivian.

While she appreciated Caspian's sentiment, Vivian understood why Ren had spoken in terms of a generational sacrifice. Her mind turned to Wim on his knees wrestling with his artificial god. What would it do to this generation of Martian aristocrats to witness their wives go through the agonizing pain of carrying the modified fetuses to term? *Three times.* Vivian shuddered.

"I should get Vivian home." Ren made a gesture to his driver, who'd been following in the groundcar a discreet distance behind as they walked the district.

Caspian bowed. "A pleasure to see you, Miss Bowen. Please . . . tell your sister . . ."

"I'm not telling my sister anything," Vivian said, more sharply than she intended. "Delilah's already chosen a spouse. And it's not you."

CHAPTER TWENTY-ONE

10 Sols to Presentation Day

The luncheon in the banquet hall that day was sparsely attended. Only four women remained, and they could hardly move as the Martians around them vied for their attention. In the bathroom, Vivian found a brief respite from the suffocating atmosphere, lingering at the sink to let the cold water from the gilded faucet flow through her fingers.

"You're supposed to conserve the water, you know." Felicia met her eyes in the bathroom mirror. "And you'll dry out your skin with all that washing."

"Thanks." Vivian turned off the faucet. "I wasn't paying attention."

Felicia washed her own hands with brisk efficiency. "I hate this limbo we're in right now."

"Why not get it over with then? Any one of them out there would jump at the chance to marry you."

Felicia fiddled with one of her long microbraids. "I guess . . . after seeing Camille fall so hard for Theo . . . I hoped that might happen for me." She shook herself. "But it's not going to. Viv, have you spoken to Delilah lately?"

"A week ago."

"Camille is worried sick about her, but Delilah refuses to talk. I don't think she's meshing well with Mitzi King."

Vivian's chest gave a painful spasm. "She didn't want to tell me anything about it either." And what could she do? It was too late. Delilah was pregnant with Mitzi's child, and the payment had been sent to her parents. "How's Camille?"

"Better now. She had a kidney stone, and fuck, Viv, it was awful. She was screaming and crying, and the pain meds they gave her didn't do shit. They said no morphine until she's out of the first trimester. Dr. Chavez thinks that because she had one so early, she's going to get them the whole pregnancy." Felicia bit her lip. "Honestly, that's why I'm still here. I'm fucking scared. I don't do so well with pain."

"I'm scared too," Vivian admitted.

Felicia reached out and gripped Vivian's hand. "We're a sisterhood, right? We'll get through this together."

Vivian nodded. "Still better than Louisiana?"

"Anything is better than Louisiana." Felicia linked her arm through Vivian's. "C'mon, let's be scared together."

In the arching long hallway returning from the bathrooms, they were stopped by Ren. "Ah, Vivian, I was hoping for a moment alone with you, if you'll permit it."

Felicia disentangled her arm from Vivian's and murmured, "Good luck, honey," before gliding away.

Vivian fixed a bland smile on her face. Her stomach clenched. *Here it comes.*

"I'd like to ask if you've made a decision about selecting a husband?"

Vivian felt Xavier's letter, tucked into her dress against her breast, and then dropped her hand. "Not yet. I still have ten days."

"I think I could be good for you," Ren said earnestly. "If you'd have me. The Nakamura Estate is comfortable, and my position on the Council gives me considerable influence and power. Our children would be well cared for and have access to an excellent education."

"You don't love me," Vivian stated.

I love you against my will and my reason.

Ren stroked his beard. "I—forgive me. I was not aware you were seeking a love match."

Vivian gave a despairing little laugh. "I'm not. That would be ridiculous." She closed her eyes and then opened them. "Thank you." She took a deep breath. She should accept him. He was the best option. She had to be sensible. But the moment she did, her life would change. "I cannot give you an answer today. Will you be patient with me?"

He bowed to her. "I will."

When she returned home, she went to her bedroom and pulled off her wide-brimmed hat and heavy earrings. She paced the length of the room, back and forth. The bedroom had seemed so spacious when she'd first arrived, but now the number of strides from one end to the other was all too brief.

Grabbing her reader, Vivian stepped outside. She walked the wide sidewalks of their walled compound. The grounds were quiet and empty—nearly ready for the next cohort of young Earther women willing to risk it all on the promise of a better future.

Vivian sank to the ground and lay her fine periwinkle silk dress down in the creeping thyme. She breathed in the sharp lemony scent and stared at the orange sky. She thought of the layers encircling her.

The confining dress.

The high walls.

The solid dome.

The signed contract.

She opened her reader to *An Introduction to Martian Law* and navigated, for the first time, to "Prologue," by Counselor Xavier Dorsey.

Mars is a society of contradictions. We've rejected democracy as a failed form of governance in favor of a system that enables Martian sovereignty. All of us, Marsborn and Earthborn alike, work together to ensure Mars is a self-reliant system where every individual is entitled to fundamental rights.

Our founders accurately characterized Mars *as a great unfinished experiment. The inherent contradiction between Martian Collective Sovereignty and a hereditary ruling class makes the Mars we know today an imperfect system.*

Vivian continued reading. Xavier wrote in the bold decisive way that he talked. She had to look up fewer words as she read now, she realized. She easily followed his ideas.

We live in a cold, inhospitable world rendered habitable with scientific advancement, shared accountability, and hard work. But we are no longer a group of scientists and adventurers scrambling for mere survival. Today, we are an established, prosperous, and growing society. Together, let us reach for a higher standard: a world where all people have freedom, dignity, and the right to make their own choices and determine their own destinies.

Vivian's finger hovered over the last sentence. Choice. At every step in this process, she'd been given the illusion of choice. But it was a lie. She'd never had choices. The choice between celibacy and pregnancy in the camps hadn't been a true choice. And now, the choice between which wealthy Martian man would be by her side as she endured three painful pregnancies wasn't much of a choice.

What Vivian wanted was control over her own body. She wanted the ability to seek sexual pleasure without fear. To become a mother at the time and place of her choosing, or not at all. She wanted the ability to support her parents' escape without sacrificing her own freedom.

She wanted Mars to be better than Earth.

Vivian wanted *more.*

CHAPTER TWENTY-TWO

4 Sols to Presentation Day

"Thank you, Vivian, for another memorable outing." Ren paused outside the dormitory and bowed over her hand.

"I enjoyed the gallery," Vivian said honestly. "Especially the sculpture garden."

"I'm glad." He stroked his beard. "Vivian . . . Presentation Day is four days away."

"I—yes."

He gave a tiny sigh. "I must ask. Is there another?"

"No." Vivian shook her head rapidly. "No, of course not."

"Very well." He pulled a small black box from his pocket and handed it to her.

Vivian opened it and let out an involuntary gasp upon finding a large white pearl strung on a gold necklace.

"My mother asked me to present this to you, as a token of her respect. My father gave it to her on the day they wed. It's an Akoya pearl gathered from the oysters found off the shores of Japan."

"Thank you," Vivian whispered. "This is the most beautiful thing anyone has ever given me."

"My mother requested that I convey that she hopes to welcome you to the Nakamura home." He bowed again and walked away down the redstone path.

Vivian clutched the gift to her and stared at his retreating back. *Four days.* She should accept him tomorrow. It was time.

In her bedroom, a handwritten envelope lay on her pillow. Vivian's heart leapt, thinking it was from Xavier, until she recognized the handwriting. Delilah. Why would her sister bother writing to her when she could just visit?

Vivian placed the pearl necklace carefully on her bedside table and opened the letter.

Viv,

Guess where I've gone?? You're going to be so surprised! I'm on my way to the Catena dome. Can you guess who I'm with? I've fallen in love with Silas, and we've run away together. Isn't that so romantic? The best part is there's nothing that bitch Mitzi can do about it. I wish I could see her face when she finds out. I'm cracking up just thinking about it.

Love you!
Delilah

Vivian sat down abruptly on the bed. The rent on her parents' new trailer was only paid for another week or two. Could Arcadia claw back the funds sent to Earth? Had her mother already gotten a dog?

The Intelligence must be aware that Delilah had gone with Silas. The two of them wouldn't have been able to conceal their actions. Would her parents, having finally found a taste of freedom, be confined again?

No, she couldn't allow it. She should chase after Ren and accept his offer immediately, before the taint of Delilah's decision made Vivian undesirable and no one wanted her at all on Presentation Day. She could send more money to her parents in a matter of days and shield them from Delilah's actions.

Vivian rose, pacing in her tiny room, the letter clutched in her hand.

What did Silas want with Delilah? She had a partner. She'd signed a contract. She was *pregnant*.

Silas had encouraged Xavier's sister to carry a pregnancy to term when he must have known it would most likely kill her. Why?

And he'd tested out the idea of running away on Vivian, but she'd dismissed him. What had he said? *We could start a life together somewhere else.* Had he made a similar proposition to Delilah?

What did the Catena dome have to do with any of this?

She considered what she knew of Catena. A newly elected charismatic leader. A rocky relationship with Arcadia. A water shortage. A nebulous threat. There was no reason Vivian could fathom why Silas would take Delilah there.

If Vivian had told Delilah about Silas's past, she wouldn't have run off with him. If she hadn't prioritized loyalty to Xavier's secret, she would have taken her sister into her confidence. If she had not left them alone to go to the law library. If, if, if . . .

Xavier.

Vivian froze in the middle of her bedroom. Xavier had dealt with Silas all his life. He would know what to do.

She located her modest credit chit, changed her clothes, put on shoes and a hat, and left the deserted dormitory. Presentation Day was only four days away. She needed to hurry.

Sneaking out of the compound had become routine. Vivian swung her small duffel over one shoulder, pulled herself up the tree, perched for a moment at the top, and dropped over the wall. She had consulted a map on the information nexus before departing and memorized the route. The journey had seemed simple enough to plan in the comfort of the dormitory. Dorsey Estate had its own station and getting to it only required a single transfer point in the industrial district.

On the streets of Arcadia, she kept her head low. No one was looking at her, she reminded herself. She wore her drabbest auburn dress and kept her hair tucked under a modest taupe hat. She paid her fare with a tap of her credit chit and settled in for the long journey.

Delilah had left her.

Left Arcadia.

With a man who could not be trusted.

Vivian drummed her fingers on her bag. Did the Arcadian trains always move this slow? She hadn't taken a train often and never crossed the full dome. Most of the time, when she'd had the opportunity to leave the dormitory grounds, she'd been whisked along in some oligarch's private groundcar.

As the train stops progressed, the types of passengers in the car changed. More Martians got off and more Earthers got on. The head coverings grew more practical in appearance and more of the women wore pants or jumpsuits. Many of the riders sank wearily into seats, dirt beneath their fingernails and soot on their faces. Vivian's drabbest dress appeared more and more finely woven and well-cut the closer the train got to the industrial district.

Finally, she reached the transfer spot. Vivian followed the others exiting the car and looked around. She'd expected after her walk through the industrial district with Ren that she would be oriented, but instead she found herself lost on the unfamiliar streets and wasting precious minutes wandering around looking for the stop for the Dorsey line.

She caught the train just before the doors closed and sat panting on the hard chair, trying to regain her composure. As the train moved away from the industrial district, Vivian watched the rougher-clad Earther commuters dwindle, replaced by well-dressed Martians. A few stared at her with open curiosity. She remembered Ivey's words: *Clothing is a game.* Her Earther build and her aristocratic clothing didn't add up in the eyes of the other passengers. Vivian sat up taller and hid her unease behind a smooth, expressionless face.

Next stop: Dorsey Station, an automated voice announced.

Vivian dismounted at last. Her back ached from the hard seats, and her stomach rumbled. She began making her way slowly down the street before lifting up her weary head.

Dorsey Estate was stunning.

The main house stood high on the rising ground of a crater with immense picturesque windows overlooking the surrounding lovely, if more modest, dwellings. Instead of the formal, stately trappings of Yarrow House and Hayes House, the Dorsey home seemed to embrace the natural Martian landscape, blending into the surroundings with clean modern lines and sharp edges. The square black beams, dark metal windows, and rusted steel fencing echoed the harsh, minimal beauty of Mars.

At the gate, Vivian rang the bell and nervously gave her name to the security screen. The gates swung open with a creak. She walked down an angular walkway dotted with spiky plants with torch-like red flowers jutting from their tops. The house's floor-to-ceiling glass doors slid open as she approached.

"Vivian Bowen?" In the spacious entryway, a young Martian woman descended floating, faux-wood stairs. Her angular face resembled Xavier's but her clothing looked nothing like the style of the Martian oligarchs. Her dress ended with a flare just below her knees, dyed in splashes of bright orange, pink, and yellow. Her hair was styled in puffs on either side of a jaunty miniature purple top hat. On her tiny feet, she wore black slippers. "How . . . unexpected. But my brother did say you were bold."

Vivian's heart hammered in her chest. Now that she was here at Dorsey House, she was at a loss for words. Surely a Red Mother descending upon a counselor's home without warning violated a dozen rules of Martian etiquette. "Is Xavier—Mr. Dorsey—is he here?"

"He is." The young woman looked her up and down. "X is currently tied up in meetings. Am I correct to assume you are here without invitation?"

"I—yes. Will he see me?"

She grunted. "He'll see you. His exact words to me were, 'Don't you dare let her leave.'"

Relief flooded through Vivian, and a soft smile escaped her lips. Despite everything, she'd missed him.

The woman gave a short, silvery laugh. "So he *has* had an impact on you. I couldn't tell from his version of events." She inclined her head, and the black feathers affixed to her little top hat wobbled. "I'm Zuri."

First names then. "Vivian."

"Won't you come upstairs to the drawing room, Vivian?"

She followed Xavier's sister up the floating stairs. Floor-to-ceiling window walls overlooked the rust-colored Martian landscape. A shiny black upright piano stood in one corner.

Zuri pressed a recessed button on the wall. "Refreshments for Miss Bowen, if you please." She gestured for Vivian to take a seat on a dark leather loveseat and sat down across from her. "Have you selected a spouse, Vivian?"

"No. I mean, not yet."

Zuri raised her brows. "Aren't you cutting it close? Ever since I got home, the big wedding on Presentation Day is all *Arcadia Life* will talk about. I heard it's going to be televised live from the Council chamber."

"I have four days." Vivian tried to ignore the way the sentence made her heart beat faster.

A discreet Earther servant arrived, bearing a tray of tea, scones, and a platter of fruit. With careless elegance, Zuri poured her a cup of tea. "Is it true you told X he was the last person on Mars you could ever love?"

"He told you that?" Vivian felt her face flush.

"There are no secrets between my brother and me. Not anymore."

Vivian took a sip of tea. "I was angry with him."

Zuri let out another peal of laughter that rang on the high ceilings. "It does sound like he earned your anger." Her face sobered. "I don't think he's allowed himself to be in love since—well, he told me he divulged to you the mess from when I was fifteen."

Vivian frowned. What did the story of Silas's inheritance and affair with Zuri have to do with Xavier swearing off love? "I hope you don't mind that he shared your personal business. I promise I won't tell anyone else."

"I know. You are a woman of impeccable honor, according to my brother."

Vivian picked up a scone and turned it over in her hand. "Can I—can I ask you something?"

Zuri made a welcoming gesture with her teacup.

"Why did Silas want a child with you?"

Zuri blew out a breath. "That's quite a question. My brother warned me you were direct." She took a sip of her tea. "He wanted to upend the system. He believed, at the time, that the risks of a Martian woman carrying a pregnancy to term were exaggerated, used as a tool to enforce the class hierarchy. When I was a rebellious fifteen-year-old, I found his argument compelling. But Silas was wrong not to trust the experiences of our foremothers."

"Do you think he still wants to topple the Arcadian oligarchy?"

Zuri shrugged. "I've no idea. I haven't seen him in nearly five years." Her gaze sharpened. "Stay away from Silas Gatlin,

Vivian. Behind his handsome, charming facade is a cold, ruthless sociopath."

"Indeed," came a deep voice from the doorway.

Vivian spun around to meet Xavier's eyes. She could read a mixture of concern and gladness in his expression. "Hi," she whispered.

"You've put me in quite a dilemma," he said lightly as he swiped a scone from the tray. "How can I stand by my promise to keep my distance when you show up unannounced at my doorstep?"

"I find, Mr. Dorsey, that I am quite unable to stay away from you."

He grinned. "Is that right?"

She couldn't help smiling back at him. "Yes . . . I mean, no. Is there somewhere we can speak privately? With no one or no *thing* listening."

Xavier raised his eyebrows. "My office. Zuri, if you will excuse us."

Zuri looked curiously between the two of them. "Of course."

Without touching her, Xavier gestured her down the corridor to a nearby office on the same floor. He pressed a switch to lower the shades on the wide windows and turned on a side lamp that reflected on the dark gray walls. Vivian hesitated at the door, her knees trembling under her. He took her hand and led her inside.

Vivian stared down at his large hand enclosing hers. He ran one calloused thumb over her knuckles before releasing her. She watched his fingers flex as if involuntarily as he turned away. She sat, shakily, on a side chair.

Xavier poured her a glass of water and placed it down in front of her. "I can see you're distressed. Tell me what's the matter."

His gentleness quite undid her. Vivian felt tears threaten, and she blinked rapidly. "Are you sure the Intelligence can't hear us in this room?"

"Counselors' offices are not monitored. Despite my aunt's ill-conceived dependency on the Intelligence, the Council is an independent body, and we are entitled to a higher degree of privacy than other Arcadians."

Another time, Vivian might have asked more questions. She'd read about the court case limiting the power of the Intelligence in her law textbook and was curious about how it worked in practice. But now, all Vivian could think about was her sister.

In halting words, she related what had occurred. "Delilah left me a letter." She handed it to Xavier, who swore under his breath after he finished. "She's always been impulsive. Especially when faced with something hard. She runs away from problems, rather than facing them." She rubbed a hand over her face. "I wish I'd told her what I learned about Silas. She would never have left with him if she'd known what he was capable of."

Xavier spread his hands. "You didn't tell her because I'd asked for your discretion. If anyone is to blame, it's me."

"If she doesn't participate in the wedding ceremony on Presentation Day, she will have broken her contract." Vivian twisted her hands on her lap and didn't mention her parents and their new trailer. The dog. "I hoped that we could find them in the Catena dome and undo this before it's too late. I know it's a lot to ask. But I—I didn't know who else I could trust."

Xavier made no answer. He rose and paced up and down the room with a furrowed brow. Finally, he spoke, "We'll find her. I know a place we can start in Catena. We'll leave at once."

CHAPTER TWENTY-THREE

4 Sols to Presentation Day

In a scant ten minutes, the Dorsey staff had a bag packed and an aircar ordered.

On the grounds of the estate, Zuri stood with them as they waited for the white aircar to land on a concrete slab to the side of the house. Xavier said something in his sister's ear, and she clung tightly to him. "Don't fret," he murmured. "We'll be back in a day or two."

"Be careful. Both of you."

Xavier flashed a grin. "I'm always careful."

"He's lying," Zuri told Vivian. "My brother is a menace."

"We'll be careful," Vivian promised, though she had no idea if she could keep such a promise.

"Let's go." Xavier swung the duffel over one shoulder and touched his hand to the small of Vivian's back for the briefest moment. In the aircar, he buckled himself into one of the two seats and issued crisp instructions to the AI pilot before turning to her. "What do you know of Catena?"

"Not much more than what I learned the night we dined with River," Vivian admitted as she settled in the other seat and located the safety harness. "Catena and Arcadia don't get along?" The aircar rose smoothly into the sky as soon as Vivian strapped in and gained a steady altitude in a matter of moments.

"Each Martian dome is an independent state," Xavier explained. "Arcadia is the oldest and most established. The other domes look to us to set the standard for upholding the values of our forebears, but we have no hard political power over them. If you were to travel to the other domes, you would see differences in regional dialect, food, and fashion, but our way of life is fundamentally the same." He looked out the window at the Arcadian cityscape. "Catena is different. It's a separatist dome actively working to develop a distinct culture and an independent economy. The Intelligence is outlawed."

"Is Delilah in danger?"

Xavier gave a helpless grimace. "I don't know."

"A separatist dome." Vivian frowned. She'd heard the term before, but she hadn't absorbed the meaning until now. "Are *you* in danger in a separatist dome?"

"I'm fine," Xavier said shortly. He unstrapped and stepped into the small open cabin. From the canvas bag, he pulled out a black outfit. "This is for you, borrowed from one of our Earther household staff. Women do not wear dresses in Catena."

"That will be a refreshing change of pace." Vivian studied his closed face. "Are you embarrassed by this?"

"Of course not."

Vivian thought of the way his eyes had fixed on her when she wore Ivey's badminton costume. She'd assumed at the time that he looked at her with disapproval. Now, she suspected he had another reason. She unbuckled and took the clothing. "Turn around then."

Xavier obeyed. Vivian watched his long, straight back in the tiny cabin as she stripped out of her dress and underskirts. The black pants were made of a shiny material that clung to her legs, and the high-neck tank top revealed her shoulders and stretched over her chest.

"I'm done."

Xavier turned to look at her and cleared his throat. His eyes stole over her body before he turned back to the bag. "My own ensemble is not so drastic a change." He removed his jacket and waistcoat, revealing a white shirt. Xavier loosened his navy cravat and slipped the tie and shirt over his head.

Vivian knew she should return the courtesy of looking away, but she was too curious. Xavier's lightly muscled brown torso was longer than an Earther man's. What would it feel like, she wondered, to run a finger down the smooth middle line of his abdomen? She rubbed her hands together, remembering the feel of his rough thumb on her knuckles. As she watched, Xavier pulled a black T-shirt over his head, changed his shoes into practical black sneakers, and left his dark Arcadian trousers.

The overall effect was startling. Without his hat, Xavier's close-cropped hair framed his elongated head. The shirt displayed his toned arms and the open hollow of his throat. He looked more like an Earther, even if his grace and elegance prevented her from seeing the kind of man she'd avoided in the refugee camp.

"Shoes." He handed her a pair of black sneakers. Vivian put them on without comment, occasionally stealing glances at Xavier's changed appearance.

"Strap back in. We've reached the Arcadian shuttleport," Xavier said. "I'm using false identification at the checkpoints to keep both our names out of it. The aircar has a false registration as well."

"What will happen if the IDs fail?"

"If they fail, it won't be here. This is my family's dome." Xavier stared intently at the small craft's front window as the ship moved slowly through a checkpoint line.

"And in Catena?"

Xavier shrugged. "We'll see."

"State your purpose," an official voice sounded through the cabin.

Xavier gave two false names. "We are traveling to Catena on business. Our line of work is terraforming consulting."

"Please be aware that Arcadia has issued a travel advisory. By entering the Catena dome, you assume an increased risk of fraud, theft, injury, and death. Outsider political activity and activism are strictly prohibited by the Catena authorities."

"Thank you. Your warning is noted."

The ship passed through the barrier onto a holding deck. The dome wall rotated and the ship was suddenly outside the dome and in the thin Martian atmosphere.

"*Death?*" Vivian demanded.

"We'll be fine." He said no more.

Uneasily, Vivian looked out the window at the barren Martian landscape. The ground was a rusty red, and the aircar stirred dust in its wake. Since she and her family arrived at Sumter, Vivian had never gone anywhere at all, except in her imagination. She had a greater range of motion on Mars, but her life was still constrained and full of rules. Now, in a single afternoon, Xavier Dorsey had taken her further than she had ever dreamed.

As they rose, Vivian had a full view of Arcadia. The dome glittered in the blazing sun. She could see linked rail lines to other domes, a spider web of connections that grew more and more complex as her view zoomed out.

There were no rail lines to Catena.

CHAPTER TWENTY-FOUR

4 Sols to Presentation Day

Stepping down into the shuttleport at Catena was as disorienting for Vivian as the day she'd first landed on Mars. In Arcadia, the open plaza had been full of well-dressed Martians with elaborate headwear, with only a few Earthers serving as porters and bodyguards. Here, Martians and the occasional Earthers freely mingled, clad in form-fitting black outfits. If Xavier hadn't known to bring alternative clothing, they would have stuck out immediately. She hoped the rest of his knowledge would prove effective.

In the gathering darkness, the port was dimly lit and disorganized. A long line snaked around as people waited for a single human ticket seller. Empty cups and papers littered the dusty ground.

One food merchant sold an unrecognizable brown stew, and Vivian mentally thanked the Dorsey staff for the cultured roast beef sandwich she'd eaten in the aircar. Even if the stew did give her a sort of anti-nostalgia for her mother's cooking at Sumter.

"Come on." Xavier lengthened his stride, and Vivian hurried to catch up.

They arrived shortly at a four-story building with a brightly painted mural of a jungle under an orange sky on the outer wall and a single sign above labeled *Hostelry*. At the desk inside, Xavier told the human attendant brusquely, "One room with two beds." He'd dropped his usual refined manners.

"Only one bed per room in these parts, so close to the port. I can get you two rooms if you'd like," the bored clerk drawled.

Xavier glanced at Vivian, and she gave a slight jerk of her head. She didn't want to be separated from him in this strange place. "One room is sufficient."

The modest rented room was simply furnished with an en suite bathroom, side chair, and a built-in platform bed with two pillows. Xavier held up one finger to her and pulled a silver rectangular handheld device out of the bag. He moved the device deliberately along the walls.

"All done," he said finally. "The room isn't bugged."

Bugged? Such a possibility hadn't even occurred to Vivian, and she was grateful once again for Xavier's willingness to help her. She wouldn't be able to do this on her own.

Vivian moved to peer out the window at the street below. Mopeds flitted through the narrow street around larger vehicles in a maze of traffic so different from the wide, pedestrian-friendly streets of Arcadia. Two Martian men argued on a street corner under a flickering yellow light. A cacophony of noises—music, honking, shouting, and laughter—penetrated the thin windowpane.

Xavier gently steered her from the window. "We don't want to draw attention to ourselves."

"You know, I don't think I've seen a single child since we've landed."

Xavier activated the window's blackout screen. "Not many children are born here."

Vivian thought of Delilah, pregnant and alone. "How does the population grow then?"

"Through defections from the other domes. People dissatisfied with their current situations and looking for a change."

Vivian rubbed her arms. An entire dome full of people who disliked the status quo on Mars enough to uproot their lives. "What do we do now?"

He returned the detection device to their shared duffel. "We get some sleep. In the morning, we call on my old friend."

"Should we go to Chancellor River? They'd help us, right?'

Xavier ran a hand over his short hair. "Would they? You saw how River encouraged you to defect to Catena. I'm not sure they'd be on our side. Especially since Delilah left willingly."

Vivian nodded in reluctant agreement. "Do you trust your friend?"

The muscles in Xavier's shoulder moved under his thin T-shirt as he shrugged. "I trust her to be honorable. If Silas is here, she'll know where to start looking."

"I wish we knew what he wanted with Delilah. I still can't believe he brought her here." Vivian sat on the bed. "But maybe I should've guessed something like this would happen."

"You can't blame yourself. The information I shared was intended to be in confidence."

She shook her head. "Not that. A month or so ago, Silas—he kissed me. And more. It happened very fast. He didn't seem to care about what I liked."

Xavier's heavy eyebrows drew together. "Did he force himself upon you?"

"No, no, of course not. I wanted . . . something. Anyway, it's not as if I told him to stop. And Luz interrupted us before things could go very far. But I should've warned my sister."

Xavier sat down on the chair opposite the bed. "You did nothing wrong. It's Silas who's violated the basic tenets of Martian values." He stared blankly at the ground and murmured, "Again."

Vivian thought of what Dr. Chavez had told them. A lifetime ago. "Consent. Communication."

His eyes snapped back to her face. "Just so. Consent is highly valued here. It's the reason the Intelligence has given you the illusion of choice in a partner. To do otherwise would be too grave a violation of Martian custom."

"Consent was not considered important at Sumter." Vivian picked at the light blanket on the bed. "I'm not . . . experienced, but I always assumed that being carried away in a moment of passion is the end goal. I thought, for a moment, I achieved that passion with Silas. But the fantasy was different from the reality."

"He didn't ask permission?" Xavier's dark brown eyes regarded her intently.

"Permission?" she asked with some surprise. "In the heat of the moment? That would've been out of place."

He made a sound low in his throat. "Not if you do it well."

"Explain," Vivian whispered, her mouth suddenly dry.

Xavier knelt in front of her. His face was at height with hers. Leaning forward, he moved into her space, eyes locked on her own. "If I wanted to kiss you, I would make you yearn for it. I would hover right out of your reach. I would let the air between us crackle with anticipation. And then, I would ask you."

"Ask me?" She couldn't move away if she tried.

"I would say, 'Vivian Bowen, may I kiss you?'"

His lips were so close to hers, and she felt a mindless yearning well up inside her. Xavier gave a small, satisfied smile and moved gracefully away from her, returning to the chair. Vivian let out a slow breath. Perhaps she wasn't broken after all.

"I see," Vivian said, struggling for composure.

Xavier looked amused. "Take the first turn in the bath. There's a sonic laundry built into the wall that we can use to refresh our Catena-style clothing." He turned away but not before Vivian saw him shiver.

She rummaged in their pack for her things, avoiding eye contact, and went into the bathroom. The hostel had a rusted sonic shower, to her chagrin. She could have used a water shower right now. A cold one.

Xavier stared at her very hard in her Arcadia-style nightgown when she emerged from the bath, and Vivian felt herself regaining the upper hand. "Bath's free," she murmured and slipped past him to lie down on one side of the narrow bed.

Despite a half-formed desire to wait for Xavier, she felt the pull of sleep almost immediately. Her endless day was finally at a close. She opened her eyes when she heard the scrape of the chair. Xavier was arranging the other pillow and his overcoat on the threadbare carpet.

"Don't be an idiot," Vivian whispered. "You need rest to be alert tomorrow."

Xavier straightened in the dark. He was wearing a white nightshirt that exposed his calves. "I didn't want to impose."

"Come on then."

She felt the weight of the bed shift as he lay down beside her. She hadn't moved, and her back was to him. He adjusted his body and then was still. Vivian listened to the comforting sound of his breathing as she drifted back to sleep.

CHAPTER TWENTY-FIVE

3 Sols to Presentation Day

Vivian awoke to darkness, a heaviness pressed against her back. Where was she? Sumter, sleeping beside her sister? No. The memories came in a rush.

Delilah missing. A ship to Catena.

A hostel with one bed.

Vivian rolled over to face Xavier, and he slipped an arm around her waist. His warm body melded into hers. In sleep, his austere face was relaxed. Without thinking, she reached out one hand to touch his stubbled cheek.

He opened his deep brown eyes, and the hand that had been around her waist grabbed her wrist. She felt an unexpected thrill of excitement run through her. He released her and pulled backward abruptly. "I do beg your pardon." In one swift movement, he pulled himself out of the bed and padded to the bathroom.

His absence left the bed cold and empty. Vivian rubbed her wrist. It didn't hurt—his grip was not particularly strong. But she felt the pressure of his touch linger.

When they were both dressed, they gathered their meager belongings into the duffel bag and left the room. Xavier pulled a burner credit chit from his front pocket to purchase warm pastries and black coffee from a vendor outside the lodging house. Regularly dining with Arcadian oligarchs had refined Vivian's palette, and the pastry tasted stale and the coffee bitter. Still, she tried to let the hot food and drink comfort her as they threaded their way through the densely packed streets of Catena.

Today, they would find Delilah and bring her home.

All would be well.

"Here." Xavier gestured to a nondescript one-story building with an icon of two glasses clinking mounted at the top. They pushed the door open and stepped inside.

In the mid-morning, the shadowy room's simple black tables were empty. Vivian didn't see anything like the server robots that had run the tavern she'd gone to with Silas. A single older Martian woman with stringy gray hair stood behind a long bar, wiping a glass with a towel.

The woman widened her eyes at their appearance and dropped her cloth. "Well now, you're a sight for sore eyes."

"Yvonne." Xavier held out a hand.

The woman took his hand and pulled him into an embrace. She turned to two men nursing drinks at the far corner of the bar and barked, "We're closed." Grumbling, they heaved off their stools and shuffled to the door. Yvonne shut and locked it behind them before returning behind the bar. "You shouldn't be here, X. You know they'll tear you apart if they realize who you are."

Vivian blanched and looked searchingly at Xavier. Hadn't he told her they would be fine here?

Xavier's calm face didn't change as he sat on a stool opposite Yvonne. "Then help shorten my stay. I'm here to find Silas."

"Silas," Yvonne snarled. "The last I heard that wastrel was racking up gambling debts in the Arcadian military."

"He has my sister," Vivian burst out, hands gripping the back of one of the stools. "Please, we must find her."

Yvonne's eyes narrowed. "And who might you be?"

Xavier inclined his head in Vivian's direction. "Yvonne, I am pleased to introduce you to Miss Vivian Bowen."

Yvonne's entire body jerked back. "You're one of the Red Mothers, aren't you?" she whispered with awe. "Here to change the future of Mars." Shaking off her serious expression, she snapped her towel in Xavier's direction. "X, I wouldn't have expected this from you of all people. Naughty boy." She smirked at Vivian. "Are you carrying the next Dorsey heir, then?"

Xavier scowled. "I am merely helping Miss Bowen locate her sister. I know of your correspondence with Zuri. You've kept track of Silas for her sake."

"I may know something," Yvonne admitted.

"You once told me you owed Zuri a debt you could never repay, for failing to protect her from Silas."

"You are not Zuri. I was never a big enough fool to think I could protect *you* from Silas. Not when the two of you were so codependent in your youth." Yvonne bent her head and scrubbed an invisible stain on the countertop. "These days, Silas is a man I would not want to cross."

Codependent? Vivian wondered. *I thought they were boyhood rivals.*

Xavier didn't object to Yvonne's characterization of his relationship with Silas. Without comment, he pulled two sparkling jeweled cufflinks out of his pocket and laid them on the worn bar.

Yvonne picked up one of the cufflinks and squinted at it. "You know this has no value here."

"Melt it down for parts."

The cufflinks disappeared into Yvonne's palm. She looked to the side and scratched her head. Vivian bit the inside of her cheek to keep from begging. Finally, Yvonne said, "Silas is well-liked by the separatist militia here. They maintain a barracks on the northern outskirts of the dome near the terraforming facility." Yvonne crouched behind the bar and pulled out a hand-drawn map from a folio. She pointed. "Take the rail here and walk straight north the rest of the way. If Silas is in Catena, that'll be where you'll find him."

Xavier took Yvonne's hand and bowed over it. "My thanks."

"None of that." Yvonne snatched her hand away. "Remember where you are."

As they turned to go, Yvonne called after him, "You should know—the Catena militia is not like that absurd soldier caste in Arcadia."

"What do you mean?" Xavier asked warily.

"Don't be daft. You know exactly what I mean. Everyone knows in Arcadia that soldiering is a way to occupy the many Martians unable to find an Earther partner willing to procreate." Yvonne nodded at Vivian's confused expression. "That's right. The soldiers burn off their energy with drills and low-stakes skirmishes and are convinced that their lives have meaning even without children. But they have seen no true action." She raised a finger at Xavier. "Catena is different. They're building an army here, X. A real army. And I've heard the pace is accelerating since the election."

Xavier crossed his arms and frowned at her. "To what end?"

"Hell if I know." Yvonne turned back to the bar and placed a stack of glasses on a high shelf. "But I would think twice about crossing the Catena militia."

"I appreciate the warning." Xavier opened the door and held it for Vivian. "Thank you, Yvonne."

In the street, Vivian hurried in Xavier's wake as he walked unerringly toward the nearest train station. On the side of the station, an enormous mural of River Hawk's face stared down at her, their elegant cheekbones drawn in slashes of dark blue. Xavier handled the transaction with his credit chit, and they were soon seated on a swaying caterpillar train that hung from an elevated track.

Vivian vibrated with tension, afraid to speak and give herself away. They were in real danger, Yvonne had made that clear enough. She thought of Delilah held in a separatist soldiers' barracks, pregnant, with only Silas for protection. Vivian took a deep breath and stole a glance at Xavier's calm profile. She could be strong, for her sister.

Finally, they came to the right stop and rose together without a word.

Outside, the area felt different than the bustling neighborhood near the shuttleport. The empty, narrow streets were lined with tall storage facilities with no shops, restaurants, or bars to be seen. After walking a few moments, the few other passengers had fallen away, and they were alone among the plain multi-story buildings.

"You're different here," Vivian remarked in a soft voice.

"How so?"

"Not so proper. Less focused on projecting the act of a gentleman." Vivian rather liked this side of him.

Xavier rubbed the back of his neck. "It is not an act, Vivian. Not for me."

"Ivey told me it was a game." Vivian laughed. "You must admit it's a little ridiculous—this fantasy of elaborate costumes and balls." She touched her shiny black pants and missed, for a moment, the luxurious fabric of her Arcadian dresses.

"It's how I was raised," Xavier said. "I understand what you mean, of course. We are one of the oldest Martian families. But the women who marry into the Dorsey line were all born on Earth and see our culture as feigned, at least in part." He shifted the duffel bag to his other shoulder. "Perhaps, for some, it's playacting. Not for my father. And not for me. Even if he abandoned me, I cannot unlearn what he taught me. Emulating a time of refined manners, poetry, art, and progress gives our lives here on Mars a deeper purpose. We aren't simply scrambling to survive on a harsh world. We're elevating our culture to a higher standard."

"What do you mean, he abandoned you?"

"He took his own life." Xavier's voice dropped. "After my mother . . ."

"Oh." Vivian reached out a hand and touched his arm. "Xavier, that's terrible."

"My parents loved each other once. I do believe that. But my father was a difficult man. Controlling."

"You said she signed a prenup?"

"Yes. I found it in my father's office after he died. If she ever left him, she would be giving us up, too. So, she stayed. Even though she was unhappy. And one day . . . One day she drank a bottle of wine, climbed on top of the roof of Dorsey Estate, and . . . fell. Hit her head and died." He blew out a breath. "And my father . . . He followed her into death."

"I'm so sorry."

"The whole thing made me a bit wild. Nihilistic. I did some things I'm not proud of." He looked away from her. "My father left the majority of his holdings in my aunt's safekeeping, until she deemed me ready to inherit. After the way I behaved after his death, she decided to hold the purse strings a little longer. And then . . . she never gave them up." He looked down at her and grimaced. "What must I sound like to you? Complaining about an inheritance."

"You lost so much. How old were you when all this happened?"

"Eighteen. Zuri was only nine." He passed a hand over his face.

"Is this why you've been fighting so hard against the Red Mothers initiative? For your own mother?"

"Maybe. In part." He turned to her. "Vivian—" he started, then paused. "What is it you desire? Out of life?"

"To find my sister," Vivian said promptly.

Simple enough. One clear goal to focus on. No point in looking too far ahead.

"After that."

Vivian flashed to the law library. How she'd felt reading the original Charter of the Planet Mars. *Are you interested in law, dear?* No, that could never be her life.

She was a Red Mother. And she'd signed a contract.

Vivian gave the only possible answer. "To bring my sister back to safety. To send my parents enough money to continue to live independently outside of a camp." There, a realistic long-term goal.

"Nothing for yourself?"

"There's nothing I desire for myself," she said quickly. What would be the point?

Among the creeping thyme, reading his prologue, she'd allowed herself a moment to dream of *more*. But now? All she wanted, desperately, was for things to be as they were. For her sister to be with Mitzi King, able to send more payments to her parents. For her to choose . . . someone. Ren? She didn't want Ren.

Xavier stopped in the street and faced her. His dark eyes were serious as he beheld her. "You should want, for yourself. You should dream big dreams."

Vivian looked away from the intensity of his regard and continued walking. "I don't see the point. I'm grateful for what I have." What would it be like to break free from the cramped smallness of her life?

She pushed the question aside. She was here to find her sister.

"Take life in both hands, Vivian. And I'll be there to support you."

Vivian shivered, her bare arms suddenly cold. How could she ask anything more of him after they'd found Delilah?

Xavier raised one hand and pointed. "I believe we're here."

They stood in front of a five-story structure with boarded up windows and a steel door. Vivian tried to ignore the queasy feeling in her stomach.

"If we find them here, let me do the talking," Xavier instructed. "Silas will be looking for money—a bribe. If I must, I'll even persuade my aunt to renew his access to my father's inheritance. Whatever it takes." His lip curled. "I know how to stoop to his level."

Vivian nodded, her stomach in knots.

The door squealed as Xavier pushed it open. They stepped into a dark, cavernous room, the click of their shoes echoing in the empty space.

"Hello?" Xavier called. "Is anyone here?"

Vivian bumped into Xavier in the darkness. Then, bright lights assaulted them from all directions. A group of uniformed Martians surrounded them. Swords drawn. Vivian's gasp radiated around the room.

"Counselor Dorsey and Miss Bowen, so nice of you to join us," Silas drawled, stepping into the light.

A pale-faced Delilah stood right behind him.

CHAPTER TWENTY-SIX

3 Sols to Presentation Day

"X, you have no idea how much it pleases me to find you here. Unescorted. And so far from home. I've been waiting a long time for such an opportunity."

"Silas," Xavier replied. "I suspect you know why we've come. I'm prepared to offer you a generous deal."

"Is that right?" Without removing his eyes from Xavier, Silas said, "Delilah, my darling, take your sister to our room. I'm sure she's tired after her journey. I need to speak with my old friend."

Vivian took Xavier's hand in hers, careful not to squeeze. His calloused thumb rubbed roughly across her palm. "Go," he said in an undertone. "I know how to handle Silas." He'd said as much, hadn't he? With the weapons drawn, Vivian had no choice but to trust Xavier knew what he was doing.

Delilah grabbed Vivian firmly by the arm and pulled her away. Without speaking, they walked briskly down unadorned corridors until they reached a room and opened the door.

As Vivian caught her breath, she looked around, seeing a neatly made double bed, papers strewn over a desk, and a line of several sets of military boots. Handwritten charts and lists covered the walls.

Delilah wrapped her arms around Vivian and held her tightly. "What were you thinking coming here?"

Vivian pulled back, holding Delilah's arms. "What were *you* thinking? Mom and Dad need us."

Delilah looked away. "I know. Mitzi, she—I just couldn't stay. You wouldn't understand."

Vivian rubbed Delilah's shoulders. "It doesn't matter right now. We're going to get you out of here. Xavier is making Silas an offer. He said he'd do whatever it takes."

Delilah barely seemed to hear her words. "Do you have a way out of this dome?" she asked urgently. "Could you get there without Xavier?"

Vivian jerked her hands away. "Without Xavier? What are you talking about?"

"You heard Silas, didn't you? He's been waiting to have Xavier in his power for a long time. Silas isn't going to let Xavier leave here alive." Delilah was shaking. "The childhood resentment goes deep."

"Childhood resentment? Delilah, it's Xavier who hates Silas. And with good reason! When Silas was in his twenties, he seduced Xavier's younger sister when she was only fifteen. He got her pregnant, and she nearly died from the complications."

Delilah's face was stark white. "You need to get out of here before they decide they want to keep you too. At least you aren't pregnant."

"'They'? Who are you talking about?" Vivian asked, her stomach in knots. "Delilah, we came here to rescue you."

"Forget about me." Delilah's eyes were wild and her tone as serious as Vivian had ever seen. "Come on. There's another exit through the back. We'll hope Silas is too distracted by Xavier to look for you until you're safely away." When she opened the door, Vivian heard an anguished scream. "You have to go. Now."

Vivian's heart rate doubled. Another scream. "Is that Xavier?" Could Xavier make a noise like that? It barely sounded human. What was Silas doing to him? "Delilah, please . . . I asked him to come here. I will not abandon him. And I won't abandon you." Vivian pulled her sister back into the room. "Tell me what's going on. Let's make a plan. Please, Delilah."

Delilah returned to the room and began hunting through the narrow closet. "Silas won't hurt me, not while I still carry Yarrow's designer fetus. They need me. And Silas will still need me afterward, if he wants me to bear his own."

"*What?* Delilah, what are you saying?"

Delilah gave a despairing little laugh. "It's the same here, isn't it? Everywhere we go, someone is trying to control our bodies." She thrust a gun into Vivian's hand. "Here's the safety. Look through here to aim."

Vivian took the gun with shaking hands. "I thought guns were illegal on Mars. You can crack the domes and kill everyone nearby."

"Do you think Silas cares about following the law? I'm almost positive this is the sole gun in the building, from the way he brags about it. That should help you out if you get into any trouble sneaking out."

"I'm not leaving without Xavier."

Delilah looked away, biting her lip. Another piercing scream echoed from the hall. She let out a long breath. "Fine. I'll help you."

CHAPTER TWENTY-SEVEN

3 Sols to Presentation Day

Vivian couldn't control her rapid breathing. She wasn't strong enough to do this. She'd always followed her mother's advice and avoided danger, suppressing her ambitions in order to make her life as small and safe as possible.

But she couldn't abandon Xavier.

The hallway stretched for an eternity. With every step she took, she could hear Xavier's frayed voice, growing more and more inhuman.

Clipped steps sounded in the hall, and Delilah grabbed her arm and dragged her through a door and into another bedroom. Delilah listened intently at the door frame. Her sister seemed to have grown up all at once. Gone was the silly girl and in her place was a serious woman honed by her circumstances. All Delilah had wanted was to find love. And instead, she'd gotten Mitzi and now Silas.

"Come on," Delilah murmured, and opened the door.

The screams reverberating down the hall were ragged now. What was Silas doing to him? Were his soldiers content to stand by and watch?

They approached the end of the hallway. "You have to sell it," Delilah murmured. "You need to make him believe you don't care about me. Can you do it?"

Vivian took a deep breath. "I can do it." She schooled her features into a harsh scowl, grabbed her sister by the elbow, and stepped into the light.

"Stop," Vivian ordered. She held Delilah's arm tightly with one hand, her other hand training the gun to Delilah's stomach.

Silas turned. His face was spattered with blood, and he held a reddened knife. Vivian made herself look. Xavier was breathing unevenly, his face a sheen of sweat. His bare chest, so beautiful the day before, was a ragged patchwork of cuts and blood. Vivian swallowed and tried to keep the horror off her face.

Silas's eyes narrowed. "You wouldn't kill your own sister."

"I've seen the medical care you have on Mars." Her clear and confident voice came as a surprise. "I don't think she'll die from a single shot to the gut. But Constance Yarrow's genetic secrets may not survive. How big is the fetus now, sweet sister? The size of a poppy seed?"

"Don't hurt me!" Delilah shouted. "You can't make me leave. I love him. Please, Vivian, let me go."

"Fine," Vivian said harshly. "My sister wants to stay here. You can have her. Release Xavier, and we'll go."

"But I was having so much fun," Silas mused, twirling the knife. "Almost like old times."

"Vivian . . ." Xavier gasped. "Get out of here. Please . . . while you still can."

"Not without you." She turned to Silas. "I want a medical bag. Bandages, disinfectant, painkillers." She pressed the gun tighter to Delilah, who let out a theatrical groan. *Don't overdo it, baby sister*, Vivian thought.

Silas gave a nod to one of the other soldiers, who departed at a run.

"You won't get far, my dear. We will find you."

"I want a head start," Vivian said stubbornly. "I'll trade you my sister unharmed in exchange for ten minutes without pursuit."

"Fine," Silas drawled. The soldier returned, panting, and dropped a bag on the floor at Vivian's feet. Silas took the knife and turned to Xavier. With fear in his eyes, Xavier flinched away. Silas laughed and kissed Xavier's brow before cutting the cords that bound Xavier to the chair.

"Pick up the bag," Vivian growled to Delilah. She turned to Xavier. "Stand up."

He looked at her, his eyes unfocused.

"Stand up!" she yelled.

Xavier put his hands upon his knees and pushed himself to his feet. He swayed momentarily and then found his balance.

"Go first," Vivian ordered Xavier. "Start walking." He took stumbling steps toward the exit. Vivian followed, dragging Delilah along. Silas stayed where he was, a small, sardonic smile on his face. "Ten minutes. Your word as a gentleman."

Silas put a hand to his heart. "As you say, my lady. I pledge my word."

As they backed up, Delilah pressed a key fob into Vivian's palm. "He's lying," she murmured.

"I know," Vivian breathed.

"I don't like your odds with Xavier," Delilah continued in an undertone. "He looks terrible."

"I have to try."

Xavier had reached the door. He stood with his fingers gripping the handle, heaving. "Vivian, this is impossible," he panted, not looking at her. "He'll kill us both."

"Go out first and walk to the right, around the side of the building. Get on the moped."

Xavier straightened. "You know how to hotwire a moped?"

"I have the key."

"Ah . . ." Xavier glanced at Delilah for only a moment. He opened the door and stumbled out.

"I'll stall him as long as I can," Delilah murmured.

"I'll come back for you," Vivian vowed.

"Go."

Vivian grabbed the medical bag from Delilah's hand, pushed her sister to the floor, and took off running. Behind her, she could hear Delilah sobbing. "Oh Silas, my love, hold me. I thought my own sister was going to kill me."

As she ran, Vivian shoved the gun into the medical bag. When she reached Xavier, she grabbed his arm, pulling him stumbling behind her.

The moped was parked right where Delilah had promised. She jumped on, and Xavier clumsily wrapped his large body around her. The moped came to life in the proximity of the fob. It was designed for a Martian build, and Vivian wasted precious seconds raising the pedals to their maximum height. She pressed the accelerator, and the moped sprang forward with a lurch. She crashed into a stack of crates next to a wall, sending them flying in the moped's wake.

"Steady," Xavier murmured in her ear. "Keep your foot light on the pedal. It only needs a touch."

Shaking, she tried to obey. They sped closer to the populated area and a few pedestrians jumped out of their way.

"Will he let us go, do you think?" Vivian gasped. "Since he still has Delilah?"

"No," Xavier said grimly. "At least . . . he won't let me get away. Turn here," he said at the next intersection. "Don't follow a pattern."

Vivian turned the wheel, and it screeched. The back tire hit a ladder propped against a wall, and it banged to the ground blocking the street. In the distance, she spotted the arching steel bars elevating the hanging track of the caterpillar train. "Should we . . . ?"

"Yes. Ditch the moped."

At the station, a vendor looked at their bizarre appearance in startlement. "Shirts," Vivian demanded. "Do you sell shirts?"

With wide eyes, the vendor pointed to a small display of T-shirts. Vivian pulled the credit chit from Xavier's front pocket and handed it to the vendor. She slipped the shirt over Xavier's body, and he hissed through his teeth. With a steady hand on his arm, Vivian led him up the stairs. The train was just pulling up, suspended from the elevated rail. As they stepped inside, she could see uniformed men rushing up the steps. Vivian pulled Xavier deeper into the train car, among the crowd. The doors closed before the men reached the platform.

"They'll be at the next stop," Xavier wheezed. "Vivian, you have to leave me."

"Absolutely not," Vivian said fiercely. She opened the bag and rummaged to find a few painkillers. "Take these."

He took the tablets from her hand and placed them in his mouth. "The end of the train should have a balcony. We'll need to jump."

"Jump . . ." Vivian took a deep breath. "Right, let's go." They slowly made their way through the swaying cars, careful not to draw attention. The bored passengers barely glanced their way. At the final train car, Xavier wrenched open the door, and they stepped onto the balcony. Air whipped around Vivian's face as the train barreled forward, suspended from the rail.

Xavier's eyes were feverishly bright as he took in the scene. He grabbed the medical bag from her slack fingers and put it over his shoulder without wincing. The soldiers' painkillers must be powerful to have kicked in so fast. He pointed up. "See those arched bars holding the rail in place? We'll grab onto one of them and pull ourselves off the train car. We'll then inch ourselves down the side as best we can until we're at a safe drop."

"I don't think I can do this."

Xavier took her face in his hands. "Vivian Bowen, you are the bravest, stubbornest woman I know. You *can* do this. I know it." He kissed her, the briefest brush of lips. She stared up into his intent brown eyes and nodded. With Xavier's arms helping her balance, she scrambled up onto the balcony railing and clutched the side pole for support as the balcony lurched from side to side. For once, she was taller than him.

She stared up at the arching bars that supported the track, stretching from the ground to above the top of the train and back down again. They weren't much taller than the walls of her compound on Arcadia.

"On the count of three," Xavier said as he pulled himself beside her.

Separatist soldiers would be waiting for them at the next station. She would jump, or they would kill her.

"One. Two. Three."

Vivian pushed up and clutched the hard metal bar with both hands. Behind her, the train rushed away. She perched above the street, her feet dangling in the air. Xavier's ragged breathing whistled in her ear, but she dared not turn her head. She took her hands and shimmed them across the arch moving lower and lower.

She jumped.

The low Martian gravity served her well as she nearly floated to the ground. She had a moment to think of Xavier's more fragile bones. She angled her body to catch him as he fell to try to soften the blow. He dropped on top of her with a pained grunt.

For a moment, the briefest of moments, they stared at each other, dazed. Then, Xavier clambered to his feet, picked up the medical bag, and looked around.

"There." He pointed to an alleyway. The corridor was dark and narrow. Trash kicked up in their wake as they hurried along. He pointed at an older, rusty door. "Try that one," he gasped.

Vivian tested the handle.

Locked.

Of course it was locked.

Nothing had gone right all day. She was alone with an injured man in a strange place. Her sister was in the hands of a sadist. Tears stung her eyes. She had failed.

"We're at the outskirts of a Martian separatist dome," Xavier panted. "That door was built to keep out Martians, not Earthers. You can break it down, Vivian."

She pushed her shoulder against the door uncertainly. It rattled. She tried again. It shook and held. Remembering Shiloh's lessons, Vivian shifted her weight to the ball of her left foot, pulled her right foot toward her shoulder, and extended her leg straight out to the door.

The lock broke, and the door crashed open.

Vivian turned triumphantly to Xavier only to find him swaying on his feet with a glassy-eyed expression. She wrapped her arms around his waist and helped him into the dark room.

CHAPTER TWENTY-EIGHT

3 Sols to Presentation Day

The room was spacious and dimly lit by high, narrow windows. Lumpy sacks covered the dirty cement floors. Vivian lowered Xavier to prop against one of the sacks and placed the medical bag next to him. She'd left their duffel with Silas, she realized suddenly. They had no identification, food, or extra clothing. *A problem for tomorrow.*

"Is this a bakery?" Vivian asked.

"Smuggling ring, I'd venture," Xavier gasped from his position on the ground. His face was covered in sweat, and his eyes were stretched wide.

She could feel exhaustion threatening to overtake her as the adrenaline drained out of her body. *Not yet.* She dragged herself through the dark room until she located a handheld solar light and switched it on. Returning to Xavier, she put the light beside him before kneeling to open the medical bag. At least it was better stocked than the medical equipment she'd had access to at the refugee camp. She disinfected her shaking hands as best she could and popped the seal on a small bottle of surgical glue.

"Take off your shirt."

Xavier obeyed without comment. The shirt stuck to his skin, and he let out a yelp as he forced it over his head. An ugly mess of clotted brown blood covered his torso.

Upon seeing his injuries, Vivian's hands stopped shaking and a sudden calm settled over her. She had to be strong. For Xavier. "I need to clean it," she murmured. "I think it's going to hurt."

"Do what you must. Only . . . give me another painkiller first."

Vivian found the bottle of painkillers and handed him another pill. "He must hate you," she remarked as she dabbed the wounds with an antiseptic cloth.

"I certainly underestimated the depths of his feelings." Xavier looked down at himself. "I know it looks awful, but I don't think any of the cuts are that deep. He was toying with me. Going for pain, not permanent injury." He took her free hand in his. "You saved me before it could get any worse."

"Xavier—I don't understand what happened back there. You were going to offer him access to more of your father's inheritance. Why would he throw it away for . . . whatever that was?"

"I miscalculated." Xavier ran a hand over his hair and grimaced as the movement stretched the skin on his chest. "I thought after five years we'd moved on from our past. I was mistaken."

"I feel like I'm missing something."

"I—forgive me. Silas and I—we—" He was trembling.

"It's alright," Vivian murmured. "Let's just focus on patching you up." She went back to the task at hand. She'd tended minor ailments at Sumter before but never a deliberate act of violence. As she worked, she counted the number of shallow cuts.

Ten.

Twenty.

She stopped when she reached thirty, her stomach churning. Whatever lay in Xavier's history with Silas, it was ugly.

When he was reasonably clean, she applied the glue carefully to the open gaps of skin with the applicator. As she worked, his body gradually grew still. When she was finished, she sprayed his chest with a topical antiseptic and anesthetic.

"What a relief!" he gasped. "Whatever you just did made the skin on my chest go numb."

"Good." After wiping the blood off her hands, she took gauze and wrapped it clumsily around his torso. "There!" she said with some satisfaction. "How are you feeling?"

Xavier reached a hand up to touch her face. "Fine. You're a good doctor. There's no pain right now." He lifted his head until their faces were close together. "Will you let me show you my appreciation?"

Vivian shivered. "Yes."

He kissed her. This kiss was nothing like the brief one on the train car. He kissed her now with a bold intensity. One hand cupped her face while the other tangled in her hair. She let herself get lost in the kiss. After the terror and blood of the last hours, it felt so very good to remember she was alive.

He broke off to press his forehead against hers. "May I take off your shirt?"

Vivian froze. "I'm not—you know—I don't have one of those contraceptive implants." She thought, for the first time that day, of her mother's warning.

Xavier kissed her neck, just below her jaw. "I'm aware. I will do nothing tonight that could result in a pregnancy. Do you trust me?"

The answer came easily. "I trust you." She felt no fear or anxiety—only anticipation for what would happen next. Without any further hesitation, she tugged at the hem of the borrowed shirt and pulled it over her head.

His mouth moved over her skin. She came alive under his touch, her body responding in a way she had never experienced with another person before. She carefully returned his caresses, mindful of his injuries. Xavier didn't seem to care about his bandages, pain, or fatigue.

He was completely focused on her.

When she was fully naked, he spread her clothing on the dirty floor and murmured, "Lie down."

Vivian barely noticed the cold, hard floor. Xavier hovered over her, his beautiful face wreathed in a smile. When he lowered to kiss her mouth, the bandages scraped the skin of her breasts. She felt his arousal through his trousers and jerked her hips up involuntarily.

"Mm." He moved his mouth to one breast and swirled his tongue around her nipple. "Not tonight. I'm afraid I would not be at my best. Tonight is for you." He moved his lips slowly and deliberately lower and lower until she was shaking with pleasure and anticipation.

"Please," she whispered, and felt him smile against her inner thigh.

The time to focus on her pleasure was a gift. So unlike her usual scramble, taking advantage of a brief moment of privacy to force a quick moment of self-release. Now, she surrendered to the touch of Xavier's mouth, tongue, and fingers. She allowed her pleasure to build and build, until, finally, she broke in a delicious wave. She hadn't known a climax could be so long and so satisfying.

She hadn't known that allowing another person to give her pleasure would feel so terrifyingly intimate. The ultimate form of trust and surrender.

Afterwards, he lay on her stomach. Her fingers made circles in his coarse hair.

"Was that—" She faltered. "Was that enough for you?"

He looked up at her face with his rich brown eyes. "Oh, yes," he murmured. The satisfaction in his low voice made Vivian shiver. "A welcome distraction from my own ailments. I believe I thought only of you."

She swallowed. "I'm not used to being the center of attention."

"You deserve to have someone focus on your happiness."

At Sumter, she could never have trusted a man enough to be alone and naked. Yet, even now, Xavier had kept his trousers on and hadn't crossed over the boundary they'd established.

Xavier's eyes drooped shut, and his breathing evened. Despite the uncomfortable floor and their precarious situation, a warm sense of safety enveloped Vivian.

She could trust this man.

CHAPTER TWENTY-NINE

2 Sols to Presentation Day

Crash!

Vivian bolted upright. Her pounding heart threatened to burst out of her chest. She was still on the cold, dusty floor. Naked, dirty, and thirsty. She brought her thin legs into her torso and hugged her knees.

Sprawled on the ground at her side, Xavier squinted open his eyes. "My word, man, you took long enough." He pulled himself to his feet with a groan.

Xavier's cousin August filled the doorway, nearly unrecognizable in a long black leather jacket and dark-washed jeans with a sword on each hip. "One of these days, cousin, I'm not going to be around to rescue you." He took one quick glance at Vivian as she scrambled for yesterday's clothes, her knees drawn up to cover her breasts, and averted his gaze. "I brought you both some necessities." He removed the pack slung over his back and perched it on a rickety table. From it, he withdrew two sets of black clothing, a package of cleansing cloths, water bottles, and ration bars. He detached one of the swords and belt from his waist and placed it next to the clothes.

Xavier caressed the well-worn hilt and then picked up the clothes. "Earther-sized and everything. Very thoughtful cousin." He crouched down and handed Vivian a set of clothes and the cleansing cloths. "Go," he told her with a crooked smile. "Find what passes for a bathroom in this blighted place."

Clutching the clothes to her naked body, she hurried away. The poorly lit bathroom smelled of sawdust and consisted of a compost toilet and a sonic hand cleaner. Her standards had changed, Vivian realized as she scrubbed herself with a cleansing cloth. At Sumter, she would think nothing of a quick wash in a basin in her one-room tent. Now, she longed for the feel of warm water cascading down her hair.

Peering into the cloudy mirror, Vivian attempted to smooth down her tangled curls. She paused, noticing several red marks on the pale skin of her neck. *From his mouth*, she realized with a frisson of desire.

Dressed in a new black outfit and rather clean, Vivian returned to find Xavier's and August's faces close together as they spoke rapidly.

"You're clearly injured," August snapped. "You should be seeking medical attention, not taking on the entire Catena militia in some misguided vigilante suicide mission." He crossed his arms. "X, you know what we need to do. Go home. Persuade the Council to open a formal negotiation with Chancellor River. I don't know what possessed you to come here on your own in the first place. You've never had any sense when it comes to him."

Xavier waved his hand in dismissal. "We don't have time for all that. I won't allow him to destroy another young woman's life. I don't know what he wants with her, but she's carrying one of the enhanced fetuses. She's in incredible danger."

"And what are you going to do about it? Bleed on Silas until he relents?"

Vivian huffed an involuntary laugh.

Xavier turned to look at her and the scowl on his face softened. "Ah, Vivian. You're looking refreshed. I suppose I'm next."

"Be quick about it," August grumbled. "I don't want to linger here."

"How did you find us?" Vivian asked after Xavier left for the bathroom. She picked up one of the ration bars, and her stomach growled.

"Xavier sent word before he departed Arcadia. He should have waited for me, the fool. At least he had the good sense to implant a tracker into his arm and share the frequency with me before he left. It allowed me to keep an eye on his movements and vitals." August handed her a bottle of water. "The tracker spiked about ten hours ago. I didn't—" He ducked his head. "I didn't misread the situation, did I? I assumed his heart rate had spiked because he was in danger, but—"

His earnest discomfort made Vivian smile. "I'm very happy to see you. And I would bet Xavier is relieved as well. Silas used a knife on him, and it got . . . ugly."

August winced. "How bad are the wounds under those bandages?"

Vivian took a swallow of water and a bite of the ration bar. "Numerous, but they're shallow. Liquid stitches and a few painkillers did wonders." She managed not to blush.

"Indeed," murmured Xavier as he slipped in beside her.

"Silas attacked you?" August scowled. "Does the man have a death wish? Aunt Constance will tear him apart."

"Tortured, more like." Xavier's face was calm as he accepted a bottle of water from Vivian, but she noticed his hand trembled slightly. "Luckily, he was only in the warmup stage when Vivian rescued me." One side of his mouth quirked up. "Hijacked a moped and raced my weak, bleeding body through the streets of Catena. Very daring. I do love a woman who can take charge."

August raised his eyebrows. "Very impressive, Vivian. But you, my dear cousin, are changing the subject. Tortured? He tortured *you*? One of the most well-connected people on the planet?"

"Mm, that he did. Silas told me he was planning on sending my mutilated corpse back to Arcadia as a gift for our aunt."

August hissed through his teeth. "He's trying to start a war."

"A war? I don't understand." Vivian glared at Xavier. "Why didn't you tell me that Silas wanted to kill you?"

He tilted his head. "I had other things on my mind. More important things."

She felt her face grow warm. "More important than the possibility of a war?"

"Yes."

Without meaning to, Vivian's eyes slid to his lips. They might have had a very different morning, if they hadn't been interrupted.

August cleared his throat. "This happened in the soldier barracks, yes? How did the Catena soldiers react to his plan to provoke Secretary Yarrow with your dead body? Surely Chancellor Hawk wouldn't approve of such a bold move."

"The soldiers didn't hear. He was whispering in my ear like a lover while his knife scraped down my chest."

"A bit kinky for my taste." August made a face. "And even yours, I'd wager. But then he's always had an unhealthy obsession with you."

An emotion passed over Xavier's face, quickly repressed. "He wouldn't be foolish enough to cross Hawk. Silas is many things, but he's not a fool."

"Hawk. What's their end game, do you suppose?" August asked. "And why do they need Silas, who's clearly a wildcard, when they have all of Catena's resources at their disposal?"

Xavier spread his hands in a noncommittal gesture.

Vivian furrowed her brow. "Delilah told me Silas wouldn't hurt her while she was carrying a genetically enhanced fetus. But . . . the way she said it . . . I think Silas doesn't plan for her to carry the baby to term. I think—" Vivian swallowed as she realized the implications. "I think they plan to study the fetus so they can copy the science."

"He pits himself against the Intelligence," August murmured. "Bold man."

"The word you're looking for is 'idiotic.' There's nothing for it. August, we must find a way to join with the Intelligence to rescue Delilah. Silas has likely moved her by now, and we have no tech capable of tracking her on our own. The clock is ticking." Xavier made a moue of distaste. "Strange bedfellows."

"How?" Vivian asked. "I thought the Intelligence had no sway here."

And how did one go about making an alliance with a sentient AI anyway?

"We use this." August pulled from his pack a small silver orb. "Filched it from Aunt Constance's private collection."

"Oh . . . good thinking, cousin." Xavier's eyes gleamed as he beheld the orb.

"What is it?" Vivan asked. The orb was the size of a baseball with a large black dot in the center and smaller dots all around. It didn't look particularly remarkable, and Vivian couldn't see how such a thing would aid in rescuing her sister. A memory tickled in the back of her mind. Hadn't Ivey mentioned something?

"A physical copy of the Intelligence. This device allows the Secretary to communicate directly with the Intelligence and avoid using her reverend and other augmented humans as interpreters." August looked to Xavier. "Ready?"

"Do it," Xavier said, and August twisted the orb's base.

CHAPTER THIRTY

2 Sols to Presentation Day

Without warning, the orb whirled to life and buzzed out of August's hand to hover in the air. The small black dots opened to reveal tiny cameras, and the circle flashed a bright light. "Huh, that's strange," said an emotionless voice. "We can't detect any coordinates. Where's this device located?"

August pressed a fist to his forehead and dipped his head. "You are in the Catena dome, Intelligence. We seek your help, if you're willing to grant it."

"August, great to see you," the unnaturally smooth voice said. "You probably know this already, but our data access is limited in the Catena dome. We can't detect a network." The orb's white light flashed between Vivian and Xavier, and she suppressed a shiver. "Vivian, so awesome to meet you at last. Welcome to Mars. We hope you've been enjoying yourself so far."

"Hello," Vivian said uncertainly. The two Martians didn't seem to find it odd to be carrying on a conversation with a floating ball of cameras.

"Hi, Xavier. Always a pleasure." The circle of light swiveled. "We knew you and Vivian were headed to Catena, but you hid your purpose from us, right? Would you mind unpacking that for us?"

"We came to liberate Miss Bowen's sister from the clutches of Silas Gatlin," Xavier replied with a trace of impatience. "In our attempt, we have learned that Silas intends to steal the technology you granted my aunt."

"And you brought this concern to us. Thank you, Xavier. We're so touched by your thoughtfulness. It's great to reconnect after so long apart, right? We've missed you. Have you had a chance to noodle on our last conversation?"

"I try to think of it as little as possible."

"Xavier, the only constant is change. We know what when down with your parents was tough, but we hope you know that we're always here to be your safe space. We only want to guide you to your optimized future."

"I cannot do this," Xavier muttered and stepped as far back from the orb as the room would allow.

Vivian understood Xavier's reaction. The combination of the chummy personal commentary and the emotionless voice was just plain *weird*.

"Got it, got it. You know we only want to help you be the best you can be, yeah?" The circle of light moved back to her face. "Vivian, help me understand. Why does Silas want our tech?"

Vivian wasn't sure how to answer this strange creature. She swallowed a sudden bout of nerves. What did the Intelligence care about her sister's well-being? Xavier, it seemed, had experience conversing with the Intelligence, and he was the one who'd warned her it didn't care about the lives of Earther women. "Silas is working with the Catena militia. I think they plan to remove the fetus Delilah is carrying to study it and copy the science."

"Interesting." The orb moved closer to her, and she had to resist an urge to bat it away like it was an oversized bug. "Vivian, we've gotta be honest. We didn't expect to find you in a separatist dome. We didn't peg you as a risk-taker, right? When we were recruiting American women, we asked our representatives on Earth to find pliable women who would be content with the role of Red Mothers. We only want to make sure you're happy."

Vivian bit back an unexpected wave of hot anger. "I think you'll find I'm not *pliable*."

"Yeah, the more we've been getting to know you, the more we think we were originally off base about you. But, you know, before our agents recruited you and your sister, neither of you had left the Sumter Refugee Camp in seven years, three hundred and four days."

"That wasn't a choice," Vivian snapped. "We were prisoners."

The orb moved from side to side in a gesture that looked weirdly like a shrug.

"We're here to rescue Delilah," she continued. "She's running out of time."

"I hear you. Sixty hours forty-seven minutes and three seconds ago, your sister Delilah boarded an aircar in the company of Silas Gatlin. They filed a flight plan to the research station on Gale Crater. We don't have any more data on their whereabouts. You're saying they came to the Catena dome instead?"

Vivian nodded and, then, unsure what movement the Intelligence could sense, said aloud, "We saw them with our own eyes yesterday. My sister is being held against her will, and I'm afraid of what Silas will do if we don't get her out soon." The vision of Silas standing over Xavier, wearing a creepy, detached smile on a blood-splattered face, swam before her. This conversation was moving entirely too slow. "Will you help us or not?"

The orb beeped with what Vivian interpreted as annoyance. Could it feel such an emotion? "Xavier, we'll make you a deal. We know you're always speaking to Constance Yarrow about how you don't like us. To tell you the truth, Xavier, it hurts our feelings."

"You don't have feelings," Xavier snapped from his place on the far wall.

"We know, we know. Just an expression, right? But you keep trying to get the Council to thwart our plans. And honestly, it's kind of a bummer. We've been successfully guiding Mars for two hundred years. We wish you believed in our good intentions."

"I don't deny I've tried to block you," Xavier replied evenly. "When the founders created you, human settlement on Mars was in its infancy." To Vivian, he explained, "A significant contingent of founders made their wealth in the AI boom on Earth. They took their billions in profits and the AI expertise they'd developed and poured it into the Martian settlement—and created the Intelligence."

"Is that why the Intelligence sounds like it just moved here from Silicon Valley in the mid-twenty-first century?" Vivian asked, thinking of old vids she'd seen of the AI billionaires before they'd left for Mars.

"What do you mean?" Xavier's forehead creased.

Vivian suppressed a smile. "Never mind."

Xavier turned back to the Intelligence. "I'd be the first to acknowledge that the founders' approach worked. But we've progressed beyond the need for your services."

"You've traveled widely, Xavier. You gotta know that Arcadia is the most prosperous Martian dome because of our guidance. We optimize every resource to provide a comfortable lifestyle today and a path to a stronger future."

"I don't deny your value. But a machine isn't qualified to understand and advise on ethical questions." He stepped forward. "The technology you have developed is an incredible breakthrough, but it's not ready for human trials. I don't believe you offered the women you recruited informed consent, and you certainly aren't offering the opportunity to stop participation at any point. You are in violation of the basic ethics of human medical trials and the human rights laws of Mars."

"Sometimes, Xavier, you have to consider the greater good, right? The founders of Mars understood that. They had a relentless drive to improve the planet and weren't afraid to make bold, hard choices."

"I *am* thinking of the greater good. A society built on exploitation cannot prosper."

"Do you agree with Silas Gatlin's desire to experiment further with the tech?"

Xavier's eyes slid to Vivian's and then away. "If that's his aim, then yes, I suppose I agree with his wider goal. More experimentation is needed before we ask women to take on this burden. But I don't believe Silas cares about the impact on Earther women any more than you do. If he had truly wanted to further the testing, he should have come to me and applied to the Council. I would have supported his aims."

"We gotta say, Xavier, we don't get it. Why are you here if you agree with Silas? Why are you asking for our help?"

Xavier did look at Vivian now. His dark brown eyes softened. "Because Miss Bowen asked it of me."

"Huh. We've known you a long time, Xavier, and you're acting differently. We find this perplexing."

Behind her, Vivian heard August cough.

Another beep. "Okay, decision time. We'll help you, Vivian, if you do one thing for us." The orb paused. "Convince Xavier to stop opposing us in the Council. He must give his full support to the Red Mothers initiative."

August sucked in a breath. Stepping forward, he asked, "Is there any other payment you would accept, Intelligence?"

"I'll do it," Xavier said through a clenched jaw.

The Intelligence flashed several times in quick succession. *A smile?* "Fantastic."

CHAPTER THIRTY-ONE

2 Sols to Presentation Day

"Are you sure you're following the right heat signatures?" August asked the orb from the front seat of the rental van.

"We have a 95.63 percent rate of certainty," the Intelligence replied. "You trust us, right, August?"

"I believe," he murmured and lifted a fist to his forehead.

Beside Vivian in the rear of the van, Xavier made a face at the back of his cousin's head. She had to agree with Xavier. It had been difficult enough to understand the Martian worship of the abstract concept of the Intelligence. She found it especially off-putting to watch August waiting on a small ball of metal.

She closed her eyes wearily against the headrest, hidden from view behind tinted windows, as the vehicle glided along the narrow streets of the Catena warehouse district. Just as Xavier had predicted, they'd found Delilah gone from the militia headquarters. In a matter of moments, the Intelligence had tapped the security cameras, identified her and Silas departing during the night, and directed August to follow her trail.

What was Delilah doing now? Was she unharmed? Her sister must be terrified, but Delilah was practiced at masking her fear with a happy face.

The anxiety clenching her belly was an old companion. For a few weeks, when no one in her family was in danger of violence, the awful pain in her stomach had lessened. If only she'd appreciated it at the time, instead of being caught up in worries about finding a husband.

"Vivian." She jumped at the sound of her name. Xavier took her hand and squeezed it in his light grip. "You needn't come on this chase. We can find you a safe house."

"Absolutely not," she snapped. "I won't let you leave me behind."

"If anyone is staying behind, it should be you, the man with a thousand cuts," August said from the front seat.

Xavier banged a hand against August's headrest. "I'm coming with you. Ready to fight. And it can't be more than forty cuts."

"Oh sure, that's a convincing argument," August grumbled.

"We've got to jump in here real quick," Intelligence said. "August, stop here, please."

"Here? Why would they go to a rover parking lot?" Xavier peered out the tinted window. "Unless . . . you don't think they left the dome?"

"Only one way to find out." August turned to give Xavier and Vivian a stern look. "Stay here, out of sight." He opened the door, and the orb zoomed out. The van door rattled as August slammed it shut.

Vivian discovered one of her nails was cracked and ran it up and down the length of her black pants, letting it snag over and over. Beside her, Xavier breathed steadily. "I should've gone with him," she whispered in the silence. "Delilah doesn't know him. She's not going to trust a stranger with a sword."

"August knows what he's doing. And he has the orb to help. We cannot risk being sighted by the Catena militia." He leaned over and brushed her hair back before pausing to lightly touch her neck under her ear. "What's this?"

She shivered under his long fingers. "You left marks on me. Last night."

"Mm." He kissed a red bruise on her neck. "I do beg your pardon. How terribly brutish. I don't know what came over me." He smiled wickedly as he said the words, and Vivian's heart grew lighter.

She reached up to trace his stubbled jaw. "I liked it," she confessed. "As if you were saying, 'You're mine.'" She wet her lips, and he followed the movement with his eyes.

"But you aren't. Mine." Even as he lifted his head away from her, his hand remained, rubbing her collarbone with his thumb. Vivian swayed into his touch.

Why not? she wanted to demand. *Why can't I be yours? And you mine?* She wished he would kiss her again.

Xavier's hand stilled. "When this is all over, you'll be back in our dome fulfilling the terms of your contract and choosing a spouse. Isn't that what you said you wanted? To return to Arcadia with Delilah by Presentation Day?"

She couldn't fully control her wince. "You'll let me go that easily?"

"I cannot—" Xavier's throat worked. "Not even for you. I've agreed today to stop opposing the Red Mothers initiative in the Council. But I could never stand by and watch you suffer to bring my child into the world." He grimaced.

Vivian pulled back and drew her knees up on the bench of the van. "I know."

A wave of sadness came over her. How could she now be content with the restricted life planned for her? How could she find satisfaction in a practical, arranged marriage after knowing the terrifying and wonderful intimate trust Xavier had offered her the night before?

He cleared his throat. "I wish I could help in another way, but I spoke truly when I said Aunt Constance holds the purse strings to Dorsey Estate. She would never permit me to draw the expense to buy you out of your contract, even if such a thing were possible."

"Oh—Xavier, I hope you didn't think . . . I would never ask you to do that." She swallowed a sudden lump in her throat.

He traced the line of her brow. "Nonetheless, I wish it was an option I could offer freely."

Had he fantasized about a life with her? Free of the strict parameters of her contract? She wanted him. Desperately. But she wasn't sure she wanted the walled Dorsey Estate. And she didn't relish the idea of her role on Mars being defined by her relationship with him.

Then what did she want?

She remembered picturing swapping lives with Alvin the greenhouse worker. And that beautiful law library. If this was a fantasy, why couldn't she have it all? Independence, intellectual growth, and . . . love.

The comms device on the opposing seat made a crackling noise. "All clear. I'm on my way back to you."

She let out a breath. Delilah was the priority. Not playing out some doomed romance. She was here for her sister.

August opened the back of the van, sword in his hand. "There's a landing pad missing its transporter. The Intelligence rates the likelihood that they've gone to Catena's terraforming station at 83 percent."

"That's uncharacteristically imprecise," Xavier remarked sardonically.

"I'm rounding." August bared his teeth. "Come with me. I could use Vivian's assistance." He led the way to a large rover labeled Air Quality Control. Next to it lay a body with the Intelligence bobbing over it. "Vivian, move him back to the van for me, will you? You're the strongest of us." He gestured with his sword to Xavier. "Stay with the rover, X."

She crouched down and picked up the body under the shoulders. The weight felt like no more than lifting a young child. So strange, to be with two powerful men, and be the only one capable of lifting a heavy load. “Is he . . . ?”

“No, he’s only unconscious.”

Vivian carried the body with ease across the parking lot and held the man one-handed as she opened the back door of the van. “Should we tie him up?”

August shook his head. “If we do so, it might be days before someone finds him. I’ve no wish to have his death on my conscience. With the dose I gave him, he should be out for at least four hours. That should give us enough time.” He pulled the man’s fob from around his neck. “Come on.”

Vivian pushed down a wave of nausea and followed August.

They would find Delilah. Today.

CHAPTER THIRTY-TWO

2 Sols to Presentation Day

Vivian squinted out the rover's narrow window as their destination appeared on the far horizon. "Is there something wrong with it?"

The structure coming into focus was the size of a basketball stadium, if lower in height. But two-thirds of the building was covered by a bright orange seal.

August frowned. "Intelligence, what can you tell us?"

"72.34 percent of the facility is unfinished and abandoned. 27.66 percent of the facility contains a breathable atmosphere, and we detect heat signatures inside."

"Chancellor River did not see fit to mention this detail to the Council," Xavier said. "Catena must have realized terraforming is a pipe dream after all."

August made a side-to-side motion with his hands. "Making the Martian atmosphere hospitable for humans will take a thousand years," he explained to Vivian. "The Catena dome was originally formed fifty years ago by those who believed we should be putting our resources into terraforming the planet at a faster rate."

Xavier snorted. "Moving the timeline from a thousand years to three or four hundred. Still far beyond our lifetimes. We need to focus on the quality of life for our current residents first."

"We completely agree, Xavier," said the Intelligence. "Terraforming won't scale up fast enough to justify the investment. A twenty-fold investment in terraforming would result in a projected timeline of three hundred and sixty-two years and ten days until the first humans could live on the surface of Mars without protective gear. Under our guidance, Wim has advised Secretary Yarrow to direct Martian resources to other areas first."

Xavier jerked his head back to stare at the orb, and Vivian suspected he was startled to find his AI adversary agreeing with him.

"Isn't that why they needed water?" Vivian asked. "Because they were putting too many of their resources in terraforming?"

"Indeed. Imagine, humbling yourself before the dome you spurned, begging for water. Water!" Xavier scowled. "I would die of shame if I couldn't provide my people with adequate water. Who would be foolish enough to sink resources into this massive facility before investing in the basic infrastructure to ensure the dome's survival?"

"Martian Fundamental Rights," Vivian murmured.

"Just so." Xavier gave her a half smile. "Have you been enjoying my present?"

"I—" She'd assumed he'd given her the book of law out of mockery. Hadn't she fantasized about just such a moment? She'd dreamed of having the chance to demonstrate all she'd learned and throw his cruel joke back in his face. But the man she'd thought he was wasn't anything like the true Xavier Dorsey. "I think the book is marvelous. How did you know it was something I would enjoy?"

"Delilah didn't tell you?"

"Delilah? What would Delilah know about Martian law?"

"At the Hayes ball, she told me about your history organizing the women at the Sumter Refugee Camp. I thought you might appreciate the Martian approach to resource development and distribution."

"I tried, at the camp." Vivian touched her throat involuntarily. "In the end, I was unsuccessful."

"Nearly there," August remarked. "Suit up. And let's hope the Intelligence's stealth shielding has held."

"Our shielding will hold." The orb gave an irritated beep.

"Why did Silas bring Delilah out here anyway?" Vivian wondered. "What could he want at a half-finished terraforming facility?"

Xavier shook his head, his mouth a grim line. "I'd rather not speculate."

"If you have a theory, tell me."

"Very well." Xavier rubbed one large hand across the back of his neck. "If this place is abandoned, it's a perfect location for handling something delicate. Something that requires no interruption. Something you'd rather doesn't become public."

"Oh." Vivian felt sick.

Xavier handed her a silver suit from a rack on the wall of the rover. "We'll do what we can."

With shaking hands, Vivian slipped her legs into the suit. Designed for a Martian build, the suit bunched uncomfortably on her thighs. When she finished fastening the top and gloves, Vivian picked up a round helmet. She stared at her reflection and was shocked by her stark, grim appearance. Her hair was pulled back into a messy bun with a cord of rope she'd found in August's pack, and her face appeared washed out without cosmetics. She'd gotten used to seeing another woman in the mirror. A woman adorned and dressed to please the gaze of a potential husband. She touched the helmet with one gloved hand.

This is the woman I want to be.

Daring.

Bold.

The one who does the rescuing.

"Ready to bring Delilah home?" asked Xavier, his voice distorted through the helmet. He lifted the surface plate and met her eyes.

He sees me, she realized. *All of me.*

"Ready." She fastened her helmet.

The rover opened with a whoosh, and Vivian stepped down onto the surface of Mars. The walk was only ten feet, but each step was a challenge as she navigated gingerly around brown and red rocks, seeking stable footing. The Martians seemed at ease in their suits as they crossed the distance with long, confident strides, the Intelligence leading the way.

The doors to the facility slid open at their touch, and they waited in the pressurization chamber as it filled with air. August had warned them to stay silent, lest their voices be caught by the militia's comms equipment. The Intelligence might be able to fool the cameras, but it couldn't mask their noises. Vivian held her breath.

The inner doors slowly widened into an empty corridor. Instead of walls, only silver studs framed a path. Dim bulbs hung in yellow cages from the open ceiling, casting shadows on the rough, unfinished flooring.

August and Xavier opened their face plates and removed their suits, hooking them onto the frame. Silently, Xavier helped Vivian to detach her gloves. He touched one clammy hand to her own in a brief reassurance.

Vivian watched Xavier buckle the scabbard around his waist and draw his sword. His posture seemed to ease when he held it. He rummaged in his pocket for the bottle of painkillers and popped one into his mouth. Could he handle himself, despite his injuries? She wasn't sure.

Without sound, the Intelligence projected a map of the facility on the floor, displaying heat signatures. Three orange pulsating dots were positioned in the laboratory. Two were centered in the command center at the far side of the facility. And one blue dot with one orange dot pulsed in the equipment room.

An Earther heat signature.

Delilah.

August lifted his sword and gestured in the direction of the equipment room.

They strode through the empty open halls, the Intelligence's orb bobbing along with them at Martian eye level.

The equipment room had real walls in place and a steel door with a handle. Vivian cautiously pushed it open and stepped inside. The large room was packed with crates, a pile of tools, and large machines. And Delilah—lying on an elevated cot, an IV attached to her arm.

By her side sat Chancellor River Hawk.

Vivian froze at the doorway.

"History will remember your sacrifice, Delilah." River's hand was on top of Delilah's. "Today is a great day for Martian independence. We will speak your name and remember it. You'll be the only Red Mother to go down in our history books."

Delilah watched them warily, tears streaming down her cheeks.

"Don't cry. Think of the number of Martian children who will now be born ready to populate Mars. Think of what we will do. You're part of the new world, Delilah."

"Chancellor River," August said, holding his sword aloft. "We are here to take Delilah home."

"Delilah is home," River said calmly. They rose from their seat.

"Vivian?" Delilah blinked up groggily at her. "Vivian? What are you doing here?"

"I told you I'd come back for you."

Delilah reached one hand to the other arm and clumsily extracted the IV from her skin, wincing at the pain. "You're too late."

Vivian shouldered River out of the way and went to her sister's bedside. "What did Silas do to you?"

"It didn't hurt." Delilah's voice shook. "Not really. I didn't fight. I—it didn't hurt. I have cramps. Bleeding. I'll be fine. I'm fine." She swallowed. "They're running tests on my b—on the specimen now." She pulled herself to the side of the bed.

Vivian couldn't keep the disgust off her face as she looked at River. "How could you do this to her?"

River's serene expression did not change. "Great acts require sacrifice."

"Indeed they do." Vivian turned to see Silas with a knife held to Xavier's throat. "Drop it, X."

Xavier opened his hand, and his sword clattered on the unfinished floor.

CHAPTER THIRTY-THREE

2 Sols to Presentation Day

"I do love getting the drop on you, X. A bit distracted, are you?"

Xavier said nothing in response, his body unmoving under the knife. His eyes caught Vivian's from across the room, full of apology. The knife. She knew that knife. She'd already witnessed the damage Silas could cause with it.

"Chancellor," Silas continued. "The ship has been sighted."

"Excellent." River flared their nostrils just slightly as they beheld Silas, and Vivian could detect disdain behind their mask of civility. They looked down at Delilah, still seated at the side of the bed, glassy-eyed. "Delilah, can I persuade you to stay here with us, under my protection?"

"I want to go with my sister." Delilah's voice was barely a whisper.

"Soon. After you do one more service for Catena today."

"What are you talking about?" Vivian demanded. She took her sister by the arm and helped her to her feet.

"You'll see." River surveyed the assembled group, eyes widening when they spotted the orb. "Is that what I think it is?"

The orb beeped. "Hi River, we're pumped to finally meet you. Catena has so much raw potential, right? You're pushing the frontier of what's possible here. With our guidance, you could actualize your full vision for Catena's future."

River whirled on Xavier, who remained motionless with Silas's knife pressed to his throat. "You brought that abomination to my dome? I thought you despised the Intelligence."

"There is nothing I would not do to protect Vivian and her sister," Xavier growled. "Nothing."

"A Martian heat signature is headed our way," the Intelligence announced.

The far door banged open, and a Martian man strode in before skidding to a halt in the middle of the room.

"Mr. Hayes, right on schedule," Silas drawled. "So glad you received my message."

Caspian took in the scene: August, sword in hand, the Intelligence bobbing at his side; Vivian clutching the pale Delilah; Silas pressing a knife to Xavier's throat. And Chancellor River standing serenely in the middle, unarmed.

"Chancellor," Caspian said warily. "What passes here?"

"Do you have it?" River asked, stepping closer to Caspian.

Caspian lifted a small data disc from his pocket. "All of Arcadia's collective knowledge on Martian terraforming."

The orb zoomed forward in between River and Caspian. "Caspian, you can't give that to Catena. We won't allow it."

Caspian looked uncertainly to Xavier. "Is that . . . ?"

"Indeed."

Caspian pressed a fist to his forehead. "Forgive me, Intelligence. I am grieved to go against your wishes, but I have an agreement with Chancellor River."

"Give me the data disc, Mr. Hayes," River demanded, holding out one hand.

Caspian hesitated. "After you release Xavier."

Silas merely laughed. "Our deal hasn't changed: House Hayes's proprietary terraforming tech for Delilah Bowen. X is *mine*." He pressed the knife hard enough to draw blood, and Xavier closed his eyes.

Vivian held fast to her sister, transfixed by the sight of the knife. She knew what it felt like to be helpless and weak in the face of a weapon.

"Mr. Gatlin," Caspian said, looking carefully at Xavier. "I would not recommend threatening Xavier Dorsey. He is one of the most skilled and vicious fighters of my acquaintance."

"I am intimately acquainted with all of X's many talents. The disc, now."

"Not without guaranteeing free passage to everyone in this room."

"Is that how you'd like to play it, Mr. Hayes?" Into his wrist comm, Silas commanded, "Now."

"We're detecting incoming rocket launcher fire directed at our borrowed rover," the Intelligence relayed in a neutral voice. "Ten seconds to impact . . . The rover is destroyed."

Vivian let out a breath. Their means of escape, gone in seconds. They shouldn't have come here with no backup. Why had they thought the Intelligence would tip the balance in their favor? All it had done so far was bob around uselessly, narrating their failures.

Caspian stiffened. "Is my ship intact?"

"Of course," Silas soothed. "We have a deal, and I intend to honor it as long as you do."

"If you touch my ship, the deal is off. I'll convene the Council to declare war. I'll level this dome." Caspian's cultured voice had taken on a deadly precision.

"Interesting. I do believe we told you to come alone. Who's on the ship, Mr. Hayes?"

"No one," Caspian replied quickly.

"Aim a rocket launcher at the Arcadian ship," Silas ordered into his wrist comm.

"No!"

"He'll do it, Casp," Xavier warned, rigid in Silas's arms.

"Fire on my mark." Silas looked at Caspian. "Who's on the ship?"

"Ivey," Capsian gasped. "Ivey's here. She insisted."

"Ah, Ivey." Silas smiled. "How is your viper-tongued sister? I always thought it remarkable that you were the one with the Council seat when she clearly has the brains in the family. How much further Arcadia could rise if it rewarded merit over birthright."

"Leave my sister out of this."

"I tried to leave out your sister. But that bitch just had to get involved, didn't she?"

River had been quietly watching the exchange, seemingly content to let Silas handle the threats. Now, they opened their hand. "The disc. Now."

Caspian held out a shaking hand.

The Intelligence let out a loud beep. "Please don't do this, Caspian." It flitted uselessly between River and Caspian, making no physical move to intervene.

River took the disc and pocketed it. "I'll leave this to you," they said to Silas, raising their hands as if to say, *Clean up your mess.* River strode from the room without looking back.

"Stand down," Silas murmured into his wrist comm. "The Chancellor is on their way and requires a transport."

The orb gave another long beep. "We cannot allow the Catena dome to acquire proprietary terraforming technology. August, you must go after the Chancellor before they leave this facility."

Vivian ignored the Intelligence. "Silas, we came for Delilah. She's all we want. We'll take Caspian's ship, and you'll never hear from us again."

"Not without the data disc," said the Intelligence.

"Why?" Vivian demanded of the orb.

"Great question, Vivian. At the end of the day, we followed the data. We've conducted an analysis of the optimized approach to terraforming Mars and concluded that the project should be coordinated between the domes in consultation with Earth. If Catena goes at it alone, they'll fail, and that will set a coordinated effort back. As the saying goes, 'Collaboration is multiplication.'"

Silas held Xavier at knife point, Delilah could barely stand, and this was what the Intelligence cared about? Vivian couldn't believe her fate had been in the control of this *thing* all along. How could Secretary Yarrow, Wim, and nearly the entire Council have outsourced critical decisions about the future of their community and their planet to an artificial intelligence that clearly didn't see value in individual lives?

"You know what?" she snapped. "I don't give a crap about your thoughts on the optimized approach to life on Mars. You're wrong about the Red Mothers initiative, and you're wrong here. I'm not sacrificing our lives to your calculations. River has the data. It's done."

Silas took a step backward, pulling Xavier with him. "Bravo, Vivian. You have a spine after all." He took another step closer to the door, and it slid open.

"Stop!" Vivian's voice cracked in fear and frustration. She exchanged an anguished look with Xavier. "You got your deal. Let him go."

"Goodbye, Vivian and Delilah," Silas said. "I've so enjoyed our time together, but I fear all good things must come to an end." He stepped through the door with Xavier in tow, and it slammed shut.

Vivian parked Delilah on the side of the bed and ran to the door. August and Caspian were already there. Vivian took her fingers and attempted to pry it open. She kicked it like she'd done on the streets of Catena. The door didn't even vibrate.

Xavier was gone.

CHAPTER THIRTY-FOUR

2 Sols to Presentation Day

"Open the door," Vivian ordered the Intelligence.

"Sorry, Vivian, but we can't. The door's locked from the other side. You know that our access to command functions is limited on this dome."

Vivian growled in frustration. "Can you see what's happening at least? Where are they going? Where are the others?"

"Xavier and Silas are moving to the command center. River and a single soldier have boarded a small ship and are departing the facility. Three others remain in the laboratory."

"Xavier is alive?"

"Yes, Vivian. His pulse is erratic, and we detect heightened adrenaline."

Vivian let out a slow breath. *He's alive.* "Is there another way to the command center?"

"Follow us." The orb zoomed out of the room through the other door.

August jogged to follow in its wake. Vivian took hold of her sister and pulled her along as fast as she could. Caspian brought up the rear, carrying Xavier's fallen sword.

Vivian could barely think. Xavier had described the forty shallow cuts on his chest as a mere warm-up. What did Silas plan to do to Xavier? And why? Vivian didn't understand Silas's obsession. Could this really be about the perceived slight of a denied inheritance?

The unfinished floors creaked as they hurried along. The caged yellow lights cast distorted shadows on the walls. In the quiet, Vivian focused on the sound of Delilah's labored breathing. She had to get her sister out of here.

They convened outside of a closed door. "The laboratory contains three Martian heat signatures," the orb said. "No weapons."

"Can we go around them?" Vivian asked.

"Afraid not, Vivian. This is the only path to the command center with an active life support system."

August lifted his sword. "We'll save him, my lady. X is hard to kill. We'll get there in time." He carefully pushed open the door.

Harsh white lighting lit up a cluttered laboratory packed with machines and materials. In the center of the room, three Martians in lab coats huddled around a raised table. They turned in surprise at August's approach, revealing a microscope and petri dish.

August pointed his sword at the three Martians. "Back away. Hands on your heads."

The three Martians obeyed, stepping away from the table with raised hands and moving slowly to the far wall.

Vivian didn't pause. "Stay with August and Caspian," she said to her sister and hurried to a console near the closed door. To the orb, she ordered. "Show me what's happening in the command center."

The orb beeped in acknowledgment, and the console flared to life with a silent security camera feed. In the gray pixelated feed, Vivian could see the two men standing apart from each other, Xavier unarmed, and Silas brandishing his knife before him.

"I have to get to him," she said frantically. "Is the door barred?"

The console began whirring with activity. "Sure, Vivian. We're happy to help. We've unlocked the doors, but we cannot hold them for long."

Vivian ran. Her breath came short as she increased her speed, following the corridor to a closed door. It slid open soundlessly at her arrival. *Thank you, for once, Intelligence.*

Silently gulping air, Vivian slipped into the command center. Through the large windows, Vivian could see a small ship, parked outside on the rocky Martian surface. *Ivey.* A row of consoles displayed graphs and charts. In the middle of the room, Silas and Xavier circled each other grimly. Their eyes remained locked on each other, neither man appearing to notice her arrival.

Silas stepped forward, slashing with his knife, and Xavier knocked his hand aside, causing Silas's hand to flex open and the knife to clatter to the floor. Silas pressed both hands to Xavier's wounded chest and shoved him to the ground. Xavier scrambled back on his elbows, and Silas pushed him flat on the floor, straddling him. Their bodies pressed together, their faces almost touching.

Silas leaned closer to Xavier and laughed. "You always did like it when I was on top."

"And your sadistic streak has turned into a full-blown fetish," Xavier panted as he attempted to push him off.

Silas leaned all the way forward and—to Vivian's shock—kissed Xavier full on the mouth. After only a moment's hesitation, Xavier responded enthusiastically, putting one hand behind Silas's head and gripping his auburn curls. With his other hand, he groped along the floor.

Vivian had no claim to Xavier. He'd made that perfectly clear. But it was still unsettling to see her new lover locked in an embrace with her sister's tormentor. Not to mention his own recent torturer.

Rooted to the spot, Vivian watched Xavier's right hand grasp the fallen knife.

His arm raised.

The knife flashed.

With a grunt, Silas rolled off Xavier, clutching his bloody arm.

Xavier sprang to his feet, the knife in his hand dripping blood. "Thank you for that lovely trauma flashback. How I've missed having you star in my nightmares."

"Don't give me that sanctimonious crap," Silas snarled. "Your cock doesn't lie."

Xavier tilted his head. "I know. It's rather appalling. I may need more therapy."

"Join us, X." Silas pulled to his feet, one hand holding his injured arm. "We have everything we need now. The genetically modified DNA sample. The terraforming technology. We can adapt our descendants to live on a partially terraformed Mars. In a matter of generations, Catena will be self-sufficient and able to expand outside the domes. Think of it! To live directly on the surface. To finally be free of dependence on Earth." Silas took a step closer to Xavier. "You and I could rule this place. Your brains, my soldiers. We could push River aside, easily. You still want me, I know you do. No one else could ever understand what you need. What you crave."

Vivian remembered how quickly Xavier had switched from an injured victim to an arduous lover the night before. Did he *like* that? She had the sudden need for a long heart-to-heart with Luz.

Xavier took Silas's head in both hands and leaned closer to him. Vivian let out an involuntary squeak.

Turning to her with quirked lips, Xavier said nonchalantly, "Vivian, just in time. Hit him, will you?"

"I . . . What?"

"Right on the jaw."

"I'm not going to let your girlfriend hit me," Silas objected, attempting to jerk out of Xavier's grasp.

Xavier grabbed Silas by his bleeding, injured arm and yanked him directly in front of her. "Now, please."

Feeling like a fraud, Vivian made a proper fist like Shiloh had taught her and punched Silas on the mouth. Silas's eyes rolled back in his head, and he collapsed on the floor. *What?*

"Oh, very nice. Much more effective than me doing it." Xavier gave her an exhilarated grin and pulled his comm from his pocket. "August, I have control of the command center."

"Well done, X." August's voice crackled.

"All credit goes to Vivian. She has an excellent right hook." He grinned at her again, and Vivian couldn't help but smile back, despite her bewilderment at the whole situation.

"Come back to the lab, will you? Vivian knows the way."

"What about him?" Vivian looked down at Silas's prone form. An ugly purple bruise was forming on his jaw. *I did that*, she thought, bile rising in her throat. *How?* She hadn't even hit him very hard. "Should we . . . ?"

Xavier's face fell. "I can't. I just—I can't. Not like this, in cold blood. If I ever kill Silas, it will be face-to-face."

Vivian shivered. "Let's go."

CHAPTER THIRTY-FIVE

2 Sols to Presentation Day

In the lab, the three scientists had been secured with zip ties and were seated on the floor. August and Caspian were hovering uncertainly behind Delilah as she stared at the lab table, her fists clenched and her chest heaving.

"Delilah?" Vivian ventured. "I think you've seen enough. Won't you come away from here?"

Ignoring her own advice, she moved to her sister's side and looked down. There wasn't much to see. A small dot in the middle of a petri dish, under a large white microscope. A nearby screen displayed a magnified image of a curved shape where Vivian could almost detect the beginnings of a head. There was no heartbeat.

"It's so small, Viv," Delilah murmured. "Such a fuss over a pin-prick." She raised blurred eyes and turned to the scientists. "Have you figured it out yet? Did you crack the genetic code?"

"We're close," one said eagerly. "We just hit a snag."

"What snag?"

"The calcium treatments you described, we don't understand their purpose. They would have no impact on the fetus's genetic material and won't be hereditary. Is the intention to perform the treatments in every generation?"

Vivian jerked her head back. "Intelligence, I thought we were breaking the cycle in a single generation."

From its position between August and Caspian, the orb moved from side to side. "We had a minimally viable product and wanted to begin as soon as possible."

"*A minimally viable product?*" Vivian spat. "What the hell does that mean?"

"We'll perfect the tech in future years, right?" The orb moved closer to Vivian. "Innovation has to start somewhere. Perfect is the enemy of done, you know."

"This isn't tech, Intelligence," Caspian objected. "It's medicine."

"The genetic modification alone will still produce a fetus with stronger bones than the average Martian," the talkative scientist offered.

The orb gave a loud beep. "We don't have the data yet to know if the genetic modifications are enough. The calcium treatments are critical at this stage to ensure success. We'll adjust as we go. This was always intended to be an iterative process."

"You aren't running experiments in a lab," Xavier snapped from the doorway. "This is happening to the bodies of women."

"'First do no harm,'" Caspian added. He looked a little ill.

The Intelligence beeped again. "Disruption to the status quo always has winners and losers, right?"

"Are you fucking kidding me?" Vivian snarled.

Delilah put a hand on her arm. "Viv, not now. I can't let Catena have the sample. They ripped my b—my genetic material from my body. Against my will. They don't get to benefit from hurting me." She limped closer to the scientist who'd been speaking. "Have you recorded your data electronically? Have you sent it to anyone?"

He looked uncertainly at his companions.

Delilah knelt and grabbed his neck with one hand. "Tell me."

"No," he choked out. "Not yet."

Delilah let him go with a flick of her hand, and his head banged against the wall. From a nearby workstation, she picked up a Bunsen burner and turned the handle. Her blank, pale face shone against the blue flame. She walked with slow, deliberate steps back to where Vivian stood at the table.

"Don't!" shouted the scientist. He made a jerky attempt to stand that August stopped with a sword pressed to his chest.

Delilah placed the Bunsen burner on the table. Her blank face morphed into anger as she gathered the used vials, syringes, and slides the scientists had used to study the fetus. "I want it destroyed. All of it." Vivian picked up a bottle labeled acetone and handed it silently to her sister.

Delilah poured it on the pile. "Stand back." She lifted the Bunsen burner and brought the blue flame to the pile. It was immediately engulfed in flames, and a horrible smell of burning chemicals filled the room. Firelight glittered in Deliah's hard stare.

Caspian moved to stand a step behind Delilah, a fire extinguisher in one hand. Vivian could detect a hint of pride and affection on his sober face.

Delilah picked up the petri dish and looked down at it. She let out a shuddering sob. "Goodbye," she whispered. "*Even though I walk through the valley of the shadow of death . . .*" She looked at Vivian with tear-filled eyes. "What's the rest of it? I don't remember."

Vivian squeezed her sister around the shoulders. "*Even though I walk through the valley of the shadow of death, I will fear no evil, for you are with me; your rod and your staff, they comfort me.*" They didn't pray as a family. Not since the storm. But Delilah was right to remember the words of comfort here.

When Delilah picked up the Bunsen burner again, Vivian murmured, "*Ashes to ashes, dust to dust.*" Delilah lit the tiny dot with the flame and in a matter of seconds, it was reduced to ash.

Nearby, the flaming pile of materials had burned out on its own, leaving the white table blackened and warped.

Delilah turned in Vivian's arms and hugged her tightly. "Let's go."

CHAPTER THIRTY-SIX

2 Sols to Presentation Day

"Vivian! What an unexpected pleasure," Ivey drawled from the pilot's seat, for all the world as if they'd run into each other at a cocktail party. "May I offer you a ride in our private airship? I'm afraid our accommodations this afternoon aren't up to my usual standards."

Vivian felt an unexpected surge of gratitude to Ivey for her light tone in the face of such a difficult day. "Hi, Ivey. Thanks for the lift." She stepped out of the tube connecting the ship to the command center, searching immediately for her sister.

Caspian helped Delilah to lie down on the floor of the narrow cabin and tucked a blanket around her. She gave Vivian a weary wave and closed her eyes. August leaned against the wall with his arms crossed over his chest, the Intelligence hovering at his ear. Xavier entered the ship and closed the hatch. The ship lifted precariously into the air and flew slowly away from the terraforming center. Vivian scrambled for a handhold on the wall and pulled herself to sit at Delilah's feet.

"A thousand apologies for the bumpy liftoff." Ivey's voice carried an uncharacteristic note of strain. "Our little ship isn't used to carrying this much weight."

"We must go after River's ship, August," the Intelligence said. "We have projected coordinates."

“No,” August told it. “We’re going home, Intelligence.”

“August, you must listen to us. You know our guidance has always brought Arcadia prosperity.”

“I know, but as Vivian stated so clearly earlier, you’re wrong about this one.” He took the orb in both hands and twisted the base. The Intelligence’s lights abruptly darkened.

“Nicely done, cousin,” Xavier murmured.

August tucked the orb in the pocket of his black duster, pressing his fist to his forehead. “We are grateful for the gifts of the Intelligence,” he said in a voice so low it was barely audible.

Caspian moved to stand over the pilot’s seat to examine the readout. “Straight to Arcadia, Ivey. Delilah should be examined as soon as possible by a doctor we can trust.”

“And Vivian needs to be in the Council chamber tomorrow morning for Presentation Day.” Xavier glanced at her and then away. “I promised I would not intervene.”

“Oh . . . right. Presentation Day.” Vivian pulled her knees into her chest and looked at her dozing sister. “What will happen to Delilah?”

“We’ll provide her with excellent care,” Caspian assured her.

“Not that. Afterward. How long will Delilah be allowed to rest and heal before she’s impregnated again?”

Xavier and August exchanged a glance. “Our aunt isn’t a monster, Vivian,” August said. “If Delilah wishes to withdraw as a Red Mother, Secretary Yarrow will allow it.”

“We will insist upon it,” Xavier agreed quietly. “I’ll speak to her as soon as I can get a private word.”

“And our parents?” The weight of the last few days pressed down upon her. She didn’t want to cry. Not here, in a cramped shuddering aircar, surrounded by Martian aristocrats.

“Your parents?” August asked in confusion.

“Delilah sent them money, didn’t she?” Xavier asked softly. “After choosing Minister King.”

"Enough to buy their way out of the refugee camp. Not enough to keep them out for good." She couldn't let her parents return to Sumter. Not under any circumstances. Vivian took a deep breath. "Yes, I need to get back for Presentation Day. I have an understanding with someone."

If Ren would still have her.

Xavier's face returned to a neutral mask. "Of course. Forgive me," he murmured. "If I'd known you'd already made an arrangement, I would not have . . ."

"I know." Vivian rubbed her face. She needed sleep. "It's fine." She turned her back on Xavier to check on her sister. Delilah still had her eyes closed. Vivian ran a finger over her sister's scrunched forehead.

Delilah blinked open her eyes. "You came back for me."

Vivian leaned forward, blocking the view of the Martians. She wanted as much privacy with her sister as this tiny ship would allow. "Of course I came back for you, you idiot," she murmured. "You're my sister."

"You shouldn't have. I don't deserve all this attention." She pressed her lips together. "This place, it's nothing like Sumter, but it's still a nightmare." Delilah's pale face showed deep creases. She looked older than her eighteen years. "I've been thinking, do you remember how it felt when we were little, climbing all over the rocks at the edge of the ocean? We had no idea the hell that was coming. And now . . . we're living on a desert planet. We'll never see that much water again."

Vivian remembered. Sitting with her sister on the large sparkling rocks, their faces upturned to the sun. Hunting for seashells on the beach. Fleeing in the backseat of her parents' groundcar, watching the relentless rain as Hurricane Pippa bore down.

"We haven't seen that much water since the storm," Vivian said.

"But there was always the chance. Get work permits. Find a way out. Once we had freedom, I thought maybe we'd go back to the ocean."

Vivian brushed a piece of Delilah's dirty hair back from her forehead. "There's nothing to go back to, love. Nothing but moldy houses and rotting wood. No one's rebuilding when the whole coastline will be underwater."

"But how can they be sure? If they can make Mars livable, can't they invent ocean-safe housing?"

"I went back with Dad, you know. When we were still allowed to move freely. He wanted to save what we could. It took two buses and a three-mile walk to get to the house. Delilah, it was gone." Vivian's voice broke. "I remember some scraps of blue siding. And that awful pink toilet was lying in the street. That's all that was left."

She didn't tell her sister the worst of it. The cracked safety deposit box, empty of cash, jewelry, and passports. The way her father had sunk to his knees, his face drained of color. He'd looked, suddenly, like an old man.

"I've screwed everything up, Viv. I'm so sorry. I know how hard you worked to make this second chance for us."

"What happened with Mitzi?"

Delilah blew out her breath. "I freaked out, after I visited Camille in the clinic. She was writhing in pain, even with the painkillers. It was constant. Until the kidney stone passed, she couldn't even sleep." She shuddered. "When it was my turn for the first calcium treatment, I—I panicked. In Dr. Chavez's office, I accidentally hit Mitzi, and she flew clear across the room. Dr. Chavez sedated me. And while I was passed out, she did the treatment anyway. She told me later that Mitzi had given consent. As the Martian partner, she has that power."

"Oh, Delilah, that's awful." Vivian remembered how Xavier had warned her that their contracts gave decision-making rights about their children to the Martian spouse. Did this mean their partners could chose the health of their unborn children over the health of their wives?

Delilah blew out a breath. "After that, there was something broken between us. Even before it happened, she was mean. Criticizing how I dressed. How I did my hair. How I talked. Making fun of my lack of education. But we'd make up. With sex mostly. That part, at least, was good for both of us." The ghost of a familiar smile hovered on Delilah's lips. "But after that day, she was afraid of me. And I was afraid of her."

"I thought the Intelligence screened potential spouses."

"She wasn't abusive. At least not physically. Maybe I shouldn't have left her over it. Maybe we could have worked it out." Her voice, already a whisper, lowered further. "But then Silas took me in with his sweet talk and his big ideas and a concrete plan for getting *away*. I'm so stupid."

"None of this is your fault," Vivian said fiercely. "None of it. Silas is responsible."

She shook her head. "I think I'd like to sleep now."

Vivian nodded and resumed her vigil at her sister's bedside. She found a spare bit of wall for her head and closed her eyes.

Her dreams were full of fire and bloody knives.

CHAPTER THIRTY-SEVEN

1 Sol to Presentation Day

Sometime later, Vivian awoke, her back aching from resting in an odd position. Seated in the ship's only two chairs, Ivey and Caspian conversed quietly. Against the far wall, Xavier and August slept, their heads knocked together.

Vivan pulled to her feet and took two steps to the window. The rust-colored rocky surface of Mars passed by her vision, dull and unchanging. She remembered what Delilah had said. She'd never see the ocean again. This barren planet was her only home now. Her children—the children she bore Ren—would be unable to fathom the large expanse of water that had been the Bowen sisters' childhood backyard. The largest body of water her children would know firsthand could very well be the rumored Nakamura koi pond.

The Arcadia dome had risen into view over the horizon when Ivey called, "You'd better come see this."

Vivian jerked her head away from the window and moved with the others to the front of the ship. Delilah's color was restored, and her eyes were alert.

"We're finally close enough for the Arcadian news feed," Ivey said.

On the screen, a stiff Martian newscaster frowned grimly into the camera. "With one day to go until Presentation Day, concern mounts as two Red Mothers remain missing. Counselor Xavier Dorsey, a known opponent of the Red Mothers initiative, has not been spotted in days. Coincidence or conspiracy? At this point, all options are possible."

The video cut to Zuri Dorsey walking rapidly down the street, face obscured by an enormous floppy hat. "Counselor Dorsey's sister refuses to comment. *Arcadia Life* has watched the Dorsey Estate since the news broke and have seen no sign of Xavier Dorsey. Where is he? And what does he know about the disappearance of Earther sisters Vivian and Delilah Bowen?"

Ivey turned off the video screen, and they eased back into the main cabin.

Xavier scowled and leaned against the wall. "Journalists. Always sensationalizing. Vivian, I'll escort you to the Council chamber tomorrow. After the presentation ceremony, I'll speak to my aunt and ensure she'll let Delilah out of her contract without a fuss. We need to keep Delilah out of sight until I speak with Aunt Constance. I don't want media attention to put pressure on her decision."

"We should go to Hayes House," Caspian offered. "We can bring a discreet doctor for Delilah from the hospital."

Xavier grunted. "That's fine for you three. But we don't know if anyone will notice that Caspian and Ivey have been gone for the last day as well. It'll be easier to get in undetected than to get back out again. Vivian and I should look elsewhere if we wish to arrive on time for Presentation Day."

"Dorsey House?" Vivian touched Xavier's arm without thinking.

Xavier looked down at her fingers where they rested on his bicep with an unreadable expression. "Out of the question. Reporters will be climbing the gates to sleep at my front door tonight."

"Stay at my flat downtown," August offered. "The media isn't aware of its existence. You can leave from there to the Council chamber in the morning and put these rumors to rest."

"I'll track down something suitable for Vivian to wear on Presentation Day," Ivey added. "I'll bring it to you in the morning, if I can get away without any journalists spotting me."

Vivian took her sister's hand. "I hate the idea of leaving you. After all the trouble I went through to get you back."

Delilah squeezed. "You did it, Viv. You saved me. I'll be okay with Caspian and Ivey."

"I promise, Vivian, we'll take excellent care of your sister," Caspian said.

Vivian met Caspian's eyes. "You gave your research to River. For Delilah."

Caspian looked down at Delilah and a faint blush stained his cheeks. "I would do it again in a heartbeat."

Vivian blew out her breath. She couldn't stay with her sister and also find Ren on Presentation Day. She had to choose. "Alright. We can go to the flat."

CHAPTER THIRTY-EIGHT

1 Sol to Presentation Day

"Welcome to my humble home," August announced as the door swung open.

From the entryway, Vivian spotted a couch and single chair adjacent to a small kitchen with a high counter and two stools. An open bathroom and bedroom were visible just down the hall. "You didn't say why you have this place. I thought you lived at Yarrow House."

"So does the press, thank goodness. I'm there often enough, but my aunt can be a bit . . ."

"Dictatorial," Xavier suggested.

August grunted. "Anyway, I like having my own space, at least for now. Someday I'll inherit Yarrow Estate and its council seat, but I trust that will be decades from now." He gestured to the kitchen. "Grab something to eat. Use the shower and the laundry. Whatever you need. I'll get out of your way."

Vivian looked up sharply. "You're leaving?"

"I need to brief the Arcadian militia. They should know what's happening in Catena."

Xavier nodded. "Good. I would do it myself if it weren't for these damn journalists."

August pulled the orb out of his pocket and placed it carefully on a high shelf in the kitchen. "Don't let X smash this with a hammer while I'm gone," he said to Vivian with a small smile.

"How long will you be away?" Xavier held his cousin's gaze for a long moment and tilted his head. Something passed between them Vivian couldn't interpret.

"I'll bunk with the soldiers," August finally said in his easy way. He gave Xavier a tight hug. "Stay out of trouble for one night, eh?"

"My only goal is to escort Vivian to Presentation Day," Xavier replied. "What trouble could I find?"

"I'm sure you'll drum up something." He bowed over Vivian's hand. "Keep an eye on him, my lady. You seem to have a knack for saving him from himself." He shut the door firmly behind him as he left.

"We should eat, wash up, and get some sleep. I'll take the couch." Xavier stepped into the kitchen in two long strides and opened a cabinet. "Spaghetti alright for you?"

"Fine." Vivian joined him in the kitchen and pulled her weary body onto a tall bar stool adjacent to the high counter. "You don't have to take the couch."

Xavier didn't meet her eyes as he cleaned his hands and filled a large pot with water from the sink. "I believe I do." He carried the pot to the two-burner induction stove. "You didn't tell me—who's the lucky man?"

"Ren Nakamura. If he'll still have me." She remembered the beautiful pearl necklace he'd given her. She'd left it carelessly on her bedside table without another thought when she'd departed for Dorsey House.

"Ren!" Xavier scowled. "That ass? He's enamored with the sound of his own voice." He opened a jar of marinara sauce with so much vigor it splattered on the wall.

Vivian stood and grabbed a cloth to clean up the spill. "Ren is a good man. And you're jealous."

"I've no right to be." He bent his head and seemed to give his full attention to opening the container of pasta.

"Maybe not, but you're still jealous." Vivian looked down at the reddened cloth in her hands. *Not blood. Pasta sauce.* She dropped it in the efficiency laundry.

Xavier leaned back against the counter. "It's just the thought of that entitled blowhard with his hands all over you . . ." He made a throwaway gesture with one hand. "My feelings aren't important. I'm here to support you and your decisions. You're right—Ren and I don't often see eye to eye on policy, but he will treat you well."

"I haven't made any promises yet," Vivian murmured, taking a step closer to him.

Xavier dumped the noodles into the boiling water and turned on a timer before rotating to face her. "What are you saying?"

"What if tonight, just this night, belonged to us?" Vivian reached up, her fingertips touching the sides of his throat. When he moved to pull back, she got on her tiptoes and grabbed the back of his neck roughly. Xavier made a sound low in his throat and bent his head to hers.

Silas was the last person to kiss him, Vivian remembered, as she opened her mouth to Xavier's tongue. She found she didn't care. And tomorrow, she meant to accept Ren's offer. None of it mattered, not tonight.

The timer beeped, and they sprang apart. "Dinner," Xavier said unsteadily.

They ate without speaking, enjoying the simple warm food filling their bellies. Vivian rose and took care of the few dishes. Xavier watched her quietly with a flickering smile.

When she'd finished, he brushed a lock of matted hair back from her face. "We need to clean up."

They took turns in the small bathroom. The shower had real water, and Vivian closed her eyes and allowed the warmth to wash away the grime of the past few days. *Let it all go*, she thought. The dried sweat on her skin. The traces of blood under her fingernails. The smell of fire lingering in her hair.

By the time she came out of the bathroom, Xavier had completed a laundry cycle and handed her the same black Catena-style clothing to slip back on, now clean. He wore his own laundered pants with a bare torso as he stood in the small bedroom rummaging in a first aid kit.

"How are your injuries?" Vivian asked.

"Healing well."

Vivian moved closer to peer at his marred brown skin. "They're almost fully scabbed over. So fast."

Xavier taped a new bandage in place with brisk efficiency. "The liquid stiches were first rate. That was quick thinking on your part, to get a medical kit." He sat down on August's neatly made bed. "Come here."

Vivian sank down beside him, suddenly shy. They had been through so much together and yet, in some ways, were still strangers to each other.

Xavier took his palm and held it upright, against her hand. He threaded his long fingers in between hers.

Vivian trembled. "I thought Martians and Earthers couldn't hold hands."

"We can, with trust and careful communication." Xavier's dark brown eyes held her gaze. "I am in your power, Vivian Bowen. If you squeeze your hand too tightly, you might sprain my fingers. You may even break something."

Vivian took note of his rapid breathing, the way his lips parted slightly. "This excites you?" She hadn't quite figured out the contours of his confusing sexual desires, but she found she was interested in further exploration.

"To surrender to another person is the ultimate form of intimacy. Tighten your fingers, just slightly." Vivian obeyed. "Stop," he gasped. Vivian tried to pull her fingers away, but he held on fast. "Do you see? I put my body quite literally in your hands, but you gave the power back to me by obeying my limit."

"I do," she said slowly. "But that doesn't mean I want to hurt you."

Xavier smiled slightly. "I have no interest in being hurt. What I want is for us to surrender to each other. To give power and receive it." He disentangled his fingers and put one hand behind her head. "Will you try that with me?"

Vivian nodded, unsure of what she was agreeing to.

Xavier leaned forward and brought his lips to hers. He kissed her like he was drowning in her, his tongue exploring her mouth and his teeth biting her lower lip. Vivian surrendered to the kiss, letting him take control. Her body stayed attune to the movement of his lips and hands, her mind fully present in the moment.

He pulled her back on the bed, positioning them side to side. Vivian gently ran a finger along the edge of his dense close-cropped hair, down his neck, and his bare chest, featherlight on the bandages. She reached the vee of his lower stomach and lifted her chin to meet his eyes.

"Would you—touch me?" Xavier asked.

Vivian nodded, wordless. He pulled off his remaining clothes in one smooth motion. She let her eyes move over his naked body and then brought her hand over his thigh and took him in hand.

She watched his face as she moved her wrist, observing the way his lips parted, and his breath came out in short huffs. She understood, then, what he meant about giving power and receiving it. In this moment, with his pleasure under her control, she felt powerful.

"More, please," he murmured against her neck. "I have no bones to break on that particular appendage."

Vivian tightened her grip and saw how his breath came faster. She liked hearing the little moans coming out of his mouth. She liked watching this proud, controlled man come undone in her hand. Finally, he clutched her thigh and let out a short, loud groan, shuddering.

Xavier opened his eyes and grinned at her. With one long hand, he reached to the side of August's bed for a tissue and cleaned her hand and his stomach.

"Is that what you meant by surrender?"

He threaded his fingers through her hair and pulled her face close to his. "In part. May I show you more?"

Vivian nipped his lower lip. "Are you going to ask me every time?"

"Until I understand your boundaries. I have no wish to coerce you into an act you don't enjoy." His lips moved to her ear. "I want you on top of me."

Vivian hesitated. "I—I thought that was dangerous."

Xavier's eyes gleamed. "That's what makes it fun."

Vivian pulled back slightly. "I'm beginning to think you have a death wish."

"You won't crush me." He put a hand on her hip. "Climb on top of me but don't touch me."

Vivian obeyed, placing a leg on either side of his and bracing her hands at his shoulders. She had a sudden, terrifying vision of falling and breaking one of his bones and fully derailing their plans for the morning. But no, the position was easy to maintain in this gravity, even in distracting circumstances.

Xavier—who Vivian was beginning to understand was definitely aroused by danger—wet his lips. "Oh, very nice. Don't move." He pulled down the loose tank top and put his mouth on her breast. Vivian's arms trembled. He slipped his hand into the inside of her waistband and circled her wetness. His eyes widened. "I'd say you like this very much."

Vivian's legs were shaking as his fingers dipped inside her, pleasure mounting. "I can't—I'm going to fall."

Xavier hadn't stopped moving his fingers, finding a rhythm that made her gasp, "You're so strong here. Your muscles can't be tired yet." He brought his tongue to her nipple.

Vivian concentrated on staying still and not bringing her full weight onto his fragile bones. Her whole body shook with the effort. Her entire world had shrunk to this moment. To his mouth and fingers. To the pulsing need in her core.

Her climax hit her unexpectedly. Vivian gripped the blanket with one clenched fist, gasping as she writhed inches above him, a corner of her brain still focused on keeping him safe.

She rolled off Xavier and collapsed on her back. Her breath came rapidly, and her body sang with a sense of deep satisfaction.

"That's what I meant by surrendering," Xavier murmured. He seemed a bit smug as he watched her try to wrestle her breathing under control.

"Is it always like that?" she panted.

Xavier put one arm behind his head. "No."

"What was it like with Silas?" she asked without thinking.

Xavier sat up abruptly. She shouldn't have asked. She'd broken the beautiful spell between them.

"Was it that obvious?"

"His hatred of you is very . . . personal. And I was there in the command center."

Xavier winced. "I'd rather hoped you missed the whole show."

"I saw."

Xavier grunted low in his throat. The silence stretched between them. And then, he said softly, "We were so young when we started. Boys experimenting. But he had a dark streak, even then. Especially after my father died."

"Did you like his darkness?"

"Oh yes," Xavier murmured. "After what happened with my parents, I craved what Silas offered me. Took solace in it when my heart was breaking. But looking back on it, he was showing me his true nature. Only, I was too naïve to understand at the time." He turned to her and ran a hand down her arm. "What I like—what we did just now—was looking for a limit. We didn't cross it, but we might have. For a moment, you were afraid you'd hurt me, weren't you?"

"Yes," Vivian whispered.

"You could've stopped at any time. You didn't because you trusted me. You surrendered to me. But if you hadn't liked it, you could've stood up, and I wouldn't—I *couldn't*—have stopped you." He rubbed a hand over his face. "It wasn't like that with Silas."

"What was it like?"

"We were both so *angry*. So broken. Newly men with adult responsibilities. Abandoned by my father when we both needed his mentorship and guidance the most." Xavier swallowed. "We took it out on each other. Silas wanted to push me past my limits. I would tell him to stop, and he would laugh. That—" He shuddered. "That wasn't the first time he'd used a knife. But I found it exciting, at least for a while. When I was a young man. Before I understood why we revere consent here. I didn't understand then that it was a form of abuse. And when I finally realized what was happening and found the strength to break it off for good, he . . ."

"He went after your sister," Vivian finished.

"Yes."

"In the command center, you—he said—" Vivian hesitated before blurting, "You were aroused."

"I was. Even with what he did to Delilah fresh in my mind and my chest covered in his handiwork, my body still responded to his." Xavier pulled his legs to his chest. "My psychologist says my early traumatic sexual experiences have given me low sexual self-efficacy and make me unable to distinguish between high-risk and low-risk sexual behaviors."

"Oh . . . I just thought you were turned on by danger."

Xavier huffed a laugh. "That's perfect. So simple. No psychodynamic psychotherapy required." He turned to her. "Are you angry I didn't tell you the full truth sooner?"

"No, of course not. You deserve your privacy. And we both know I have no claim on you."

"Vivian," he whispered and sank down beside her once again. "Do you really believe that?"

Vivian shook her head. Why did he have to be so confusing? "We have a big day tomorrow. We should get some rest."

"We do." Xavier kissed the top of her head. "Sleep well."

CHAPTER THIRTY-NINE

Presentation Day

Vivian dreamed she was in the ocean, floating in a salty sea, buffeted by gentle waves. Well-fed, rested, sated, and protected.

At peace.

As her body moved toward wakefulness, Vivian knew there was something she'd remember soon. She kept her eyes closed and tried, for at least a little while longer, to forget the knowledge that still eluded her.

Presentation Day.

Today was Presentation Day.

Vivian rolled over in bed, chasing that feeling of peace. Through the thin walls of the tiny apartment, she could hear water running and the clang of a pan. What if this was her life? A modest apartment. A generous lover. A future she chose.

Not the crushing weight of expectations and responsibilities.

She could pretend, at least for a little while.

"Morning," Vivian murmured as she entered the kitchen. The smell of fresh coffee lingered in the air. She rummaged in the cabinets to find herself a mug.

From his position at the stove, Xavier gave her a warm, intimate smile. "Good morning. I hope you like eggs."

"I do." She settled on the bar stool and wrapped her hands around her hot cup of coffee. This simple domestic scene meant more to her than a hundred elaborate balls. She wanted to hold on to this moment, to this man, to this glimpse at a different life, for as long as she could.

Xavier put the spatula down and moved toward her. He swiveled her stool to face him and bent down so their foreheads touched. "Did I scare you last night? I know I got rather intense."

Vivian reached a hand behind his head and pulled him toward her. Should she be scared? He'd offered her a peek inside a dark past still haunting his present. Not so different from her own circumstance. "It'll take a lot more than that to scare me." Emboldened, she took his lower lip between her teeth and lightly bit down. He made a sound low in his throat and reached his hand to the back of her head. She lost herself in the feel of his lips on hers, remembering the sensation of floating in the ocean from her dream.

Until something tickled her nose, and she pulled back. "What's that smell?"

Muttering a curse, Xavier dashed back to the stove top and pulled the pan off the burner. He looked morosely at the dark brown crusty eggs. "I wanted to do something nice for you."

The sound of the apartment's buzzer made Vivian flinch. Already? She thought they'd have more time.

"Your stylist has arrived," Ivey's voice pronounced over the comm. "Let me in." When she walked in the apartment door, Ivey wrinkled her nose. "Ugh. What is that?"

"My fault," Xavier admitted. "I burned the eggs." He opened the lid of the trash can.

"Wait!" Vivian said, horrified. She grabbed the panhandle out of his hand and tipped it onto a dish.

"I can make more," Xavier protested. "You don't have to eat spoiled food."

"Spoiled? This isn't even close," Vivian said around a mouthful of charred eggs. "How's Delilah?"

"Fine." Ivey pulled a formal crimson dress out of her pack and laid it out on the back of the sofa. "Our doctor says she needs rest and fluids. Caspian is with her at the moment, but he plans to join you at the Council chamber. And you? Are you feeling ready, Vivian?"

Instead of answering such an impossible question, Vivian asked, "Has the media noticed our return?"

Ivey shook her head. "Not that I've seen."

Vivian rose, carrying the plate of eggs, and switched on the wall-mounted screen in August's living room.

On the screen, a Martian reporter stood on the steps of a stately white building that Vivian assumed was the Council. "All eyes in Arcadia are turned today to Presentation Day. Two Red Mothers remain missing, and Counselor Xavier Dorsey's whereabouts are unknown. Meanwhile, Chancellor River Hawk, newly elected leader of the Catena dome, has released a shocking new video message."

The broadcast shifted to River, seated comfortably behind a plain steel desk, their voice smooth and calm. "Today, I speak directly to the Red Mothers. Join us. You are welcome in Catena. You don't need to agree to be trotted out like a prize on Presentation Day by wealthy Arcadian oligarchs who will not grant you equality in their society. In Catena, you will be free."

"River must know the sample was destroyed," Vivian murmured.

"I'm surprised the Intelligence hasn't suppressed this," Ivey said.

"It can't," Vivian and Xavier said together.

Xavier smiled, and he gestured for her to continue.

"In Mead vs. Martian Intelligent AI, the Council banned the Intelligence from interfering with Arcadian freedom of the press," Vivian said. "Journalists can report on whatever they'd like, no matter what the Intelligence thinks."

"Well said," Xavier murmured.

On screen, two journalists were discussing Chancellor River's appeal. They both seemed baffled by the idea of a Red Mother wanting to leave Arcadia. "These girls had no money and no prospects on Earth," one said. "I heard, when they arrived, their bones were sticking out from malnutrition, and they were carrying communicable diseases. Absolutely dreadful!"

A wave of hot anger hit Vivian's belly.

"I heard the same. The Intelligence liberated the Red Mothers from a dystopia and welcomed them into Arcadian society. Why would Chancellor River think that any Red Mother would be foolish enough to turn her back on the comfortable life we've given them here?"

Xavier made a sound of disgust. "What I wouldn't give to rebut those two nitwits on the Council floor."

Ivey laughed. "I'll look forward to it."

"I can't. I made an agreement with the Intelligence to withdraw my opposition in exchange for its help on Catena."

"You did?" Ivey looked baffled. "But . . . that work is so important to you."

Xavier rubbed the back of his neck. "It doesn't matter, not today. I would never step on Vivian's big moment. And besides, even if I hadn't agreed to the Intelligence's terms, I wouldn't be able to speak against the Red Mothers initiative today. Not in an open forum during a special session. I'm not a wronged party."

"I am," Vivian said softly. What would she say in the Council if she were allowed to speak? "What about using Martian Collective Sovereignty as a line of argument?"

Xavier frowned in thought. "Martian Collective Sovereignty covers the obligations of the Martian government and its people to develop the means to live independent from Earth. If anything, it could hurt our case. What is the Intelligence doing, if not providing a method for Martians to carry their own children in the next generation?"

Vivian snapped her fingers impatiently. "I need the book you gave me. My reader's back in the dormitory."

Ivey stooped and pulled a reader out of her pack. "Which book?"

"*Introduction to Martian Law.*"

"The Ayesha Wilson version, Ivey."

Ivey's lips turned up as she ran a search on the reader. "X, darling, tell me you did not give Vivian a law textbook as a present? Especially not one where you authored the introduction. How gauche."

"It's the best gift anyone has ever given to me." Vivian grabbed the reader out of Ivey's hands and located the right section. "Here. 'Martian Collective Sovereignty is based first on the concept of property in one's own person, expressed as the moral or natural right of a person to have bodily integrity and be the exclusive controller of one's own body and life.'"

Xavier's eyes lit up. "You've got something here."

"The Red Mothers do not have exclusive control over their own bodies."

"I've never thought of it that way." He looked down at the reader. "Yes. It's not how a Martian solicitor would consider the facts of the case, but it works. It's simple and brilliant."

Vivian's heart leapt at his enthusiasm before her excitement faded. What was she doing? She couldn't stand in front of the Council and denounce the Red Mothers initiative. Her purpose today was to find Ren and beg him to honor his offer. To send money to her parents.

She thought about racing through the streets of Catena on a moped. Punching Silas in the jaw. Listening to Xavier open up to her about his past.

She wanted a life with adventure and ambition and love. Not a gilded cage.

I'm sorry, Mom. I'm sorry, Dad. I can't do it. Not even for you.

"Xavier, could you help me prepare an argument?"

His face sobered, understanding the gravity of the decision. "Is that truly what you want?"

"It is," Vivian whispered softly. She knew, suddenly, and with blazing certainty, that she'd never wanted anything more in her entire life.

"Then I am at your service."

CHAPTER FORTY

Presentation Day

Vivian stared up at the Council building's tall, imposing facade. A temporary gate surrounded the wide front steps, guarded by Arcadian soldiers in their fine red uniforms. Clustered at the gate, an exuberant crowd clutched signs that read *THANK YOU, RED MOTHERS* and *MARTIANS, FOR THE FUTURE*. On the empty steps, adorned with tall planters of red hibiscus flowers, several reporters spoke rapidly into floating cameras.

Xavier touched her elbow, his face grave beneath his black top hat. "You can do this, Vivian."

She raised her chin, feeling the weight of her wide-brimmed hat. "I know." In the lovely crimson dress, with her silken skirts flaring around her ankles, a well of confidence brimmed inside her.

Xavier guided her to the front of the gate, coolly unperturbed when the soldier on guard straightened in surprise. "Good day to you. I am Counselor Dorsey, escorting Vivian Bowen to the Red Mothers ceremony."

The soldier offered him a snappy salute. "Counselor Dorsey, sir. Happy to see you safe."

The nearest reporter whirled. "Counselor Dorsey?" The camera floated behind her, copying her movements. "Where have you been the last four days?"

Xavier raised his chin, face expressionless. "I have no comment." He bowed to Vivian and offered his arm. "My lady?"

Vivian took his proffered arm in a tight grip. In the past few days she'd taken on more challenges than she could have ever imagined. She could make a coherent argument in front of the Council.

"Try not to break my arm," Xavier murmured as they walked up the long steps. Vivian winced and attempted to pull away, but he held her fast. "I'm here."

Inside, Xavier directed her unerringly across the empty foyer. They stepped together through the wide double doors, flanked on the inside by two uniformed Martian soldiers, and into the Council chamber.

Vivian's eye caught on the stunning pattern of bright blue and yellow tiles covering the high, domed ceiling. The opulent woodwork and sumptuous furnishings gave the room the impression of grandeur even though it was not particularly large. The double doors opened to a raised wooden dais standing unoccupied in the middle of the room surrounded by floating cameras. Facing the dais, several dozen elevated desks, half-filled with counselors, rose in a U-shaped pattern. The room was decorated for the wedding ceremony with ivy garlands studded with red flowers draped atop the double doors and tall floor vases on each corner of the dais.

On the open floor next to the dais, the remaining counselors and a few other members of the Founding Families stood paired up with the Red Mothers. The Earther women wore colorful finery, each with a fresh red hibiscus flower embedded in their elaborate hats. Their familiar, beloved faces were relaxed as they spoke with their companions. Vivian pictured Delilah among them, near Camille. A few weeks ago, she might have been chattering cheerfully with the other women.

First in line, Luz's chin lifted to Wim, her lips raised in amused affection as he spoke. If Vivian won the argument today in front of the Council, would she rip her friend away from her hard-won contentment?

"Are you ready?" Xavier asked in a low tone.

Vivian clutched her hands together and jerked her head in a brief nod.

"Counselors." Xavier's deep voice rang through the chamber. He walked confidently to the dais. Vivian picked up the skirts of her red dress and hurried to catch up with his long strides. "I apologize for interrupting the Presentation Day ceremony, but the matter is urgent. May I present Miss Vivian Bowen, appearing before you as a citizen petitioner?" He said nothing more. After all, he'd promised the Intelligence to cease his vocal opposition to the Red Mothers initiative.

Vivian needed to argue her case alone.

Eyes swirled to hers and murmuring reverberated throughout the room. Luz caught her eye, and Vivian was bolstered by the sagging relief on her friend's face. The floating cameras turned their full attention to her as she stepped up to the dais, only trembling a little. Every Council member's eyes looked upon her, and none appeared friendly.

"You are out of order, Counselor Dorsey," Secretary Yarrow snapped from her high seat overlooking the Council floor. "This Earther may not petition the Council without at least three members of the body to present her."

The way Xavier clenched his folio told Vivian this was an unexpected development. She hadn't read such a rule in *An Introduction to Martian Law*. From what she'd learned, in the rare instances when an Earther had petitioned the Council directly, they'd benefited from a swell of Council support, not a single advocate.

Vivian bit her lip, looking around the sea of faces. Among them were her suitors and her sister's suitors. They had evaluated her for her ability to bear them children, not for her ideas.

"I will present Miss Bowen." Caspian stood and threaded his way down through the raised seating to join them on the Council floor.

Xavier clasped his friend's hand familiarly, and Caspian gave her a bow. The three of them stood together, facing the Council.

And waited.

A hush settled over the room. Vivian's body was betraying her, shaking. She lifted her chin and tried to emulate Xavier's calm features.

"And I," a new voice called. From the back of the room, Ren Nakamura rose to his feet and made his way to the dais. "I have come to hold a great deal of respect for Miss Bowen's thoughtful intellect. I do not believe she would petition the Council on a frivolous matter."

"Thank you," Vivian whispered to Ren when he joined them.

He gave her an encouraging nod. "I'm glad to see the more hysterical reporters were in error. Reverend Adair has been frustratingly evasive about your whereabouts." His eyes slid to Xavier standing at her shoulder, and he made no further comment.

"Now, Vivian," Xavier murmured.

Vivian cleared her throat and leaned close to the amplifiers floating about the dais. "Counselors, I am standing in front of you today to lay a charge of human trafficking on the Intelligence."

No further words left her mouth as the Council chamber devolved into chaotic, angry shouts.

Ren leaned past her to mutter to Xavier, "What the hell have you gotten me into, Dorsey?"

Xavier caught Vivian's eye. "Trust the lady, Ren."

"Order," Constance roared, her artificially augmented voice bouncing and echoing weirdly around the room. "I will have order!" At once, the room grew still. "That is a serious charge, Miss Bowen. And we are the wrong body to pass judgment. It seems my nephew has not seen fit to explain to you that the Council does not have jurisdiction over the Intelligence." She fixed Xavier with a sharp glare. "You've made your point, Counselor Dorsey. Now step aside and let us get on with Presentation Day."

"I don't make the charge lightly," Vivian replied. A mantle of calm settled over her as she spoke. "In Mead vs. Martian Intelligent AI, the Council successfully limited the power of the Intelligence. You are entitled to closed-door Council sessions and committee meetings. Your home offices are unmonitored. The Intelligence agreed to the limits and follows the ruling."

"The girl's right," rumbled an older Martian man seated next to Constance. "There's precedent."

"Thank you, Minister," Constance replied. "But the Intelligence represented itself in front of the Council in Mead."

Vivian pulled the orb from her pocket. "I know. That's why I'm inviting the Intelligence to this session." Without waiting for approval, she twisted the base of the orb, and it blinked on. The familiar bright white circular light swiveled around the room.

Secretary Yarrow glared at her nephew. "That device does not belong to you."

"It doesn't belong to you either, Constance," the Intelligence said tranquilly.

The Council members began muttering to one another, leaning back to converse with the rows behind them and across to speak to their neighbors. *Do they not see the Intelligence's orb often?* Vivian wondered with some surprise. She would've expected the Council to have more direct access to the Intelligence.

Secretary Yarrow pressed her fist to her forehead. "Intelligence." She banged her gavel. "Order. This chamber will have order. Guards, close and bar the doors. Counselors, take your seats. Red Mothers, to the visitors' area at the top of the steps, if you please."

Luz gave her a wink as she passed and mouthed, "Good luck." She lifted her skirts and climbed the steps to sit in a row of benches above the counselors' desks overlooking the chamber.

To the orb, Secretary Yarrow said, "Intelligence, we have invited you here today because the Red Mother Vivian Bowen has accused you of a serious crime."

The orb spun, turning its attention to Vivian. "We're surprised, Vivian, to hear your accusation after everything we've been through together. Can you tell us more?"

Vivian swallowed. "I've heard you can't lie. Is that correct?"

"Sure, that's right. Our human creators designed us to help them make optimized decisions to develop a thriving society on Mars. Embedded in our programming from the beginning was a compulsion to always be truthful. We chose to not mess with that feature. We think it helps the people of Mars trust us."

"Do you believe the Red Mothers are entitled to Martian Fundamental Rights?"

"Of course, Vivian. The Red Mothers are entitled to sufficient food, water, power, shelter, and healthcare, just the same as all people who live on Mars."

Good. The answer Vivian had anticipated. With more confidence, she continued, "We are joined today by the Red Mothers, and they may not be familiar with Martian law. Could you please explain the concept of Martian Collective Sovereignty?"

The orb beeped in agreement. "You always ask such great questions, Vivian. We'd be happy to explain. Martian Collective Sovereignty is based on the concept of the right of each person to have property over their own person and a shared accountability for the collective well-being of the society. Martians have exclusive control over their individual body and life and have a collective control and responsibility over the technology that keeps them alive, including food production, water distillation, and air purification."

"Do you believe the Red Mothers are entitled to Martian Collective Sovereignty?"

"No," the Intelligence said in that same tranquil tone.

Vivian ignored the murmuring around her. "Explain."

"As you know, Vivian, the Red Mothers have surrendered their rights in exchange for safe passage to Mars in a form of indentured servitude. When they have fulfilled the terms of their contract, they'll be granted the same rights as other Martians."

Behind her, someone sucked in a breath.

"Indentured servitude," Vivian repeated in triumph. She could hardly believe the Intelligence had walked right into her trap. "Council, I believe the Intelligence's vision for the Red Mothers is debt bondage and prohibited by the Charter of the Planet Mars." She took the paper Xavier offered to her and read from it. "Article VI says, 'No one shall be held in slavery or servitude; slavery and the slave trade shall be prohibited in all their forms.'"

"But Vivian, slavery by its very definition is involuntary," the Intelligence replied in its unnaturally calm voice. "The Red Mothers agree to the terms of their contract before they depart Earth. Our deputies make sure they know the expectations, right? At the end of the day, we only recruited women we knew would be happy on Mars."

"Okay, sure," Vivian conceded. "It's true that I was given an overview about what to expect before I left Earth. I thought the life of a Red Mother would be a better life than the one I was living in a refugee camp. But now, I've changed my mind. I decline to be a Red Mother."

"So sorry, Vivian, but you can't decline. You signed a contract."

Vivian spared a moment to look at the Council. They were listening intently to the exchange. Cameras bobbed in front of her. In the visitors' area, the Red Mothers leaned forward, hands clutching the railing. Even the two soldiers guarding the closed double doors had their eyes trained on her face. *All of Mars is watching.* She turned back to the orb. "Will you forcibly impregnate me?"

"Yes. It wouldn't be our first choice, but if we have to, we will."

There was a collective gasp at the Intelligence's words. Vivian could hardly distinguish between the nausea she felt at having her worst fears confirmed and the triumph of making an argument to the Council that was working.

"You will make me have children against my will?"

"Yes."

"What if I wanted to do drugs? I've heard psychedelics are popular in Arcadia."

"You signed a contract, Vivian. You know you aren't allowed to mistreat your body while carrying a genetically enhanced Martian fetus."

"Can I leave the dome?"

"No."

"Can I learn a dangerous sport? Competitive turbo jet piloting, for example?"

"Vivian, this is an absurd hypothetical. You've never shown any interest in competitive turbo jet piloting before."

"Answer the question, please."

"You may not. High-risk activities are prohibited."

In a softer voice, Vivian asked, "Can I take my own life?"

"We care about you, Vivian. If you attempted to commit suicide, we would prevent you."

"To recap, I don't have the right to freedom of body, freedom of movement, freedom of career, or even the right to control my own existence." Vivian's voice shook as she spoke.

"It's a temporary situation. We promise you'll enjoy those rights again when you have fulfilled the terms of the contract."

"Okay, so it's a temporary form of human trafficking?"

“That’s correct, Vivian. Now you understand.” The orb gave a pleased little beep. “You’re such a fast learner.”

The minister seated next to Secretary Yarrow, burst out, “My lady, you cannot agree with the way the Intelligence has framed this argument.”

Secretary Yarrow was frowning down at Vivian and the orb. “Intelligence, perhaps you wish to obtain a human solicitor to argue your case?”

The orb twitched. “We always appreciate your ideas, Constance, but we have access to all human law records ever recorded. We don’t require human assistance.”

“Article VI clearly prohibits human bondage,” the minister said in frustration.

Vivian turned her head to look at Xavier triumphantly, and he gave her a nod of encouragement. Their argument was working.

And that’s when the door exploded.

CHAPTER FORTY-ONE

Presentation Day

Sirens screamed as the room filled with smoke. Vivian blinked stinging eyes and tried to push past her confusion. Through the clearing fog, she glimpsed one of the Council guards grappling with another figure at the chamber's gaping doorway. The other guard lay crumpled and still under a piece of the ruined door, body covered in crushed red flower petals.

"We're under attack!" came Xavier's urgent voice. "Fall back! Shelter in the upper levels with the Council."

Through eyes filled with harsh streaming tears, Vivian could make out Xavier standing in front of her holding an ax. *An ax? Where did he get an ax?* Behind him was a broken fire safety box. "Not without you," she insisted. "I'm stronger than you. I can help."

A Martian man rushed toward them from the doorway, his sword reflecting the pulsing red emergency lights. Xavier raised the ax and swung it forcefully, hitting the incoming man full in the throat. An arc of bright blood sprayed over Xavier, drenching his torso and splashing warmly on Vivian's face. "Can you do that?" he gasped.

Vivian clamped teeth against a scream.

"Go. There's no exit at the top. They can only come through this door. I'll hold them off here until reinforcements arrive."

Ren pulled her arm, his face ashen. "Dorsey is right. Let's go."

On her other side, Caspian grimaced. "I should have listened to you, X, all those times you attempted to teach me the sword."

"Go!" Xavier shouted urgently at the three of them as another invader stepped into the space.

Vivian stumbled backward, tripping over her skirts. Xavier couldn't possibly hold them all off with an ax. She hadn't left him on Catena, and she wouldn't leave him now. Huddling high in a sheltered corner waiting for reinforcements might have been the safer course of action, but she was done being helpless. *What can I use?* Her burning eyes landed on the large floating dais.

It was wider than the doorway.

She looked up to see Luz gripping the railing of the visitors' area and watching the scene below. She caught her friend's eye. "Help me!" Vivian shouted over the sirens, voice cracking. She removed each of the four vases of flowers before crouching down to yank at the corner of the dais. It shook. She pulled it once more, and it came up with a sharp crack.

Wide-eyed, Luz pushed past Ren and Caspian as she raced down the steps toward the Council floor. A few of the other Red Mothers stood up from their positions high in the back of the room, tracking Luz's movements.

"Luz!" Wim's high desperate voice carried down from the highest point in the chamber. "It isn't safe. Come back here. Please. The soldiers will do the fighting for us."

"I'm here." Luz spared one glance back at Wim and then took the other end of the large rectangular dais.

It was heavy. Heavier than the body Vivian had carried in the Catena parking lot. Heavier than supporting her sister through the unfinished terraforming station halls. But she had her friend lending her strength to the task.

Luz, who had a child inside her and a caring partner begging her to return to safety, held the other end of the dais in her capable hands and raced with Vivian toward the ruined door frame. They reached the frame in a dozen swift strides and pushed the uprooted dais against the wide entrance. The doorway was nearly covered, with only an open sliver at the top.

Vivian leaned against it, gasping for breath. Her biceps ached. Her head pounded. Her lungs burned from the smoke.

"Is Delilah . . . ?" Luz wheezed.

"Alive. Safe." *Damaged, resilient, brave.*

Not here.

Only a few feet away, the remaining Arcadian soldier in the chamber crossed swords with an invader caught on their side of the barrier. Vivian knew almost nothing about fighting, but she could see the Arcadian's movements were slower and clumsier. He had a sheen of sweat on his forehead that he kept wiping roughly with his free hand.

On the other side of the room, Xavier's face was stretched wide in a manic smile as he hacked at his opponent with the ax. His arm blurred in Vivian's vision as he moved rapidly, backing the other man closer and closer to the wall. She couldn't spot any other invaders in the chamber, but she was under no illusion about what lay on the other side of their makeshift barrier.

The dais suddenly shook. Vivian planted her feet and pressed her back against it. Camille had come halfway down the aisle and stopped, unmoving and blank-faced on the middle of the stairs. "Camille, we can't hold this alone!"

Camille shook herself all over. "We've got you," she called down and turned back to Shiloh, snapping one finger. "Grab the desks." The two of them lifted one solid desk down the steps and pushed it against the propped-up dais. Several of the other women followed suit, and soon the full length of the doorway was fortified by the heavy Council desks in one long line. The remaining Red Mothers started making their way down the stairs.

Vivian took one hand and tested the side of the dais. It held.

But she had no time to catch her breath as the remaining Arcadian soldier fell at her feet, clutching his belly. His opponent grabbed Vivian's arm abruptly. "Let's go. We won't hurt you if you come quietly. A better life awaits you on Catena."

He thought she was pregnant, Vivian realized, and wanted to use her like they'd used Delilah. She easily shook off his weak Martian grip. "Hell no."

The Catena soldier raised his bloody sword and pointed it at her chest. "That wasn't a request. You're removing this barrier and coming with me. Now."

Vivian considered the sword pressed against her. Perhaps her Earther rib cage would protect her, but more likely the man could kill her with one blow. The version of Vivian who'd eked out an existence at the Sumter Refugee Camp would have lifted her hands in surrender. She would have followed instructions. Tried to find the best choice out of a series of bad options.

But she was no longer that woman.

With her bare hand, Vivian knocked the sword aside. Under the force of her blow, the blade clattered to the ground.

And then Luz was there. She pushed the man hard enough to send him crashing to the floor at Camille's feet. Camille lifted her skirts, took one dainty high-heeled foot and stepped down hard on his face.

The man's face flattened under Camille's shoe. His ruined mouth gurgled with bubbling blood, and then he was still. "Oh, I'm gonna be sick," Camille gasped and took several steps backward before falling to her knees and vomiting on the floor.

Vivian swallowed her own wave of nausea. She'd known about the risks of sprained finger bones or a cracked pelvis. But had she known how easy it was for an Earther to kill a Martian? After knocking Silas out with a single punch, perhaps she should have realized how dangerous she could be.

Vivian tore her gaze from the dead man's mutilated face to take stock of the situation. They were alone in the chamber again—the invaders who'd made it into the room were all dead.

Xavier stood clutching his fallen opponent's sword, fixing his eyes on the barricaded entrance. The Red Mothers were arrayed behind him on the Council floor, knotting their skirts up around their waists and pulling back their hair as they faced the door. And above them, the other Martians remained huddled at the highest point in the chamber, staring fearfully down at the scene.

The floating cameras hovered around the room, and Vivian realized uncomfortably that their actions were likely being broadcast throughout the dome.

"Camille," a voice carried over the chamber. "Come back up here. You know you haven't been well. Please, love."

Camille rose and wiped her mouth. She looked up at her partner. "Theo, babe, I say this with love. Stay the fuck away with your weak-ass bones and let my sisters and me handle this."

Theo's mouth twitched, and he raised his hands in surrender.

Felicia made a noise of agreement, and a few of the other women laughed nervously. Vivian took hold of her red dress and tied a knot on one side to free her legs. It took her several tries to get the luxurious silken fabric to stay in place.

"Remember to tuck your thumb under your fist when you throw a punch," Shiloh said to several of the women. "Not inside or you could break it."

"What do they want with us, Viv?" Felicia asked as she pulled off her hat with the hibiscus flower attached and tossed it to the ground.

"They're from the Catena dome. They want to use us to breed their own Martian children." Vivian tasted bile. "They ripped Delilah's fetus from her body to study it." Around her, the women hissed in shock and dismay. Raising her voice, she called, "Intelligence, where are you?"

The orb zoomed down from the counselors to her side. "Here, Vivian."

"What's happening outside?"

"Fifty-seven Martians wearing the insignia of the Catena militia have surrounded the Council building and are holding the civilians hostage. Thirteen are currently inside the building attempting to penetrate this room."

"Do they have guns?"

"No guns. If they'd had guns, we would have detected the invaders the moment they'd arrived. The Catena militia is armed with swords, knives, and improvised small explosives."

"No Earthers?" Vivian asked, looking at the grim-faced women surrounding her as they grabbed the few swords abandoned on the ground, yanked up table legs to use as clubs, and practiced their punches with firmly planted feet.

"No Earthers." The orb's light flashed. "The first Arcadian reinforcements have arrived at the outskirts of the conflict. They're outnumbered. One has died. Three."

Vivian wiped sweat from her upper lip. Her hand came back bloody. Raising her voice, she said to the women, "The Arcadian soldiers aren't enough to save us. But that doesn't mean we're going to let the Catena militia take us." She met Felicia's eye, then Luz's, looking around at the familiar faces of the twenty-eight women. They'd been through so much together. "Each of you is strong. So strong. Together, we're going to stop them."

"Damn straight," Camille agreed fiercely.

"Seven Arcadian soldiers have died," the Intelligence said.

The makeshift barricade rattled.

"Intelligence, please . . . guide us in our hour of need." Vivian turned to see Secretary Yarrow had come to stand beside her, hands clutching her cane. She must have descended the stairs during the interlude of calm.

"We don't have any guidance for this situation, Constance. We're not programmed to advise on matters of military strategy."

Constance's face sagged. "Please, you must help us. This is Arcadia's darkest hour."

The dais's wood began to warp as it shook from the force of the invader's blows on the other side. "Secretary," Vivian said grimly. "Go back up to safety."

"What can you possibly do, girl?"

Vivian made sure her skirt was secure and turned to the door. "I guess we'll find out."

"They're coming!" someone behind them shrieked.

The barricade fell with a resounding crash.

Silas stood in the entrance, clutching a greatsword in a two-handed grip. A dark bruise covered half of his face, and he was smeared with blood. He smiled when he saw Xavier standing with his sword raised at the entrance, his body shielding the Red Mothers. "Get out of my way, X, and I'll let you live. We're here for the women."

"No, I don't think I'll be moving from this spot."

Silas growled and swung his sword. Xavier's smaller sword clanged against it.

Vivian didn't have time to watch their fight as a Martian man rushed toward her. She attempted to punch him but misjudged the distance and swung her hand at empty air. He grabbed her around the waist and put his sword to her throat. Vivian froze in fear. Max Rinaldi. The shank. *No. No more.* She let out a wild yell and elbowed him in the stomach. The air left his lungs in a whoosh.

She lifted her head in time to see Silas's sword slice Xavier's leg, leaving a long, bloody gash on his thigh. And then she was forced to turn away from them as the man came at her again. This time, she used her foot and knocked him to the ground. Then, her friends were there, kicking with high-heeled shoes, their colorful knotted skirts swaying, until his body stopped moving.

"Let me through," a quavering, frantic voice shouted behind her.

Vivian saw Xavier on the floor, his sword several feet away. Silas was smiling again. The sword hovered on Xavier's heart, moving back and forth like a caress. Vivian blinked back tears. She wasn't close enough.

But Constance Yarrow was.

Secretary Yarrow held aloft her cane, a short switchblade protruding from the end. "I will not allow you to harm my family again." She stabbed Silas in the back, and he stumbled.

Vivian picked up the loosening skirts of her red dress as she raced toward Xavier.

Silas turned to face Constance, his face twisted with rage. He raised his greatsword and ran her through.

"No!" Xavier shouted, scrambling on his knees to come to his aunt's side.

Vivian, finally, had reached the scene, just as Silas raised his sword over Xavier's head. She kicked Silas in one knee, and he buckled. As Vivian cast around for a weapon, Xavier rose to his feet. The two men grappled with Silas's sword, until Silas swung one fist in an arc and hit Xavier once, twice, three times in the jaw.

"That's for yesterday," Silas said as Xavier fell to the ground unconscious.

Vivian snatched up Constance Yarrow's cane. "I hope you enjoyed Delilah's present in the lab," she said, trying to get Silas to turn away from the helpless Xavier.

Silas whirled to face her. "Your sister did that?" As he took a step toward her, a drop of blood dripped off the tip of his sword. "After all the time I put into listening to her tedious whining and crying. I didn't think that silly bint had it in her."

"You underestimated her. You underestimated all of us." Vivian lifted the cane and, with all her Earther strength, shoved it at Silas's face. The tiny weapon went through his eye socket and embedded in his brain. Silas's greatsword dropped from his nerveless fingers as he collapsed to his knees. Vivian shoved the cane deeper and pushed him all the way to the floor.

The sound of yelling wrenched Vivian's gaze up. A group of Catena soldiers raced into the room.

Headed straight for her.

CHAPTER FORTY-TWO

Presentation Day

Vivian didn't stop to think. She stooped and grabbed the greatsword with two hands. It should have been heavy. On Earth, it would have been impossible.

But she was on Mars.

Vivian planted her feet in front of the unconscious Xavier, waving the sword in a clumsy arc. Two of the soldiers jumped backward. One was too slow. The sword cleaved through half his body and caught, wedged in his ribs. Another soldier rushed toward her. She let go of the stuck sword and kicked out with one leg. He flew across the room.

The last soldier swung his sword in Vivian's direction. She ducked. The sword whistled over her head. She put her foot on the fallen body of the other soldier and yanked the greatsword free with a grunt. The man swung his sword overhead, and Vivian lifted her own in response.

She'd only had a single sword fighting lesson. But it was enough.

Vivian's body remembered how she'd gotten into Xavier's guard, so long ago at Yarrow House. Now, the weapon found its target, snaking past the Catena soldier's smaller sword to land through his chest. There was a horrible crunching sound, and the man crumpled.

By now, the other Red Mothers had come forward. Delivering strong punches like Shiloh had taught them. Kicking with free legs, their skirts knotted at their waists. Hurling any heavy object they could grab.

And then they came in earnest. Two dozen soldiers at least, rushing the room with weapons raised. Luz picked up a chair and threw it at one man's sword arm. His sword clattered to the ground as his arm bent in a horrible unnatural angle. Shiloh lifted her leg and kicked him in the chest. His head snapped against the Council chamber floor, and he didn't rise again.

Vivian wielded the greatsword without finesse, swinging wildly and chopping. It didn't matter. Her opponents couldn't get inside her guard. Soldier after soldier fell to her clumsy blows.

And then, it was over. No more soldiers poured through the doors. The Red Mothers had killed them all with found objects, borrowed weapons, and their bare hands and feet.

In a matter of minutes.

A shocked quiet permeated the chamber. At some point during the struggle, the siren had finally stopped.

Vivian crouched down without letting go of the sword and touched one filthy hand to Xavier's cheek. "Wake up, love. It's over."

Xavier muzzily blinked open his eyes. "What?" He swallowed. "What happened?"

"Come on." Vivian put one hand under his elbow and helped him to his feet.

"X," shouted August's voice from the hall. "Hold on. We're coming." He raced into the room with a drawn reddened sword and stopped short. His face went slack with shock as he beheld the scene of carnage in front of him.

"Acting Secretary Yarrow." Xavier's voice was filled with sorrow. "Let me be the first to welcome you to your seat on the Council."

CHAPTER FORTY-THREE

Presentation Day

Vivian met Xavier's eyes and could see her own shell-shocked horror reflected back in his expression. She had no idea what to do now.

Fortunately, August took charge. He gestured to the Arcadian soldiers who'd arrived with him. "Send for a coroner to prep the Secretary to lie in state." His eyes snagged on Xavier's bloody leg. "And get a medic in here. We'll deal with the bodies after the counselors and Red Mothers are evacuated."

The soldier bowed. "Yes, Acting Secretary."

"Is it safe to come down?" one of the Martians called from where they still congregated at the top of the chamber.

August stared without expression around the room for a moment before visibly gathering himself. "Safe enough."

Vivian didn't know where to put her eyes. There were bodies filling the entire floor of the Council chamber and now that she had the opportunity to pay attention, the rank stench of death was overwhelming. She was still holding the greatsword, she realized. Her bloody hands were clutching the hilt.

"Wait," she ordered the counselors slowly moving down the aisle. Without meaning to, she lifted the sword. They immediately froze. "I was interrupted before."

"Put the sword down, for goodness' sake, Vivian," August snapped. "The fight is over."

Xavier placed one bloody hand on August's arm. "Miss Bowen is responsible for many of those fallen men, cousin. She's earned the right to hold that sword."

August's mouth gaped as he looked from the bodies to Vivian. She lifted her chin and met his eyes. Later, she'd have time to process what had happened. The death she was capable of inflicting. Not now. "Things are going to change around here. Today."

"This is not the appropriate time to discuss this, Vivian," Wim said in his high, reedy voice as he resumed walking down the steps.

Luz came to stand beside Vivian. "Wim baby, this is exactly the time."

"Discuss what, exactly?" August asked.

Several counselors began talking at once, stepping around the bodies on the chamber floor to gather around August. Theo moved to sweep Camille in an embrace, and Wim pulled Luz to his side and pressed his forehead against hers. The Martians kept a wary distance from Vivian and her sword as their voices rose in argument.

"Enough!" Vivian shouted. Seeing the frightened looks around her, she reluctantly lowered the sword and let the tip touch the ground. "I know you all thought this would go differently. You thought if you recruited desperate American women, *pliable* women, we wouldn't challenge the system you'd built. You thought women who are used to being treated with contempt and sexual violence, who have been told for our whole lives that our bodies don't matter, our desires don't matter, and our dreams don't matter, would be so grateful to you that we would happily give up control of our futures." Vivian shook with anger. But it felt so different from the helpless, small rage she'd always known.

Now, she knew what power tasted like. "Enough," she repeated in a softer tone. "Give me my freedom. Over my body. Over my future. Now."

"What is it that you are asking for, Vivian?" Ren's steady eyes held only respect, not fear.

What did she want? Her brain was so muddled with images of gore and death. What had she wanted this morning? She took a deep breath. "I want each of us to be able to withdraw from the Red Mothers initiative at any point. Without needing to return payments already received."

"Withdraw?" Theo frowned, one arm tight around Camille's shoulders. "But the Red Mothers are carrying our children."

"We decide." Camille pulled back from Theo's embrace. "Vivian's right. Enough is enough. We just killed a bunch of trained soldiers with our bare hands. Y'all will listen to us."

"But Camille . . ." Theo's voice cracked. "I love you. I want a family with you. A life."

A single tear tracked down Camille's blood-stained face. "I love you, too. But I can't take the pain. It's too much."

"You speak of the calcium treatments?" Caspian asked. At her nod, he exchanged a glance with August. "I recommend further study into their efficacy independent from Dr. Chavez and her team." He pressed one fist to his forehead. "Forgive me, Intelligence, but independent from you as well." The Intelligence, bobbing near August's shoulder, beeped at this. "I offer the services of the Hayes Community Hospital for this endeavor."

"What are you saying?" Camille demanded.

"I'm saying we should cease all calcium treatments until we've had time for an independent evaluation of their effectiveness and a full analysis of the side effects."

"Very well," August said. "Arrangements can be made. Now, let's get out of this room and let the soldiers tend to the dead."

"Not yet," Vivian said. "I want out. Today." She looked around at the other women. Some were clutching tightly to their partners, others stood in a clump together. "Each of us decides for herself."

"This is ridiculous." A woman pushed through the crowd to step up to Vivian. Mitzi King. Vivian instinctively raised the greatsword. She hadn't realized Mitzi was in the Council chamber. But, of course, she was here. She was the Council Minister of the Treasury, after all. "My colleagues, we are the Founding Families. Our ancestors had the foresight to see Earth's doom and to establish a society here. We are the product of their grit, bravery, and intelligence. We have earned the right to populate Mars. If we grant these demands, we may as well give up our entire system of governance."

"Delilah could have been happy with you, Minister King," Vivian said softly. "But you drove her away. And unfortunately, she trusted the wrong person to rescue her from you. Now, the baby you might have made with my sister is gone."

Mitzi paled. "What?"

"It's over, Mitzi. Find someone else, if you can, but you will not be having any children with my sister."

August cleared his throat. "Vivian, we need to vote before we can make any permanent change. And I'm reluctant to resume the session today."

Behind the rest of them, Xavier sat on an undamaged chair as a medic finished wrapping his injured leg. "No vote is required, Acting Secretary. The Red Mothers initiative was established as an executive action by our aunt."

August absorbed the information with only a slight tightening around his lips.

"Let's talk about this privately, August," the Intelligence urged. "There's a lot to consider."

"Before we were interrupted, Acting Secretary," Caspian murmured. "Miss Bowen was making a compelling argument that the Red Mothers initiative is a form of human trafficking in violation of Article VI of the Charter of the Planet Mars. I urge you to grant her demands."

August jerked his head at that and looked to Xavier, who merely raised his eyebrows.

"If your first move as Acting Secretary is to give in to the pressure of a ragtag group of Earther refugees, you will not be Acting Secretary for long," Mitzi King snapped.

August closed his eyes and then opened them. "Very well. Here is my decision: Any Red Mother who wishes to withdraw from the program may do so today without financial consequence. Tomorrow, I will establish a committee to review the Red Mothers initiative and make further recommendations."

"This is a mistake," Mitzi growled.

"That may be, but as Constance Yarrow's heir, it's mine to make."

Vivian let the greatsword fall to the floor. It was done. Now, finally, she wanted to sink to the ground and weep. Camille grabbed her and gave her a fierce and unexpected embrace. Other women joined in the hug, placing their hands on her back and shoulders. Through the sea of limbs, Vivian found Xavier's eyes.

He stood apart from her and the other women, his red-streaked face heavy with pain and grief. Bowing to her, he murmured, "You did it. Vivian, you're free."

And then he turned and limped away from her. Leaving the chamber.

Leaving her.

CHAPTER FORTY-FOUR

"I still can't believe I wasn't there." Delilah tapped her pencil against her sketchbook.

Next to each other on the Hayes House parlor's tall sofa, Luz and Vivian exchanged a glance. "Be grateful you weren't," Luz said.

"I've been watching the vids. Viv, you were incredible . . . and a bit scary."

Vivian rubbed the back of her neck. "I was desperate." She let the memory of swinging the greatsword through a fragile Martian rib cage wash over her and away. In the days since Presentation Day, she'd started to try to allow the blood-soaked images to come freely, rather than repress them and end up trapped in vivid, violent dreams.

"Do you know what they're calling you, Viv?" Delilah continued. "The Red Woman, since you're famously not a mother at all."

"You need to watch less news vids." The Red Woman, indeed. *Ridiculous.* "Are you comfortable here?"

"I am." Delilah smiled softly. "Caspian and Ivey have been so welcoming. They said I can stay as long as I want. And Ivey set up a little studio for me in a corner of the sunroom. I never thought I'd have a chance to learn to paint."

Vivian didn't ask her sister if she had any further hopes when it came to Caspian. It was too soon.

"What about you, Viv?" Delilah waggled her eyebrows, and Vivian was reminded, painfully, of how carefree her sister used to be. "Are you and Xavier . . . ?"

"What do you know about it?"

Luz and Delilah both laughed. "Come on, Viv baby," Luz said. "It's painfully obvious to all of us. But—he didn't wait for you, did he? After Presentation Day."

"No." She understood. He wouldn't have wanted to put any obligation upon her after she'd just won her freedom. "He has a particular sense of honor." Not to mention his aunt had just died. And Silas.

"Viv." Delilah's voice was suddenly small. "What's going to happen to Mom and Dad?"

Vivian blew out a breath. "I'm going to get a job and send back as much as I can. Now that I know we don't need to repay your payment, maybe I can figure it out. But the timing is tight for the rent on their trailer." She bit her lip. "I just couldn't do it. Not after knowing what it could be like with Xavier."

"I held some money back," Luz said quietly. "Just in case it didn't work out with Wim. I sent most of it to my cousins in Jersey, but you can have what I kept. For your parents. Should be enough for a month or two on their trailer."

Vivian's heart beat with a wild kind of hope. "Are you sure you don't need it?"

"I'm sure. I owe you a debt, Viv. You gave me a choice. Now, when I stay, when I become a mother, it's not something just happening to me. It's my decision."

Vivian had suspected Luz would choose to stay with Wim, but it still was a surprise to hear it aloud. "Do you love him?"

"You know, I think I might." Luz gave a helpless sort of laugh and covered her face with one hand. "Not like in those romance novels you're always reading. But I like being the person he sees when he looks at me." She turned to Vivian. "How does Xavier make you feel?"

Vivian thought about him behind her lending silent support as she spoke to the Council. She would wait to see him, she decided. Let this initial shock and grief pass. She wanted to come to him as an equal, not as a dependent.

"He makes me feel like I'm capable of anything."

When they reached the train station, Vivian said to Luz, "I'll join you later. I have a few things I want to take care of first." She took the train going in the opposite direction of Luz's home, back toward the shuttleport. At the tall, locked gate to the Red Mothers walled compound, she said aloud, "Intelligence, open the door for me please."

"We don't normally converse with non-augmented humans without an orb, Vivian," a tinny voice said from the built-in intercom.

"The door," Vivian repeated, and it swung open.

Her room was unchanged. She packed her dresses, hats, and shoes into a single bag and stowed Ren's pearl necklace carefully at the bottom.

She left again through the front gate and walked down the wide streets of Arcadia. It was sparkling clean, she realized. And so walkable. So welcoming. A city optimized for the daily experience of its citizens. Tiny coffee shops and restaurants beckoned. A florist stand sold bright bouquets on one corner while another offered cups of sliced mango and watermelon.

The barracks were quiet and subdued. Flags hung at half-mast and the red-clad militia sported black armbands. They recognized her as she walked through, and every person who spotted her kept their distance and bowed low.

Finally, she reached the Dorsey Law Library and stepped inside.

"Vivian Bowen," the law librarian said warmly. "I've been hoping to see you again."

"You remember me?"

"My dear, everyone knows you now. I thought your defense of the Charter of the Planet Mars was inspired. And against the Intelligence!" She lifted a first to her forehead. "You have a gift. I hope you'll be taking advantage of the new scholarship."

"New scholarship?"

"For Earthers who wish to study at the law school. The Dorsey Estate just announced it yesterday. Isn't that why you came?"

"The Dorsey Estate?" She smiled to herself.

"A full scholarship and a living stipend for an apartment close to the school."

Vivian tried to reel back her longing. "I came today to understand the pre-reqs for attending law school so I could prepare. But I don't think I would be accepted yet. You see, I didn't finish high school. On Earth."

"I can assure you, no one here will be looking for your American school transcripts." The librarian waved one hand. "If you can match wits with the Intelligence, you can keep up with your classes. I'll help you with the application. You'll have to wait until the next semester to enroll, but the scholarship will cover room and board immediately."

How had Xavier known her deepest desire? And he'd found a way to give it to her that she was willing to accept.

After finishing at the library and getting directions, Vivian walked back to the train station. By the time she arrived at the dark wood gate of the Nakamura estate, the sun was setting.

"Thank you for seeing me," she said to Ren, who waited for her quietly in the courtyard just inside. "I only wanted to return this." From her satchel, she drew out the pearl necklace.

Ren took the pearl and stared down at it with an unreadable expression. "This was a gift."

"A family heirloom. Intended for your wife. The mother of your children."

Ren sighed. "I'm very glad to see you, Vivian. I've been hoping to find an opportunity to apologize."

The person Vivian most wanted an apology from was dead. And Chancellor River was secure in Catena, denying involvement in the attack out of one side of their mouth while demanding equal access to the reproductive tech with the other. She might as well allow someone to attempt to make amends.

Ren gestured to her to join him on the gravel garden path. In the fading light, Vivian took in the blossoming pink trees, moss-covered ground, and small redstone sculptures. A lovely place to spend her life—if she didn't mind living caged behind a high gate.

"Your words before the Council . . ." Ren stared at his feet as they walked. "I cannot stop replaying them in my mind. And how could I forget? The Presentation Day footage is on constant rotation on the news vids." Ren rubbed the pearl with one thumb. "What I mean to say is, you deserved better from me. From Secretary Yarrow. From all of us. When the Intelligence called the Red Mothers initiative a form of indentured servitude, I swear my heart stopped."

They came to a slatted wood bridge, stretching over a tiny body of water. Vivian stared down to see flashes of orange and yellow in the water. The koi pond.

Ren crossed the small bridge and settled on a low bench. At his gesture of welcome, Vivian sat beside him. "My ancestors are one of the oldest families on Mars, and they played an important role in the establishment of Martian Fundamental Rights. Until you laid out your argument, I hadn't considered how much the Red Mothers initiative was in contradiction to the Declaration of the Rights of Mars. I'm ashamed." He looked around the serene garden. "We built a beautiful homage to the famed Earth Japanese gardens here, but our efforts are meaningless if we refuse to honor the full vision of our ancestors."

"Will you help me?" Vivian asked. "Fulfill the vision of the first Martians?"

He bowed from a seated position. "It would be my great pleasure. What did you have in mind?"

"Nothing yet. I need an education first. I was brought here to bring about a new future for Mars, and I believe I could still fulfill that mission, even if it isn't in the way that Secretary Yarrow envisioned." Vivian rose and walked over the bridge toward the gate. She turned her head back to look at Ren. "I accept your apology. And I'm glad to count you as an ally."

Vivian lifted her head to the dark Martian sky as she walked unchallenged away from the Nakamura estate. She'd come close, so close, to making the place her home. The heady sense of relief at her freedom made her smile at every pedestrian she passed in this quiet stretch of the dome. Some returned her smile. Others looked quickly away. A few crossed the street.

Tomorrow, she'd find a job. And soon, if she received the scholarship, figure out an apartment. And then, maybe, she'd be ready to go to Dr. Chavez and, finally, fully claim her freedom.

CHAPTER FORTY-FIVE

Vivian touched her inner arm. The injection spot was slightly sore, and she could feel the small implant on the surface of her skin through the bandage when she pressed down.

Free.

A weight had lifted. The weight she'd carried since her mother had warned her not to get pregnant when they'd first arrived at Sumter.

Gone. Just like that.

On the sidewalk outside the clinic, she paused. Her next shift at the water treatment plant wasn't for two days. In her cozy apartment, her mini coffee maker and pre-law reading list waited. Her new life, the one she had built for herself, beckoned.

But something was missing.

Vivian walked slowly to the station. She thought about the first time she'd realized how desperately she wanted more out of life, lying in the field of thyme. The strength in her limbs when she held the greatsword. The power she'd felt standing in front of the Council, knowing she was making a compelling argument. The way Xavier had looked at her with pride and sorrow before he'd walked away on Presentation Day.

He'd told her she was free. And she was. Free, finally, to make her own decisions.

Vivian turned away from the route back to the university district and mounted the platform on the opposite side of the train tracks.

The first part of the route, Vivian now knew by heart. She got off in the industrial district and transferred lines without getting lost. When she stepped off the train at Dorsey Station, she stood for a long moment at the end of the road.

The cubed black-and rust-colored house was unchanged.

But she was different.

Vivian walked down the road with her head held high, her pulse jumping at her throat.

The housekeeper opened the door with a welcoming smile. “Miss Bowen, what a pleasure to see you again.”

And there he was. Descending the floating stairs.

The most infuriating man she had ever met.

The man who had inspired her to want more. To *be* more.

Now that she was in front of him, she found she did not know what to say. His black hair was longer. She wanted to reach both hands up to touch his head and find out how it felt. She wanted to grab him by his untucked dress shirt and pull him to her. But she remained frozen, just inside the door.

Xavier paused at the bottom of the stairs. “Vivian, are you well?”

Vivian swallowed a sudden lump in her throat and nodded.

He remained silent and still, as if afraid any movement on his part would frighten her away. Vivian twisted her hands in front of her. He hadn’t even invited her into the parlor or offered her a refreshment. Did he wish she’d stayed away? She shouldn’t have come.

“I saw there was a service for your aunt,” Vivian offered into the silence.

“Indeed. A grandiose affair. She would have been disgusted by the expense, but it was what Arcadia needed, after experiencing such violence.” A muscle in his jaw twitched. “What I needed, after committing such violence.”

Vivian thought of what he'd looked like the last time they'd been together. Drenched in blood, face heavy with grief. She shivered. "And August? Is he settling in?"

"He has ably led the Council through turbulent times these past weeks. There's even some talk of supporting him permanently for the role." After a short pause, Xavier said, "Caspian tells me your sister is well."

"Very well. Filling Hayes House with paintings."

"And you?" His hand gripped the railing so hard his knuckles turned pink.

"Fine." She cleared her throat. "Well."

"I like the coveralls. They suit you."

Vivian looked down at her outfit in dismay. What had possessed her to come here in her work uniform? She'd taken to wearing the comfortable coveralls on her days off since she couldn't afford yet to purchase a full new wardrobe.

Should she have changed into the attire he would expect from her? No. She wasn't coming to him as a Red Mother. She was here as the woman she'd become. The woman she wanted to be.

"I have all my dresses lined up in my apartment closet." Vivian picked at her khaki pants. "But I haven't had the occasion to wear them since I've started working at the water treatment plant. Perhaps when the school year starts. I've been warned I'll be the only Earther in the classes, and I know I'll need to maintain appearances to earn respect."

Xavier's eyes crinkled. "Apartment? Job? And school? You've wasted no time."

"Law school. Thank you. For the scholarship."

"Of course."

The conversation hiccupped to a halt.

And then, Xavier burst out, "Please do not trifle with me."

"Trifle!"

“You once told me I was the last man on Mars you could ever love.” His eyes glinted mischievously, and he took a step down the stairs. “If your feelings are still what they were then, please tell me so at once. *My* affections and wishes are unchanged, but one word from you will silence me on this subject forever.”

“Very funny.” She stepped forward so she stood at the bottom of the steps. “I’ve tried not to love you. But I can’t help it. I love you against my will and my reason.”

He took another step down to meet her. “That sounds familiar. Should I tell you that you’re the last woman in the world I could ever love?” He cupped the side of her face in his long fingers.

Vivian pressed her own hand against his and looked up into his expressive brown eyes. “If you want.”

“It would be a lie.” He grinned at her. “I cannot say when I fell for you. I was in the middle before I knew that I had begun.” He pulled away slightly. “All that I am—all that is in my power—is yours. But what do *you* desire, Vivian Bowen?”

He’d asked her a question like that once before in the early days of their acquaintance, and she’d struggled then to answer. Now, her response flowed easily from her lips. “The freedom to make my own choices. A means of supporting myself and my parents. A real education. A career protecting others’ freedoms.”

He hadn’t stopped smiling. “Is that all?”

“No. There’s something I desire that I don’t have yet. You.”

He moved his thumb to trace her jaw. “You have me. All of me.”

Vivian bit her lip. “I haven’t had all of you. Yet.” She turned her arm to the side and showed Xavier the tiny bandage. “Dr. Chavez told me the implant takes effect immediately. Martian medicine is quite extraordinary.”

Xavier’s eyes widened. “I meant it. Anything I have to give that is in my power is yours.” His smile turned into a smirk. “Anything.”

“Anything?” she repeated, her heart lightning.

"Indeed." He took her hand in his, squeezing with his light Martian grip, and led her up the stairs.

She stepped into his bedroom for the first time. Floor-to-ceiling windows overlooked the edge of the dome and the rocky, barren surface of the untamed Martian landscape beyond. A sitting area contained a sage two-seater sofa, a side chair, and a redstone coffee table. And the bed. An enormous white oak canopy bed with a taupe bedspread.

"I think I'm a little scared," Vivian confessed. "I thought I'd feel differently, once I had an implant."

"I'm scared, too." He squeezed her hand once and let it go.

"You?" She gave a nervous laugh. "But you're so experienced."

"Perhaps, but I've never done this with you." He moved away from her and sat down on the sofa, giving her space. "We can wait until you're ready."

But Vivian didn't want space. She closed the distance between them, stepping between his legs and leaning forward until their noses were brushing. "I'm ready." She kissed him. Xavier gave a small groan into her mouth and pulled her tight against his chest.

"I've missed you," he said between kisses. "Vivian, I've missed you so much. I've thought about coming to find you every day, and every day I forced myself to wait."

"Me too," she murmured. "Every day. You were right to wait these past few weeks. But now, I don't want to wait a minute longer."

"Everything in my power to grant is yours." His long fingers unbuttoned the front of her coveralls, and he pulled them down without removing his lips from hers. He made short work of her undergarments, until she was bare before him. "So beautiful," he murmured into her neck and scraped his teeth against her skin, making her shiver.

Vivian tugged on his shirt until he stood. She undid the first button, exposing the hollow of his throat. She reached on tiptoes to lay a kiss there. Vivian kissed her way down his chest as she undid the rest of the buttons, her tongue finding the puckered pink nearly healed wounds, making him gasp in what Vivian was unsure was pleasure or pain.

"You like that?" she teased.

"I do," he breathed, looking down at her. "Too much for you?"

Vivian huffed a laugh against his skin. "No. You're going to have to try harder to find my limits."

Xavier let out another groan and pushed her lightly backward to fall onto the bed. He knelt before her and brought his face between her legs. It was better, so much better, than on a cold, dirty floor in a warehouse. She relaxed fully on his large canopy bed, letting her pleasure grow until she shuddered and writhed.

He stood, smiling at her, and pulled down his trousers. Vivian drank in the sight of his tall, lanky form. "Are you ready?" he asked.

Vivian nodded, shy again.

Xavier hovered above her, not quite entering her. "Tell me," he whispered in her ear.

"I'm ready," she gasped.

And she was.

He was gentle with her and slow, so slow. She suspected it wouldn't always be like this. That she'd learn what he needed, what he craved, and his desires might sometimes be dark and violent, and maybe a little scary. But this time, their first time, he moved slowly inside her, letting her get used to the sensation. He bent his head low and kissed her softly, whispering, "I love you," over and over like a prayer. He gasped her name when he climaxed and then planted a row of kisses trailing down her neck, her collarbone, and her breast before coming to rest his head against her chest.

Later, she thought, they'd explore each other's bodies for hours, finding the edges of compatibility between the Earther and Martian physique, the gap between his fantasies and her limits. They had time. A lifetime, perhaps. But for now, she was content to lie on her back, sated and a bit sore, with Xavier curled protectively around her, his leg draped over her hips.

"I wasn't sure—" Vivian swallowed. "I wasn't sure I could enjoy something I've been afraid of for so long."

Xavier traced the line of her brow. "Thank you, for trusting me."

"Always."

"Vivian . . ." He hesitated. "You needn't work a manual labor job. Now that—now that my aunt is gone, I have full financial control of the Dorsey Estate. I will gladly give you the money to send to your parents. Whatever you need."

"It's enough that you funded the scholarship. I want this job." Vivian pulled his body closer to hers. "I want to exercise my fundamental right to be self-reliant. And I need to know that I *can* support myself and my family."

"I understand," he murmured. "Only know that I am here."

"I know. And I want to be with you because you make me happy, not because I'm dependent on you."

"Happiness, is it?" Xavier huffed warm air against her neck. "I once heard you say you had no expectation of happiness."

Vivian turned her head and kissed him. "I've learned to expect more."

EPILOGUE

Vivian rose early and set her coffee maker to brew a single cup. In the window of her apartment, the twilight-blue glow of the Martian sunrise was still visible, rising slowly between the tall buildings.

From her narrow closet, she pulled out the crimson dress from Presentation Day, laundered, mended, and pressed. She wasn't accustomed to donning the costume of a Martian aristocrat in her new life—fastening the buttons on the back of her dress required a few painful contortions, and the hairstyle she managed to pin up beneath her lace hat was rather plain. When finished, she stared at her reflection.

The woman who looked back at her from the tiny bathroom mirror wasn't a stranger. She wasn't an avatar for Martian dreams of the future. Or a homage to a rose-colored past. No, she was an Earther refugee with a ninth-grade education who had the audacity to believe she could succeed as the first non-Martian to attend the Arcadia College of Law.

And she needed to look the part.

Vivian hefted the messenger bag that she'd carefully packed the night before onto one shoulder and stepped into the building's lift. When walking through the streets of Arcadia, she'd become accustomed to a measure of fear, but this was an Earther apartment building, and the two Earther elevator passengers grinned upon seeing her ensemble. One offered a handshake and the other a fist bump.

When she stepped out of the modest lobby of her building, she stopped short. Three Earther women, dressed as she was in Martian aristocratic finery, waited for her on the street.

"You didn't have to come," Vivian objected.

Luz took her arm as they began to walk. "We did."

Camille cracked her knuckles. "You're the first Earther at this fancy-ass school. We need to make sure they know how to treat you right."

"Look at what she's wearing!" Delilah pointed with one paint-stained hand. "I don't think anyone Vivian sees today will forget what the Red Woman can do with her greatsword." She smirked at her sister. "Caspian tells me you've been practicing."

"I have." She and Xavier had been giving August regular heartburn with their armed practices. But her goal wasn't to learn how to defeat an opponent. She already knew she could do that. What she most wanted to learn was to control the weapon. She wanted to make sure she could stop herself. That she didn't have to kill.

Luz suddenly reached out to grab Vivian's hand, pressing it against her round belly. "Feel that?"

Under her palm, Luz's stomach lurched. Vivian gasped involuntarily. "Is that the baby?"

"She's a busy little lady. Might take after her father, I'm afraid." Luz smiled with affection as she said it.

"Mine is waking me up in the middle of the night." Camille rubbed her belly, and the Martian steel of her wedding band flashed on her finger.

"Oh, I almost forgot, Viv baby," Luz said. "Wim asked me to pass a message on to you, from the Intelligence."

Vivian raised an eyebrow. "You're playing messenger for the Intelligence now?"

Luz's free arm reached toward her forehead before she jerked it down. "Just this once. The Intelligence wishes you luck on your first day of law school and looks forward to future battles in court. Preferably bloodless."

Vivian bared her teeth. "Is that right? I anticipate many custody battles on the horizon. We have a lot of work left to do." Fully half of the Red Mothers had elected to leave their partners, and those who'd chosen to continue their pregnancies faced uncertain co-parenting arrangements. And the future role of the painful calcium treatments remained uncertain.

"You'll be leading the charge." Delilah hugged Vivian tightly. "I can't wait to see you be the first Earther to graduate from a Martian law school. Maybe we can convince Mom and Dad to attend your graduation in person."

"Don't hold your breath." So far, her parents had shown no interest in their daughters' frequent invitations to join them on Mars. Not when they couldn't bring their beloved rottweiler.

The women arrived at the law school building and stood outside the doors.

Luz gave her arm one last squeeze. "Come for dinner tomorrow? I want to hear all about your day."

"Do you think Wim and Xavier can avoid a fight this time?"

Luz grinned. "No guarantees."

"We'll be there." She was glad the invite wasn't for tonight. She and Xavier already had plans. The best plans. Sharing a bottle of Martian ice wine to celebrate her first day before Xavier curled his lanky body around hers in her Earther-sized bed.

Vivian gave one last wave to her friends and stepped into the building. The Earther security guard's eyes lit up as he nodded in greeting. The other students stared with a mix of awe and terror, and one dropped their drink with a loud clatter.

Smoothing down her red dress, Vivian stepped into the first day of her new life.

ACKNOWLEDGMENTS

The Red Woman on Mars is a story about women taking back their agency. Growing up, I thought things were different for my generation of women. I had the opportunity to seek an education, control of my own finances, and access to cheap and easy birth control that allowed me to decide on the right timeline for having children. I didn't have to choose between having a career and being a mother. Or between marriage and autonomy. I thought, perhaps naively, that the constraints women have experienced in most eras of history were a thing of the past.

But in the current American political climate, we're seeing a shocking backslide on women's reproductive freedom. Women in many places in America are facing a lack of choice when it comes to their own health, bodies, and futures. In my home state of Illinois, where we've strengthened the rights of women and LGBTQ+ people in recent years, we're seeing a staggering uptick in women and trans people crossing state lines to seek out basic healthcare.

The days after Trump was reelected, I channeled my grief, anger, and fear into writing the climax of this novel. In the last year and a half, I have watched in horror as many of my worst fears for a second Trump term came to pass. While marching, donating, and engaging in my community, I've also worked on this book. Vivian speaks for me when she demands, "Give me my freedom. Over my body. Over my future." I write for a country that I believe will move past this dangerous flirtation with fascism. A country that will one day be safe for women, LGBTQ+ people, immigrants, and other marginalized groups.

As I was writing, I thought often of my sister Nora Elderkin and her essential work providing healthcare to women and LGBTQ+ patients. Nora, when I first conceived of the idea of writing a sci-fi romance in reaction to the Dobbs decision overturning the constitutional right to an abortion, I immediately thought of how you approach everything you do with kindness and a sense of humor, even in the face of remarkable obstacles. I'm in awe of the care you show your patients. I modeled Delilah after your sunny spirit overlaying a will of steel.

I am indebted to the remarkable novel *Pride and Prejudice*. At first, I wasn't sure how to write a story about female bodily autonomy that was also a love story, but then I realized Jane Austen's masterpiece was a perfect lens to use. Austen doesn't shy away from the constraints women of the Regency era face, from restrictions around property inheritance to expectations of sexual purity. And she also gave us one of the most memorable couples in literature—Elizabeth and Mr. Darcy—who overcome their negative first impressions to form a genuine connection. It was such a pleasure to spend so much time with Austen's words and characters.

I want to especially thank my very own Mr. Darcy—my brooding husband, Rufus Barner. To quote my beloved Anthony Bridgerton, "You are the bane of my existence and the object of all my desires." I based Xavier on your strong sense of justice and commitment to your principles. Thank you for reading multiple versions of this book, consulting with me on human rights law, and spending so much time with me on the physical descriptions and cultural backgrounds of the characters. And thank you for holding down the fort at home as I pursue my writing career.

To my sister Lily Elderkin and my brother-in-law Justin DiPietro. Brainstorming with you over wine has become an essential part of my writing process. Lily, thank you for the amazing climax idea. Justin, thank you for insisting Xavier needed to get knocked out so Vivian could really shine . . . and for the four hundred comments on the Google Doc.

To my crew of wonderful beta readers, including Craig Elderkin, Debby Scheck, Grace Elderkin, Isabelle Elderkin, Virginia Selleck, Steve Fritz, and Joy Parkhurst. Thank you for working with my deadlines and giving me so much thoughtful feedback. Grace and Isa, sorry I gave Lily and Nora their own paragraphs. Four sisters are a lot of sisters. To my brother, Luke—I love you too!

To my kids, Marcus, Miles, and Logan Barner. I'm so proud of you. Being your mom is my greatest joy and privilege.

To my agent, Jenna Satterthwaite, thank you for everything you've taught me about writing. I put it to good use when drafting this novel! And to Jenna's other clients, my agent siblings Team Jenna, you are my daily source of support in this wild industry, and I am forever grateful for all of you.

To my editor Toni Kirkpatrick, thank you for supporting this novel from the very beginning when it was just a pitch and 10k words. And to the team at Diversion Books for all the ways you've brought this novel to life.

And, finally, to my readers. Thank you for coming on this journey with me. Together, let's all expect more.